THE COMPLETE ADVENTURES OF

THE MOON MAN

VOLUME 6: 1935–36

THE COMPLETE
ADVENTURES OF
THE
MOON
MAN
VOLUME 6:
1935–36

BY

FREDERICK C.
DAVIS

INTRODUCTION BY
ANDREW SALMON

 ALTUS PRESS / 2017

© 2017 Altus Press • First Edition—2017

EDITED AND DESIGNED BY
Matthew Moring

PUBLISHING HISTORY
"Introduction" appears here for the first time. Copyright 2017 by Andrew Salmon.
"Homicide Dividends" originally appeared in the November 1935 issue of *Ten Detective Aces* magazine.
"Robe of Blood" originally appeared in the December 1935 issue of *Ten Detective Aces* magazine.
"The Whispering Death" originally appeared in the January 1936 issue of *Ten Detective Aces* magazine.
"Corpse's Plunder" originally appeared in the March 1936 issue of *Ten Detective Aces* magazine.

THANKS TO
Mike Clagett and Andrew Salmon

CONTENTS

ANDREW SALMON

INTRODUCTION

PULPSMITH EXTRAORDINAIRE Frederick C. Davis earned his reputation with the astonishing variety of tales he turned out over his career. The vast array of plots he was able to mine from the concept of the Moon Man has been well on display over the course of this reprint series. We're almost at the end of the line with regards to the original tales, and if you've made it this far, you've seen the series evolve while, at the same time, sticking firmly to the basic premise.

This volume presents an action-packed quartet of tales which are variations on a theme. So far in the series we've seen subsets of stories: there are the basic Moon Man vs. the police action-ers which are to be expected as well as the Moon Man black-mailed or merely threatened with the revealing of his secret identity. There is also a substantial group of stories where the Moon Man goes up against crooks who are cutting into his efforts to alleviate the sufferings of the poor of Great City as opposed to crimes he himself commits as the Robin Hood of the pulps. Stories where the two worlds of Stephen Thatcher collide as the criminal Moon Man has to *prevent* crimes in other words. The Red Six Saga (Volume 2) is the ultimate example of these sorts of tales. And it's the Moon Man against the criminal denizens of Great City in all of the stories pre-sented here.

Perhaps this easing of the Moon Man away from his law-breaking original concept and into a true hero was an attempt to widen the character's appeal. Or, perhaps, Davis just wanted to shake things up and keep things fresh. Who can say?

Now don't think for one second that the adventures stray from the pathos and angst which are a major part of the fun of the Moon Man. No, it's here in spades even 30 tales into the canon. And we wouldn't have it any other way. Over the course of this volume, we'll see Steve, Sue, Ned Dargan, Gil McEwen in peril both physical and spiritual. The fragile globe the Moon Man wears is a microcosm of his headlong race along the razor's edge and that world can shatter in a heartbeat!

"Homicide Dividends" kicks off the proceedings with a stash of $200,000 hidden—in the police station. The Moon Man's two worlds are brought together as Detective Steve Thatcher must prevent the money from being reclaimed by the crooks and steal it himself, as the Moon Man, to help the needy of Great City.

There's more flat-out action than plot twists in this one but when Steve's fiancé Sue gets kidnapped and used as leverage against her father Detective Gil McEwen, Davis takes us into interesting territory. Thing is, the crooks have poison gas and they'll use it on the cops in the station if Gil doesn't let them reclaim their stolen loot. And they wouldn't think twice of using it on Sue for that matter. But Gil will do whatever it takes to stop them and get the Moon Man whom he blames for the crime regardless of the consequences to Sue or anyone else. With Sue's life at stake, it bears repeating—whatever it takes. Now that's dedication to duty. The Moon Man also loses his regalia yet again, which is an interesting recurring event as the ways he gets it back can be quite inventive.

In "Robe of Blood," the Moon Man is pitted against arsonists burning down buildings to hide their crimes. Except at the outset, they've set a place on fire while the Moon Man was robbing it himself. Gil risks his life diving into the burning house to capture the Moon Man and is almost killed in the process. A man dedicated to the law? Or is it obsession? He's been hunting the Moon Man for years now and is getting desperate. And so is Sue who puts her foot down about the Moon Man once and for all. We've seen her anxiety grow in past tales and she has all but demanded the Moon Man go into eclipse, Here, things come to a head. Either Steve hangs up his globe for good or she won't marry him. Torn in two directions, he has no choice but to comply. He locks up his Moon Man regalia and gives her the key.

But then Gil is captured by the arsonists and only the globed gladiator can save him from a fiery death. Sue's decision on this matter goes a long way to illustrate how the strain of the Moon Man is affecting everyone around him and the desperation is running high. Broken hearts and lives in dangers—it's a hot time in Great City!

The theme continues in "The Whispering Death" where Stephen Thatcher can only numbly watch one of his best friends murdered in cold blood by a gang of thieves with "whisper weapons" that kill silently as they rob the cash prizes from the conclusion of an air race. And then Steve and Gil are almost killed in the resulting shoot out. Vowing revenge for his dead friend while the Moon Man wants that stolen $25,000 prize money for the widow, Steve is on the warpath. He'll join the gang to get the job done if he has to. When his part of their next job involves blowing up the communications center of the police station he readily agrees, planning to double cross the gang before that can happen. But these aren't common crooks he's dealing with and they draw a noose round the Moon Man he might not wriggle out of.

By the time this one winds up, the Moon Man, Gil McEwan and Mark Keanan, a series regular at this point, will be reluctant comrades-in-arms against the gang where double-dealing can have catastrophic consequences with one slip. By the time all is said and done, the Moon Man will lose his outfit yet again but will take on folk hero status in Great City.

"Corpse's Plunder" rounds out this quartet of tales with a gang of gas-masked thieves who steal a priceless diamond necklace at the funeral of the deceased Mrs. Ashworth Pend-leton who is to be buried with the bauble.

The Moon Man has retrieved his outfit from under the watchful noses of the police and has no interest in the diamonds other than returning them to the recently departed Mrs. Pend-leton. But he does have his globe set on the money the thieves will get for fencing the necklace. Ned "Angel" Dargan plays a critical role in this one, which is a nice change of pace. The climax provides a nice twist on the locked vault gag we saw back in "The Dial of Doom" (Volume 5) where Steve's service revolver was locked in a safety deposit book belonging to the Moon Man. This time Sue is locked in the bank vault with evidence that proves, beyond any shadow of a doubt, that Steve Thatcher is the Moon Man. There's nowhere to run this time and Gil, Steve Thatcher, Mark Keanan, armed police *and* the thieves are all waiting anxiously in and around the bank for the time-lock to open the safe door so Sue can get out. Steve, desperate for the Moon Man to do something, is shocked to learn his globe of Argus glass was shattered in an earlier scrape! Is this truly the end of the Moon Man? How is the Steve going to get out of this one? The answer will surprise you.

Frederick Davis is in the top tier of purple prose purveyors and the inventiveness he brought to this series stands the test of time. The original tales of the Moon Man may be winding down but the Moon Man will not be going softly into that good night. So buckle up, the Moon Man is on the prowl and Great City is a powder keg. Action and melodrama await!

HOMICIDE DIVIDENDS

CHAPTER I

BLUE CARNAGE

POLICE HEADQUARTERS drowsed at two o'clock in the morning. Keeping the graveyard watch in the desk room, Sergeant Sullivan yawned over the book. Blue-shirted men blinked sleepily at their cards as they fumbled through a game of pinochle. An occasional routine alarm droned out of the radio room to the squad cars prowling the city. Little usually happened in headquarters during the small hours of the morning—but tonight these men were destined to hear the blasting of killer guns.

The door swung open. Detective Sergeant Stephen Thatcher, garbed in trim tuxedo, came in with a very pretty girl. He was clean-cut, lithe, the son of the chief of police. The girl in white satin, whose gloved hand rested snugly on his arm, was his fiancée and the only daughter of Gilbert McEwen, ace sleuth of the Great City plainclothes division. They laughed happily together, walking toward the stairs—until the blast of the first shot startled them.

Steve Thatcher and Sue McEwen had spent the evening dancing at the famed Stratosphere Club. Delightfully weary, the tinkling music echoing in their ears, they had driven toward headquarters on their way home on the chance that Gil McEwen might be working late. Lights gleaming in the chief's office had told them McEwen was laboring at routine detail. They had stopped to pick him up—but it was fated that they would not reach his office together tonight.

Cracking reports froze them. One muffled explosion, then two more, thumped from the rear of the corridor. Steve Thatcher gazed alertly at a closed door while blue-shirted men turned alarmed from the card table in the desk room. A groan of intense pain penetrated the hush that followed—a moan from a point below. The patrolmen were reaching for their service gats, and Thatcher was starting apprehensively toward the door when, abruptly, it slapped open.

The face of the man who stumbled into the hall was a red horror. He tottered as he groped, blinded by blood flowing over his eyes. Murderous bullets had horribly mutilated his features. His brother patrolmen loped in dismay toward him as Steve Thatcher sped. They caught him as he slumped. Thatcher snatched the gun from one of them, started down the stairs leading into the basement—and again heard the thunder of blazing guns.

Sue McEwen shrank back as Thatcher vanished beyond the door through which a dying man had lurched. Quick steps sounding above her drew her anxious gaze. Her father was springing down from the floor above. The startling concussions had brought Gil McEwen from the chief's office in a rush. He snagged his service gat into his hand, staring in grim amazement at the bloody man on the floor. An outraged question crowded to his lips, but he did not speak. Guns thundering below sent him bounding into the basement.

A spotted red trail had turned Steve Thatcher to the closed door of the furnace room. He had thrust through into darkness torn by spanging slugs. The door was standing open when McEwen whirled to it. Bullet flame slashed the gloom beyond as he stared. On the iron platform, just over the sill, a blue-shirted man was lying face down, motionless, his back dark-spotted where bullets had drilled. McEwen snarled as he leaped over the still figure into the dark turmoil of storming death.

Flashing flame showed him Steve Thatcher backed to a wall, firing swiftly. Black figures were crowding toward an open door in the far corner. They pushed out as McEwen's gun whipped lead. Thatcher sprang at his side when running footfalls sounded in the alley behind headquarters. Whining bullets barred their way as a motor roared. Their guns blasted a challenge while they leaped up. Thatcher was strangely conscious of a sheet of newspaper, blown past him by the wind, as they twisted toward a sedan that was speeding into the street beyond.

McEwen's last bullet lashed at it. A dull clanging sound told him he had hit the car. It vanished instantly in the gloom. McEwen glanced desperately in search of another car, but no other was in the alley. He sprinted toward the street. A growl of grim exultation broke from his drawn lips when he saw a radio roadster just turning into the headquarters garage. Two sleepy patrolmen were bringing it back from the midnight tour. McEwen's growl jerked them to alertness.

"Into the next street! Chase that car! There's a bullet scar on it! Get after it, by damn!"

The roadster shot away as McEwen loped back. Now lights were shining through the windows of the furnace room. Steve Thatcher had hurried in. He stood, gun in hand, in smoky air, as McEwen tramped to his side. They gazed stunned at the patrolman lying dead at the inner door, at another figure, garbed in civilian clothes, sprawled in death at their feet.

The hum of a racing motor throbbed into the hush—the radio roadster speeding after the car in which merciless killers were escaping.

STEVE THATCHER and Gil McEwen eyed each other in stunned bewilderment. They looked dazedly around the furnace room. A row of black iron doors and boilers stood in the brick wall at one side. At the other were rows of empty ash cans. Two coal bins stood in the corner. It was like a thousand other heating plants—not in use now because the weather was warm. Nowhere was there a hint of the reason why armed men had sneaked into it to kill.

McEwen gripped the shoulder of the man in civilian clothes lying at his feet. He turned the corpse face up. He saw lean features marked with an ashy pallor. The close-set eyes were shut, the thin mouth gaped. A single bullet in the chest had dropped him with an automatic in his hand. McEwen peered grimly into the dead face and blurted in bewilderment:

"Lew Reddock! I thought he was in stir. How the devil did he get here?"

McEwen sprang up the iron steps that led to the inner door. He shouldered past the blue-shirted men who had stopped to stare at a dead comrade. Thatcher, following the grizzled veteran, found his tuxedo was bullet-torn in two places. McEwen was rapidly climbing the stairs when his daughter hurried in dismay to Thatcher's side.

"Steve—are you hurt?"

"Didn't touch me. Listen, Sue. I've got to stick with Gil. Do you mind taxiing home alone? All hell's broken loose—I can't leave now."

"Of course not, Steve. Please be careful!"

Thatcher sprang up the stairs. Passing the radio broadcasting room, he heard McEwen's voice rasping inside. An alarm was being flashed to every prowl car in the city to look out for the fleeing killers. Thatcher hurried on, to the rogue's gallery and fingerprint section. His expert knowledge of the system led him at once to the file containing the picture of the crook lying dead in the basement.

Gazing at two photographs, he recalled the details of a sensational crime of eight years previous. Lew Reddock and Tony Kroth had engineered a startling robbery. They had beaten down a bank messenger and escaped with loot of two hundred thousand dollars in cash. McEwen had directed the police drive that had netted Reddock weeks later. Kroth had slipped out of the state, and had not been picked up since, but Reddock had gone up the river. Recalling that the loot had never been recovered, Thatcher intently studied the pictures of the two crooks—the one unaccounted for, the other lying dead in the headquarters furnace room.

He hurried down again. McEwen was now in the lower hall, bending over the patrolman who had staggered through the door. When Thatcher came to his side, McEwen straightened with a solemn wag of the head.

"Poor guy," McEwen said bitterly. "He's gone."

Sergeant Sullivan rasped: "Mike Chappell and Dave Abbott—they both got it, lieutenant. Mike was able to talk a little before he went, but—" He stared around, stunned. "They were playing cards with the others just a little while ago. They went down to the washroom together. After we heard the shots—

"Mike managed to say he and Dave heard suspicious sounds in the furnace room. They opened the door to investigate. Bullets came at' em, before they knew what was happening. Dave dropped right there. How Mike ever got up those stairs, wounded as he was, I don't know! Hell, lieutenant, what does it mean? Who were those men? Why did they come in here, and why did they kill?"

McEwen snarled: "I'll find out!"

Thatcher strode angrily down the basement stairs, carrying a flashlight. Grim-faced men were carrying Dave Abbott from the platform where he had fallen dead. Thatcher stooped over Reddock and minutely examined the convict's pockets, but found nothing. His light flashed over the pavement as he went along the alley. The beam revealed no clue. Thatcher was turning back when a galvanizing thought flashed through his alert mind.

His probing light swung to the base of a telephone pole. A wrinkled, soiled sheet of newspaper was clinging to it, held by the wind. Thatcher carefully peeled it away. Sight of a dark glistening on the page speeded his heart. A touch of his fingertips told him it was fresh blood. The grit of the alley concealed a fact which this torn bit of paper revealed—that one of the fleeing crooks was wounded.

Eyes narrowed in thought, Thatcher strode out of the alley. He folded the page into his pocket as he crossed to a cigar store on the corner. His shrewd mind fitted jig-saw clues together as he spun the dial of the telephone. The number he called was one known only to him and two others. A cautious question answered:

"Boss?"

"Angel." Thatcher kept his anxious voice down. "I'm looking for a cop-killer who is wounded. It's probably serious enough to force him to go to a doctor. He can't go to a reputable physician, because the law requires them to report all gunshot wounds. That probably means he'll seek out Doc Axler. Axler specializes in treating crooks and keeping his mouth shut. You're not far from his place now. Start watching him, Angel, and report back the instant you have something."

"Okay, Boss!"

Thatcher smiled tightly as he slipped from the booth. He had a clue which he intended to keep for his own. He had called a hunted criminal to his assistance—Ned Dargan, ambassador extraordinary of the notorious crook known as the Moon Man. His mind hummed with a plan for catching the cop-killers outside the law as he hurried back to police headquarters.

TWO DEAD patrolmen had been carried into the first-aid room. Their living comrades, still stunned, were staring and mumbling blasphemy. Cold fury beat in Steve Thatcher's heart as he climbed to the chief's office. Gil McEwen's hard voice was snarling through the open door:

"Sullivan, get hold of Bruley. No matter where he is, by damn, I want him brought here as soon as he's found. Hurry it up!"

Thatcher followed as McEwen tramped out. The leather-faced veteran hurried into the rogue's gallery room. As he probed into the file which Thatcher had already consulted, he rasped:

"I found out a minute ago Lew Reddock was released from the state prison early this week. I had word today Tony Kroth is back in town and keeping under cover. Bruley told me that, and he probably knows more. By damn, I'll sweat it all out of him!"

Thatcher turned back to his own office.

Closing the door, he took a special file from his desk. For years he had kept notes, on every important case that had broken in the city—special data, plus his own observations, which were not to be found in the official records. He brought out a pack of newspaper clippings concerning the messenger robbery eight years previous. His intent eyes stopped on a paragraph that speeded his mind:

> Reddock's conviction leaves unsolved the mystery of what became of the loot. The two hundred thousand in cash is still missing. Rumors from the underworld hint that, while the police were hunting for him immediately following the crime, Reddock lost it all by gambling. Others insist the missing Kroth carried it out of the state. Another theory, probably nearer the truth, is that the two crooks hid the loot somewhere with the intention of later returning for it.

Thatcher thrust the file back into the drawer as the desk telephone rang. The cautious voice of Ned Dargan whispered over the line. Thatcher made sure McEwen was not near, satisfied himself that the phone sergeant was not listening in, and signaled: "Go ahead, Angel."

"I beat it right over to Doc Axler's house, Boss. Soon as I got there, Axler came out with another man. The other man moved as though in pain. I traced 'em to a house at 50 Bergen Street. They're there now."

"Keep watching, Angel! Wait in the car in the alley. We're playing for big stakes—use every care. I'm on my way."

Thatcher left his office quietly. Pausing at the head of the stairs, he saw McEwen again in the chief's office. As he started down, two uniformed men ran up breathlessly. He waited, listening, as the pair strode to McEwen. They gestured sheepishly while the gray-eyed veteran glared, and blurted:

"The car got away from us, lieutenant!"

McEwen snapped up. "By damn, that's fine! That's beautiful work! You were right on the heels of a dirty bunch of cop-killers, and you let 'em get away. A swell bunch of men I've got under me! Get out of here—and on your way, stop in the radio room and tell Brady to repeat the alarm for the car with the bullet dent in it."

Thatcher hurried down as the men obeyed. Quick steps took him out the entrance, to his roadster at the curb. Its motor sang smoothly as he turned it across town. He took the most direct way to Bergen Street. Turning again, he clicked off the head-lamps and into the next alley. He stopped silently behind a roadster sitting in the gloom. As he slipped from the wheel, a stocky man with a cauliflower ear and no neck ducked from the other machine—a man for whom all the police of Great City were searching—Ned Dargan.

"They're still in there. Boss."

Thatcher nodded grim satisfaction as he unlocked the rumble seat of Dargan's roadster. He brought a black bundle out of the compartment. Unrolling a long, black robe, he shook it over his shoulders. He pulled black gloves on his hands. While Dargan watched anxiously, he lifted the hinged halves of a gleaming, spherical glass mask. When he affixed it over his head, it wrought an amazing transformation.

Steve Thatcher, detective sergeant, son of the chief of police, became the notorious criminal known as the Moon Man.

CHAPTER II

RADIO TRAP

THE MOON MAN was wanted for a long list of sensational robberies. He was wanted for three daring kidnappings, including that of the jurist before whom he must come to trial if ever he were snared by the police. He was charged with a murder of which he was innocent. Repeatedly the Moon Man had defied the police, and repeatedly the relentless McEwen, the avowed enemy of the infamous criminal, had sworn to send him to the chair.

Steve Thatcher had dared break the written law in order to serve the higher command of human mercy. Ned Dargan had helped the Moon Man loyally because he knew every cent of "the Boss's" loot went to the needy who must have it or perish. Sue McEwen had faithfully kept the secret of the man she loved because its revelation would mean utter tragedy. Yet, in spite of the dread danger that threatened, the Moon Man was risking an appearance tonight.

The wave of his black-gloved hand signaled Dargan to wait at the cars. He shifted the cushion of his roadster and turned away carrying a tire tool. With the utmost caution he lifted the latch of a gate in the mesh fence, and slipped through. He was a phantom figure in the gloom as Dargan anxiously watched—a silver-headed spectre that vanished in the shadows near the house.

The Moon Man turned silently to two sedans sitting in the driveway. His spherical mask glimmered as he circled them. Its mottled surface seemed opaque as a mirror from the outside, but the Moon Man could see through its sheen as clearly as though it were fashioned of finest crystal. His breath whizzed past the deflector inside the sphere as he scanned the polish of both cars. When he drifted back to the house he was certain neither had been used by the killers escaping from headquarters.

His black robe rustled faintly as he paused at a window. He gazed into a dark room, at a line of light shining beneath a closed door. A vague suggestion of voices carried to him. His silver head bowed while he slipped the thin edge of the tire tool into the crack of the window-sash. His supple muscles bunched as he bore down, skillfully levering against the latch.

A sharp snap of breaking metal stopped his breath. He backed, dropping the tool, leveling his automatic. The whisper of voices had ceased. A tense moment passed, until they sounded again. Lungs burning, the Moon Man straightened, reassured that the snap of the latch had aroused no alarm.

His black-covered fingers pried at the frame of the window. He slid it upward, inch by inch, without sound. He brought himself up and vanished across the sill. Straightening in the dark room, automatic steadied, he drifted toward the door beneath which the chink of light shone. Pausing, gleaming head lowered, he heard a subdued, twanging voice which he recognized at once as that of the police announcer at headquarters.

The radio in the next room repeated the alarm: "Calling all cars… all cars. Special instructions from Lieutenant McEwen. All patrolmen are ordered to make a thorough search for a sedan bearing a fresh bullet sear. Men on duty at all roads and bridges are to maintain vigilance. Sedan to be reported directly to Lieutenant McEwen immediately if it is found. All cars… all cars."

The radio switch snapped. A throaty chuckle sounded. A drawling voice said as the Moon Man intently listened: "Let 'em find it. It won't tell 'em anything. We're going ahead with the rest of our plan no matter what special orders McEwen may give."

Another voice asked: "You sure the cops don't suspect what we're after, Tony? Sure you know exactly where it is?"

The question told the Moon Man that one of the men in the room was Kroth, partner of the dead Reddock in the sensational robbery of eight years previous. The same sinister voice answered:

"I helped Lew put it there, didn't I? I can go to the right spot with my eyes shut Don't worry about that detail. We played in tough luck tonight, with those two cops busting in on us, but nothing's going to stop us now. I've got the next move mapped out, and all of headquarters isn't going to stop us."

The Moon Man recognized the peculiar nasal quality of the next voice. If was that of Nate Lorsh, notorious "fixer" of the underworld, whose hand was in a dozen evil rackets whose power was far-reaching and malevolent. Lorsh's presence chilled the Moon Man's nerves because it confirmed his suspicion that a criminal coup of sensational proportions was under way.

"They'll be watchin' that place from now on. Remember, Reddock never got out with us, and they may put two and two together. The next time I might get a bullet in the brain instead of the arm. It's got to be a damn' good plan before we dare—"

Tony Kroth snarled. "It can't fail. Don't worry—we'll get that money. If it means killing a dozen more cops, we'll get it, and stay clear. The next time we leave that furnace room we'll have two hundred grand to split between us!"

In the darkness behind the closed door, the Moon Man straightened with grim elation.

IN HIS office at headquarters, Gil McEwen was angrily pacing the floor. His heels hammered back and forth until the telephone jangled. He snatched up the receiver to hear Sergeant Sullivan report from the desk room. "Bruley's coming up."

Facing the door, gnawing on an unlighted cigar, McEwen waited until hesitant steps sounded in the hall.

His eyes shone with contempt at the stealthy man who sidled in. McEwen was a grim dog of the law who never left a trail. He was ready to use any means possible to get his man, but he revolted at the thought of using a stool pigeon. The fact that he had called in "Sneak" Bruley, undercover contact man between the police and the underworld—one of a treacherous breed hated by both—meant he was going to stop at nothing to trap the killers who had invaded headquarters.

"Well?" he snarled.

A jangle of the telephone kept the shifty-eyed man silent. Again McEwen snatched up the receiver. His steely eyes glinted as he listened to a rushing report:

"This is Hale, lieutenant—car 43. We've just spotted the sedan with the bullet scar. It's standing empty near the Apex Building. Dark blue, two-door, red wire wheels, last year's model. Probably it's been stolen, maybe bought secondhand. If—"

McEwen snapped off the patrolman with "Watch it!" He rattled the hook and rasped orders to Sergeant Sullivan that would immediately begin a search of the records and a hunt for fingerprints. He turned away frowning, growling to himself: "That won't come to anything." His narrowed eyes bent on the timorous Bruley and lighted savagely.

"What do you know about the car the killers used?" He described it swiftly. "Was it stolen? Bought? Which? By damn, you know you're here to talk!"

Bruley gulped: "I heard about that car. It came off a second-hand lot. Nate Lorsh got hold of it through a couple his side-kicks. Usin' false names and—"

"Lorsh!" McEwen whirled to the desk and flattened a loose-leaf book in which the names, addresses and known haunts of all the city's public enemies were listed. "You're staying here,

Bruley. If you try to leave this building, I'll slap you into a cell. By damn!"

Bruley winced away from him as he slammed out of the office. McEwen went down the steps three at a time. He thrust into the adjoining headquarters garage and ducked into his coupé. He pressed the accelerator hard when he twisted into the street, and whacked the horn button as intersections sped past.

Turning alertly into Bergen Street, he slowed. Lights out, motor off, he rolled along the curb toward the house of Nate Lorsh. Heavy shadows covered the coupé when McEwen slipped out of it. He trod silently into the yard, easing his service gat into his hand—unaware that hidden eyes were watching his movements.

The alert ears of Ned Dargan had heard the gritting of tires in the gutter. Out of sight in the thick darkness of the alley, he saw Gil McEwen steal across the lawn. Cold dismay filled him—a desperate impulse to warn "the Boss" that the merciless detective was near—but already McEwen was gliding along the wall of the house. He stared, transfixed with dread, as the detective paused at the window through which the Moon Man had entered.

McEwen's cold eyes narrowed with astonishment. The raised sash gave him a moment's hesitation. He sensed a swift darkness inside. Gun leveled, McEwen heard muffled voices beyond the door at the far side of the black room. He waited no longer. Silently, quickly, he climbed in.

He straightened, finger ready on the trigger of his gat, eyes probing the gloom—but he did not know that the notorious crook he had sworn to send to the chair was standing almost within arm's reach—the Moon Man.

The Moon Man had heard McEwen's quiet steps in the grass. He had turned in alarm from the connecting door to see McEwen stealing toward the window. Chilled, he had backed toward another door in the side wall. He had eased through it an instant before McEwen had climbed over the sill. He stood now in the close darkness of a closet, tensely listening to the detective's stealthy movements.

The Moon Man heard McEwen cross to the other door, drawn by the guarded tones of the men in the room beyond. A moment passed while McEwen stood there listening. Heart pounding, the Moon Man ventured to twist the knob of the closet door. He silently opened it a crack. His silver head bowed, he watched McEwen turn away. McEwen brought a small torch from his pocket, blinded the lens with his fingers, probed the thin beam into the corners.

The ray shadowed a telephone. The flash blinked out as McEwen alertly stepped toward it. The Moon Man saw him lift the receiver. In cold dismay he heard a whisper so faint it could not carry into the room beyond: "Police headquarters!" McEwen's gun watched the connecting door while the call went through. Then:

"McEwen. Listen carefully. I'm in Lorsh's place, Fifty Bergen. Signal the squad cars in Section J. They're to surround the house. Signal extreme caution—the cop-killers are here. Snap it through, by damn!"

The Moon Man stood with imprisoned breath burning in his lungs, trapped in the blackness of the closet.

McEWEN STRAIGHTENED from the telephone. With stinging eyes, the Moon Man saw him back away from the connecting door. He knew that even now McEwen's alarm was flashing to the squad cars near the house. Armed patrolmen would be surrounding it within two minutes. McEwen was grimly awaiting their arrival, planning to snare a gang of predatory crooks—but he did not realize he had the Moon Man in the net. He suspected no lurking presence in the black room until—

"Raise your hands, McEwen!"

McEwen stifled a gasp as a gun pressed hard to his back. He twisted to see that a faceless, phantom figure had materialized behind him. Intent on the voices in the next room, he had not heard the Moon Man's panther step. He stared in furious amazement for one breathless instant. Then, possessed by an unreasoning fury, he wrenched around and drove his gun toward the fragile mask of the Moon Man.

The Moon Man darted aside. The gun slashed past the precious shell. A black-gloved fist drove out in a desperate blow. It smashed squarely into McEwen's face. The detective sprawled against a chair. He drew up with a snarl of rage, turning his gun. On tip-toes the Moon Man frantically went at him. His knuckles exploded between McEwen's eyes with blinding power. As McEwen dropped he whirled.

The crash of the chair had hushed the voices in the next room. The Moon Man knew the crooks were taking alarm as he climbed over the sill. He dropped out while McEwen struggled up. Driven by a wild anger, McEwen lurched. The Moon Man's shining head was a clear target outside the window that swiftly drew his gun. The darkness rocked with two guns crashing at the same instant.

The Moon Man darted along the wall, hearing muffled shouts inside the house. Doors slammed as he sprang across the yard. Turning quickly at the gate, he glimpsed McEwen crowding out the window. He fired again, with careful aim. The slap of his slug in the window frame drove McEwen back. He sped through the gate as a gasp came from the gloom:

"Boss! Quick!"

The Moon Man sprang past Dargan's roadster. "Clear out, Angel!" He snapped open the door of his own car as Dargan scrambled into the other, while heels swiftly pounded the porch of Lorsh's house. Guns cracked while he slipped behind the wheel. He saw men swarming into the yard, McEwen again retreating from the window as slugs shattered the panes. The detective's guns challenged the crooks leaping toward the two sedans while the Moon Man kicked the motor of his car into action.

Dargan's spurted ahead. The Moon Man raced behind him to the street. They turned in the same direction, then, at the corner, swung apart. Both sped through shadowed gloom. Both swung again at the next intersection in a desperate attempt to escape the neighborhood. The fading hum of the motors was blanketed by the thunder of the shooting at Lorsh's place.

Eight men were crowded into the two sedans that backed swiftly into the street. Howling engines jerked them away. McEwen, leaning out the window, flung a wild bullet at them. He leaped out as they sped from sight. Racing to the sidewalk, he glimpsed a squad car speeding from the opposite direction. His wild shout sent it even more rapidly toward the corner as he ran.

Fusillading guns flashed from the fleeing sedans. Bullets screamed along the street. The windshield of the radio car became instantly transformed into an opaque pattern of cracks. The driver leaned out, gripping the wheel in one hand, aiming his Police Positive with the other. His pull on the trigger sent a slug whistling high into the sky. He slumped, head lolling and dripping red.

The car lurched crazily toward the curb. The patrolman at the driver's side made a wild grab at the wheel—too late. The front tires jounced over the curb. The bumper cracked against a stout tree. The car leaped back, twisting with all four wheels off the ground. It came down with a wrench and spilled sideward. It rolled over with a rending crash while McEwen stared in dismay.

He wheeled into the glare of approaching headlights. A second prowl car was racing in response to his alarm. Its jammed brakes squealed as McEwen gestured and shouted. His orders sent it backing around, roaring toward the other intersection, past the corner and out of sight:

"The Moon Man! That way! Go after him, by damn! Grab that crook!"

Yet, even as McEwen tramped the injured man squirming out of the demolished roadster, he told himself grimly that the Moon Man had already escaped.

OTHER CARS came spinning toward 50 Bergen Street. Mc-Ewen's orders sent searching men into the house. He snarled a call for an ambulance over the telephone. He flashed an alarm to the headquarters radio room that Tony Kroth and Nate Lorsh be picked up on sight. Leaving the place in charge of other plainclothes men, he tramped grimly to his car.

His teeth ground on an unlighted cigar while he drove to the turreted headquarters building. He looked in the desk room to hear Sergeant Sullivan say: "Those two cars haven't been spotted yet, Gil," and nodded angrily as though he'd expected it. He climbed the worn stairs and found Detective Sergeant Mark Keanan in the chief's office with Sneak Bruley. With threatening finger leveled, he charged at the timorous stool pigeon.

"You know more about this than you've said, by damn! You can tell me what's behind this and who's in it! Open up! Spill the works! I'm listening!"

Bruley licked dry lips. "I don't know nothin' more. I swear I don't."

McEwen's fist clenched on Bruley's lapel. "We've got a charge standing against you. I'll slap you into jail and keep you there if you don't talk. Come on! What is it?"

"I ain't goin' to tell you!" Bruley backed against the wall fearfully. "I don't want a bullet in my guts. Goin' to jail will be better than that. You can put the light on me—anything—I won't talk. I'm tellin' you—you ain't goin' to get it out of me!"

McEwen's fingers balled to drive a blow into Bruley's greasy face. He dropped his hand, stepping back, lips curling with contempt. "That's it, is it? You know all about it, but you're afraid to tell the truth. I won't dirty my hands by pounding it out of you, you sneaking rat. What's the use of throwing you into the jug? You'd be free again in no time. All right, Bruley. Clear out!"

The door opened before the stool pigeon could reach it. Detective Sergeant Thatcher stepped in. His face was drawn, his eyes anxious. He had heard McEwen's rasp through the door, and now he stepped aside to allow Bruley to slink past. He closed the door as Mark Keanan asked:

"You're not letting it go with that, are you, Gil?"

"Damn' right I'm not!" McEwen's eyes gleamed shrewdly. "He meant what he said—he wouldn't talk—but I'm not through with him. Keanan, your job is to shadow Bruley. Start keeping an eye on him right now. Watch every move he makes, because he may give us a lead to the cop-killers. Go ahead, by damn!"

Keanan went out the door quickly. He was as dogged a crook hunter as McEwen. He had worked grimly at McEwen's side with an unswerving determination to beat the Moon Man. Steve Thatcher had reason to believe Mark Keanan would play the gamble for all it was worth. He closed the office as Keanan went down the stairs after Bruley, and turned anxiously to face McEwen.

McEwen's teeth were driven deep into his cigar. A new gleam had come into his burnished eyes. He said in a voice that crackled:

"I don't need a stool pigeon to tell me the Moon Man's behind these murders!"

Thatcher's voice went tight and dry as he protested: "That's not like the Moon Man, Gil."

"I don't put anything past that fancy crook. I know he's behind this thing. I followed a lead to Lorsh's place tonight, and the Moon Man was there. He gave those filthy crooks a chance to get away. This is his job, and this time he's gone too far. I've sworn a thousand times to send the Moon Man to the chair, and this time I'm going to do it!"

Steve Thatcher said wryly: "Perhaps you're right, Gil." A new plan forming in his mind turned him back to the door. Mc-Ewen's heels were hammering the floor when he went down the stairs. His searching glance along the lower corridor told him Bruley was gone, with Keanan after him. Pushing through the entrance, Thatcher saw a police car, with the detective at the wheel, rolling slowly past the intersection.

He hurried to his roadster, still watching. When Keanan's machine passed out of sight, he started up. He turned, went two blocks, and stopped. Keanan's car was still traveling slowly. Another square ahead. Sneak Bruley was shuffling along. Keanan spurted when Bruley turned, and Steve Thatcher swung again from the curb to follow them both.

His blood rushed cold, with a dread recollection of McEwen's grim threat to send the Moon Man to the chair, as the slow double chase led him far across the city.

THATCHER SAW Bruley climb a grimy stoop in a squalid roominghouse district. As the stoolie vanished through a door, Mark Keanan left his car. Keanan was stationed in a dark shop entrance, across the street, when Thatcher turned his roadster past the corner. Thatcher alighted quickly, entered a cheap drug store, stepped into the telephone booth. The number he called was that of the hideaway of the Moon Man's accomplice.

"Boss?"

The voice of Ned Dargan brought a surge of relief to Thatcher's heart. "You got clear, Angel! Good! Listen carefully. I need you again. Come to the corner of Ash and Spruce Streets. I'll be waiting for you. Bring a roll of adhesive tape from the medicine cabinet. Get that? Hurry it, Angel!"

Mark Keanan was still in the dark doorway, keeping watch on Bruley's room, when Thatcher walked past the intersection. Climbing into his roadster, he turned at the next corner, then again into the alley. He slipped out at a point from which Bruley's room was invisible, but he could see nothing of Mark Keanan. He walked back to the corner and waited. In his hot impatience each minute seemed interminable. His eyes lighted when, at last, a familiar roadster turned the corner.

His gesture to Dargan sent the car swerving to the curb. As he walked past, Dargan fell into step with him. They turned into the alley and paused at Thatcher's machine. Thatcher murmured: "A dangerous step, Angel—but we've got to take it," while he unlocked the rumble compartment. As he lifted out the black bundle of the Moon Man's regalia, Dargan's eyes widened with anxiety.

"Hell, Boss! What're you going to do?"

Thatcher shook the black robe over his shoulders. "Get information." He pulled on the black gloves. "With two hundred thousand as the objective." He fitted the fragile glass mask over his head and drew his automatic from a slit in the cloak. "Mask yourself, Angel." Now Steve Thatcher's voice had the muffled quality of the Moon Man's. "Follow me."

He whispered instructions as Dargan followed him to the mouth of the alley. A handkerchief was tied across Dargan's face when he paused, and a revolver was in his hand. They searched the gloomy block and made sure it was deserted—except for Keanan, sheltered in the doorway. The Moon Man ventured out, gliding with quick steps, toward the spot where Keanan stood.

He appeared before Keanan's startled eyes as if by the power of black magic. Keanan gasped and grabbed for his gun. The Moon Man and Dargan sprang at the same instant. Dargan's fist clicked to Keanan's jaw as the black-gloved hand of the Moon Man clamped over Keanan's mouth. Together they fought the detective during a tense, breathless moment. When the Moon Man drew back, Keanan was sagging in his arms, stunned by the ex-pug's trained fists.

Another glance along the street showed them it was still clear. They lifted Keanan and carried him quickly into the gloom of the alley. Dargan twisted the detective's arms back, stripped adhesive tape from the roll he had brought, and bound Keanan's wrists. He banded Keanan's ankles, strapped Keanan's mouth, rolled the detective to the base of a black brick wall. He came to the side of the black-robed figure at the entrance of the alley as the Moon Man whispered: "Excellent work, Angel!"

Keanan was squirming dazedly, striving to break loose, when the Moon Man and Dargan darted across the bleak street. He saw them bound up the stoop and thrust open the door Bruley had entered. As they vanished, he peered around grimly. A moment passed before he saw the two empty milk-bottles standing on the sill of the door across the alley.

The Moon Man's robe rustled softly as he went with Dargan down the yellow-lighted hallway. They paused at a door which Steve Thatcher knew to be that of the stool pigeon's room. The Moon Man's gloved hand tested the knob, then raised to knock. The soft tattoo brought a quick, startled sound out of the room. A whisper came through the panels: "Who is it?"

The Moon Man commanded: "Open the door."

A key scratched in the lock. A foot braced the door as it opened an inch. Sneak Bruley's narrow-set eyes peered out and widened at sight of the silver-headed figure. In stark dismay he stood motionless. The Moon Man's shoulder thrust hard against the panels. Dargan pushed through beside him. They closed the door swiftly while Bruley retreated in abject fear. Two gleaming weapons covered him as the Moon Man's muffled voice came:

"You're going to talk!"

MARK KEANAN breathed fast as he lay in the grit of the alley. Eyes narrowed on the milk bottles standing in the doorway, he wrenched over. Kicking his bound legs, squirming, he rolled himself until the opposite wall stopped him. He strained to a sitting position, then slid himself along. He reached with an effort into the doorway and gripped the neck of one of the bottles.

His first, stiff swing smashed it against the sill, he brought the sharp edge against the bands of tape at his wrists. His breath whistled with the prolonged effort of sawing the straps. Watching the door through which he had seen the Moon Man vanish, he kept it up until the sticky strips parted.

He peeled his wrists apart, exultation shining in his eyes. He winced with pain as he stripped the gag from his mouth, then unwound the stuff from his ankles. Jerking up, he hurried to the street. He had had no opportunity, after the Moon Man's swift attack, to get his gat out of his holster, but now he brought it snugly into his hand.

He sped across the street to the door that had blotted away the Moon Man. He went in with slow, silent steps, weapon leveled. He noted elatedly that a telephone booth stood at the rear of the hall. He was moving toward it when a faint, muffled voice turned him toward the door of Bruley's room. He poised outside it, intently listening.

The voice was saying: "They've got another place. They're hiding somewhere in the city now. Where is it, Bruley?"

The husky whisper of the stool pigeon answered: "They'll kill me if I tell you."

The muffled tone challenged: "You'll wish for death, after we finish with you, if you don't speak up."

Keanan kept his position during a moment of silence. Once Bruley sobbed. Lowering himself cautiously, Keanan brought his eye near the key-hole. He saw a section of the room, a ghostly figure in black robe and globular mask. His finger pressed ready on the trigger as Bruley blurted: "It's in the basement of the old Shipper's Restaurant. If they ain't scattered, they're usin' it. That's all I know. I swear to heaven I can't tell you any more!"

The murmuring voice of the Moon Man answered: "That's quite enough, Bruley, thanks. I advise you to keep strictly quiet about our visit. Thank you again—and good night."

Keanan's heart pounded as he straightened. He heard the flapping of the black robe as the Moon Man strode toward the door. The heavier footfalls of Dargan were following when Keanan alertly stepped back. His gun was leveled, his eyes grimly slitted, when the knob turned. Suddenly the door flashed open and the Moon Man stepped into the line of Keanan's weapon.

"Raise your—"

The report of the Moon Man's gun blasted into Keanan's command. The bullet ripped through the sleeve of the detective's coat as the Moon Man sprang out. Keanan wrenched away, swinging his gat to fire again, but the swift attack of the masked criminal was a storm that overwhelmed him. A black-gloved hand gripped his wrist at the instant he fired. His bullet splintered into the floor no less swiftly than Dargan's fist cracked to his chin. Keanan spun, blinded and dazed, hearing swift footfalls through the haze of his mind.

When he staggered up, he saw the fearful Bruley slinking out the front entrance. Doors had opened along the hall and terror-stricken eyes were staring out. Upstairs a woman screamed for the police. Keanan ignored the chorus of alarmed voices as he sprang to the door after Bruley. He leaped out, searching the street. Then, his shrewd mind planning a strategic move, he loped back to the telephone booth.

He spun the dial to the number of police headquarters and snapped at the Phone Sergeant: "Give me McEwen!" When McEwen's rasping answer came, Keanan's words rushed: "I spotted the Moon Man-grilling Bruley! He's slipped away—but never mind that! Listen, Gil! The Moon Man forced Bruley to tell him where the crooks have a hideout. The basement of the old Shipper's Restaurant—got that? They may be there now—and the Moon Man's heading for it!"

McEwen roared: "By damn! We'll grab that crook!"

"We've got a chance to grab 'em all if we play it right! The cop-killers and the Moon Man, too. What's more, Dargan's with him. We can surround that place with squad cars and trap them so—"

"I expect a lot of help from the prowl cars after what happened tonight, by damn!" McEwen retorted sarcastically. "Listen, Keanan. We're going after this for all it's worth, but carefully. We'll spot that place before we plan the next move. Meet me in Seagram's place, near it—understand? Wait for me there—then, by damn, we'll nail that gang and the Moon Man!"

"On my way!"

Keanan shouldered out of the booth. He ignored the startled inquiries of the undershirt men and the unkempt women in the hall as he tramped to the door. With his hand still clamped on his Police Positive, he hurried toward his car—grimly promising capture and the electric chair for the Moon Man.

CHAPTER III

KILLERS' LAIR

STILL CHILLED by the narrowness with which he had escaped Mark Keanan's bullet in the rooming-house, Steve Thatcher turned his roadster into the gaudy neon glow of a street that lay far from the turgid stream known as Murder River. His orders had sent Dargan rushing away while he had sped, robe and mask off, in the opposite direction. Satisfied that Keanan had not signaled a chase, he now approached that location of the killers' secret hideaway.

He turned into a darker street and braked at the curb. Watching carefully, he brought a black case out of the rumble compartment. Making sure he was not observed, he packed the fragile mask into it with the robe and gloves and automatic. He was finishing the task when headlamps beamed around the corner. A roadster rolled in the gutter and stopped behind Thatcher's.

Ned Dargan quietly slipped out of it. He walked at Thatcher's side to the corner. Turning, they gazed at dark windows on which flaked lettering read *Shipper's Restaurant.* They went on to the entrance of the adjacent store. Peering in, Thatcher saw it was also empty. While Dargan warily watched, he tackled the old lock with his skeleton keys.

The rusty bolt drew back. Dargan stole into the musty darkness behind Thatcher. They groped to a rear door. Again Thatcher's master keys came into play. He opened the way into a court littered with rubbish. They glided to a fence, listened, climbed over. When they paused they were facing the rear entrance of the abandoned eating-place.

The new lock on the door verified Bruley's information. On the inside the windows had been freshly painted black. Listening alertly through the panes, Thatcher felt sure the hideout was not occupied. He returned to the door, realizing the lock was a formidable opponent. He selected a thin steel pick from the leather key case and worked with painstaking care.

After minutes of trying endeavor, he straightened with a sigh. The door opened under pressure of his hand. He leveled his gun in one hand, his torch in the other. The light shafted across the room. It contained only a table and chairs and a recently installed telephone. Thatcher went to the instrument at once and noted the number affixed to it.

"Skip out, Angel," he directed quickly. "Get to the nearest pay station and call this number. Leave the case. Make it fast—they may come into this place at any minute!"

Dargan's eyes reflected wonder and anxiety as he complied. Thatcher remained in the open doorway, listening. A series of slight sounds enabled him to follow Dargan's movements through the gloom. His nerves burned as he waited, an eternity passed before the ring of a bell shrilled in the dark room.

Instantly Thatcher lifted the receiver. "Okay, Boss!" came over the line. He instructed Dargan: "Stay at the phone. Drop enough money in the box right now to pay for an hour's service. You'll be able to hear everything said in this room. Hurry it, Angel!"

Thatcher removed a pencil from his pocket as donging sounds issued from the receiver, indicating Dargan was slotting coins at the other instrument. He pushed the point of the pencil under the receiver hook and broke it off. The small wedge of wood kept the line open when he pronged the receiver. Eyes shining with satisfaction, he whispered "I'm leaving now, Angel!" and stepped out the door.

He allowed the bolt to click into its socket. Carrying the case, he groped to the rear of the fenced yard. A pile of old boxes offered him shelter. Covered by the shadow, he opened the case. Because Detective Sergeant Thatcher could know nothing of this place—because Mark Keanan had spotted the Moon Man with Bruley—he brought up the robe and mask. One moment transformed him into the notorious, silver-headed criminal.

Even as he fitted the globular mask over his head, he heard the rattle of a padlock on a hasp. Alertly he watched a gate swing open in the fence flanking the street. Two dark figures darted into the yard. As they went to the rear door of the building, two others followed. The Moon Man watched while they went into the hideaway. After the door closed, there was silence. No light gleamed through the thickly painted panes, but the Moon Man knew the quartet of crooks had entered into evil conclave.

The Moon Man waited tensely, expecting others of the ruthless band to appear at the gate, but it did not open again. He glided across the yard. He drifted to a stop near one of the windows. His silver head glimmered as he listened. He caught only a few intelligible words in the baffling confusion of low voices—but he knew Ned Dargan, at the other end of the telephone line, must be hearing it all distinctly.

While the Moon Man remained motionless in the gloom, the tones of the men in the hideaway became edged with anger. The heat of an argument made their words louder. Now able to hear clearly, the Moon Man listened with caught breath. He identified Lorsh's nasal twang:

"It's too much of a risk! We'll have McEwen after us like a madman. You better get hold of Novik and tell him to lay off or—"

Tony Kroth's sharp voice cut in: "By this time it's already done. I'm running this show, Lorsh, and I'm telling you we've got McEwen where the hair is short. He runs the police, doesn't he? His orders go. He's going to back down and play dead, I tell you, when he finds out we've snatched his girl. If he makes a move against us now, he'll get her back dead!"

DISMAY STABBED the heart of the Moon Man. His incredulous mind echoed Kroth's ominous words as he straightened. *McEwen snatched his girl—get her back dead!* A desperate urgency turned him away from the window. He was starting in frantic haste toward the inner fence when a new alarm came out of the darkness.

A lowered, rasping voice spoke near the gate. The footfalls of two men gritted near it. An unseen hand silently pushed it against the bolt that held it fast. The Moon Man poised during a moment of tense silence, until the grating voice spoke again:

"Break it down!"

McEwen!

A powerful jar shook the gate as the Moon Man gripped the top of the fence. The dry crackle of splintering wood came while he pulled himself up. His silver head lifted into the gleam of the corner light. He balanced anxiously, ripping his robe from a nail that had caught it. Another strong thrust through a splitting crash from the gate. The Moon Man moaned as it flew from its hinges.

Gil McEwen charged in, his gun glittering in his hand. Mark Keanan dashed after him, weapon bared. They stopped short to peer dumbfounded at the ghostly figure poised on the fence. McEwen's gat roared out a bullet that whined within an inch of the Moon Man's fragile mask. Keanan's slug drilled the wood at the Moon Man's shoulder as the phantom criminal dropped.

"After him!"

Suddenly light flashed across the yard. McEwen, sprinting toward the inner fence, twisted to see the rear door of the old restaurant opening. Silhouetted figures came crowding through, guns glittering. Instantly the bulb in the room went out. Hard faces were limned by the flame spitting from four leveled muzzles. McEwen and Keanan leaped into a dismayed retreat as the four crooks mobbed toward the broken gate.

The Moon Man heard the battle break as he thrust in the rear door of the adjoining store. He whirled in and drove the bolt into its socket. Darting to the front windows, he saw startled men running. The thundering guns were swiftly spreading an alarm. In a moment, the Moon Man knew, prowl cars would rush to the spot with sirens screaming. He spun back, lifting black-gloved hands to his spherical mask, while weapons clashed behind the buildings.

He halved the globe and lowered it quickly. He whipped the black robe over his shoulders and jerked off the black gloves. Bundling the regalia, Steve Thatcher glanced around quickly. He had been forced to abandon the case in the yard behind the restaurant. He sought a hiding-place as he crossed the empty store, urged to frantic haste by the jarring reports and the cries in the street. He stuffed the bundle beneath an empty box in the corner, then sped again to the entrance.

He slipped out, pulling his hat low, and hurried away from the center of the gun storm. Cutting across the street toward the opposite alley, he glanced back to see men with guns in their hands fleeing past the intersection. Gil McEwen, gat spitting flame, appeared at the corner. The detective spun toward the entrance of the store which Steve Thatcher had just left. Thatcher waited to see no more. Sheltered by thick darkness, he sprinted.

His breath rushed as he rounded to his roadster. The splitting concussions were less frequent when he started swiftly from the curb. The mask he had left in the empty store was the only one in the world, and Steve Thatcher knew it could never be replaced, but now he gave not an instant's thought to the danger of Gil McEwen's finding it. A consuming concern for Sue McEwen sent him past corners at top speed with his horn constantly blaring.

He whirled on whining tires into the quiet street where Gil and Sue lived. He bounded from the car at the curb, heart chilled with apprehension. The front entrance of the modest house was standing open, fanning light across the porch. Rushing through it, Thatcher saw a hat-tree overturned in the vestibule, a rug kicked into a heap in the hall beyond. He stopped short, heart pounding in the ominous silence, and called:

"Sue! Sue!"

He strode into the living-room and saw with aching eyes that a chair had been crashed to its side in a struggle. Sue's hat and coat were lying on another. Thatcher's heart pounded with wrath as he gripped up the telephone receiver and spun the dial. When the phone sergeant at headquarters answered he snapped:

"Flash the radio room! Special call for Gil McEwen. Sue McEwen has been kidnaped!"

HEAVY HOPELESSNESS weighted Steve Thatcher's heart as he turned from the instrument. He despaired of finding a clue to the girl's abductors as he made a rapid search. Grimly, intent on following the only lead he knew, he hurried out to his car. He sent it speeding back across the city, toward another section of unpretentious homes.

When he braked in front of a small house he noted eagerly that lights were shining through its windows. His knock on the door brought a quiet step. He whispered, "Okay, Angel!" and a safety chain rattled loose.

Dargan turned as he shouldered in, eyes filled with dread. He began:

"Boss, I heard 'em say something about snatching Sue! Listen, Boss, if—"

"They've already snatched her! Did you hear where they're keeping her, Angel? Tell me what came, over the wire!"

"They never mentioned it, Boss. I hoped they would, but they didn't. They said plenty else—about a raid on headquarters.

They're going to pull it off tomorrow night. They said nobody can stop 'em, because they'll use poison gas if—"

Thatcher stared.

"Something called Lewisite, Boss. I don't know what it is, but they've got bombs filled with it. Kroth said there's enough to kill every man in headquarters. I heard something about masks to protect themselves. They're going to use Sue somehow, too. Boss, if we don't get her back—"

Thatcher's lips thinned. "Go on, Angel! What else?"

"It's going to come off after midnight. Kroth said McEwen has got to follow orders or else. They're already wanted for murder and kidnaping and it can't go any worse with them if they kill fifty more men. They're prepared to do it, Boss—with the stuff called Lewisite—if the cops put up a fight."

Thatcher gripped the knob.

"Til at's all I got, Boss. I heard shots, but then nothing more was said. You know you can count on me for anything, Boss. Never mind about the chances of me getting grabbed. I'll go to the chair gladly if only we can get Sue back."

"Bless you, Angel." Thatcher smiled grimly. "I'm going to need your help—badly. We'll match Kroth's tactics, and stop at nothing to get Sue safely out of their hands. Stay here, Angel, and wait for a call."

Thatcher left the house quickly. Once in the car, he U-turned to retrace his last course. A chill of apprehension persisted in his heart as he sped back toward the McEwen home. A car sitting at the curb in front of the house told him the radioed message had already brought McEwen. He hurried in the entrance to find the hard-faced detective standing with clenched fists in the living-room.

"I'll get those rats!" His steely eyes glinted at Thatcher. "Did you see 'em, Steve? Have you any idea where they've taken her?"

Thatcher answered bitterly: "I haven't a lead, Gil. I came here and found her gone. Listen. I think we can be sure of one thing.

She's being held, but they haven't hurt her. They're going to use her against you, somehow."

McEwen snarled: "The Moon Man! He planned this! He's done this to me!"

Thatcher watched in dismay as McEwen turned in icy fury to the telephone. The spinning dial ticked off the number of police headquarters. The detective's face showed black, haggard lines as he growled: "Radio room!" Then:

"Listen. Keep the alarm going to every squad car in town. Keep every road and bridge watched. Call every man off leave and put 'em on the job. I'm coming to headquarters to take charge of this myself."

His shoulders sagged as he turned back to Thatcher. He opened one of his clenched hands and looked dazedly at a wadded sheet of paper. He uncrumpled it, stared grimly at the message printed on it. Growling deep in his throat, he handed it to Thatcher.

"Found it on the desk," he rasped. "They left it here when they snatched Sue. You're right, Steve—they're trying to use her to force me to back down—but they're not going to get away with it. By damn, they're not!"

Steve Thatcher read the single sinister sentence with stinging eyes:

> *If you do not follow our orders to the exact letter it will cost your daughter's life.*

A POLICE car brought plainclothes men to the McEwen home. They efficiently began a search for clues as McEwen trudged out to his coupé. A fingerprint expert was dusting the door-frames with aluminum powder when Thatcher went to the roadster. He trailed McEwen to headquarters and strode up the stairs at McEwen's side. Mark Keanan was waiting in the chief's office, his lower left arm bandaged.

"We bagged two of 'em at the old restaurant, anyway, Gil," he reported dryly. "Heyman and Radin. They're both on their way to the morgue now. The others skipped—no sign of 'em. And—" he added grimly—"no word about Sue."

McEwen's eyes became thin steel lines. "Listen. I've doped out what's behind all this. I know why those killers sneaked in here last night and why they're planning to come back. They're after the two hundred grand—the loot of the messenger robbery eight years ago."

Steve Thatcher's lips curved wryly, for he had suspected the crooks' purpose at the very beginning and, as the Moon Man, he had verified their desperate plan.

"At the time the robbery was pulled," McEwen went on, "this headquarters building was going up. I've checked up the construction company's records. The night Reddock and Kroth grabbed the two hundred grand, the late shift working here laid the cement floor in the furnace room. Stick with me, both of you."

McEwen signaled Thatcher and Keanan out of the office. As they went down the stairs, into the lower corridor, he continued:

"Reddock and Kroth kept under cover together a few hours after they pulled the job." McEwen opened the basement door. "They knew I had the dragnet out so they decided to hide the loot and separate." Thatcher and Keanan followed him down. "Maybe they didn't know what this building was, because only the foundations were laid." Standing on the platform where Patrolman Abbot had died, he snapped a switch.

"The fact is, they sank two hundred grand in the soft cement of that floor, and it's been there ever since!"

They descended the short flight of iron steps, stood in the cool quiet of the big room, and studied the floor. During the years it had become grayed with coal dust and marked by scraping ash cans. A black stain indicated the spot where Lew Reddock had fallen dead. Yet there was no indication anywhere of the booty which McEwen believed—and Steve Thatcher knew—to be concealed beneath it.

"For eight years," McEwen rasped, "two hundred thousand in cash has been buried under this room, and we haven't suspected it until now. Only Reddock and Kroth knew about it. Kroth waited, to risk coming back for it, until Reddock got out of stir. They couldn't pull the job alone, so they split others in. They might have gotten away with it tonight if Abbott and Chappell hadn't heard them breaking in."

McEwen looked intently at the floor as he moved back and forth.

"Somehow they are connected with the Moon Man—the slickest crook in the country. He's already demonstrated he knows his way around headquarters. I'm positive he's cooked up the whole devilish plan. He wants a fair slice of that two hundred grand—and he's already killed two cops and snatched my girl in order to get it!"

Steve Thatcher gazed appalled at McEwen's hardened face—gazed and could not speak. McEwen grated on:

"All the money is in old style bills, bigger than the banknotes we're using now. The Moon Man's probably dickered with a fence for getting rid of it. In any case, he can arrange to turn it in, in small amounts, at scattered points, without exciting suspicion. We can't get at him through that money because none of the serial numbers are recorded. That leaves us just one move—to keep the Moon Man from ever getting his hands on that loot."

Thatcher protested huskily: "While crooks are holding Sue, we can't—"

McEwen did not hear. "Digging up this room, and getting the stuff ourselves first, would spoil the play. The Moon Man would learn of it and never come back. Our gamble is to leave it exactly where it is, untouched. We know nothing about it—have no idea what they're up to—understand? Then the Moon Man will come back. Then, by damn—"

"Hell, Gil!" Thatcher blurted. "Are you going to try to trap those crooks here while they're holding Sue as hostage?"

McEwen's jaw squared. "Steve, I know what Sue means to you. She means even more to me. If anything happens to her—" He broke off, throat tight, eyes narrowing. "She wouldn't want me to back down on her account—and if she did, I couldn't do it. This is the biggest chance I've ever had to grab the Moon Man, here, right in headquarters. That's my job, and I've got to face it. I'm going to do my damndest to grab that crook. Steve— even at the risk of losing Sue."

He turned with fists clenched. His heels gritted hard over the cement which concealed the bait of the trap he was setting for the Moon Man. Cold despair filled Steve Thatcher as he watched McEwen, inexorably determined, tramp grimly up the iron stairs and out.

CHAPTER IV

HEARTBREAK HOSTAGE

THROUGHOUT THE next interminable day, Steve Thatcher and Gil McEwen remained at their posts, constantly hoping for a report that Sue McEwen had been found and was safe—but no word came. The cunning snatchers had left no clue to her hiding-place. They lurked under cover so deep that the searching hands of the police could not reach them. McEwen and Thatcher personally captained the relentless search without result. When evening lowered the girl was still the captive of the hidden killers.

It was nearing midnight when Steve Thatcher, anxiously approaching the door of the chief's office, heard McEwen's heels beating back and forth across the floor. Going in quietly, he found Mark Keanan slumped in a chair, face drawn with dread. McEwen paused, toothing a cigar, as Thatcher proffered a plain sealed envelope.

"A kid just brought it in, Gil. I questioned him, but all he could say was that some man on a downtown corner gave it to him to deliver. I let him go. It may be something important."

McEwen savagely ripped it open and drew out a folded sheet. His gray eyes sharpened at neatly typed lines. He stood rigid, furious red flooding his face, peering at a message signed with a cryptic symbol.

> *My dear McEwen:*
> I send this warning in the best faith, in the earnest hope that you will heed its every word.

The crooks headed by Tony Kroth and Nate Lorsh plan to return to headquarters sometime after midnight tonight for the buried loot. They will not stop at wholesale murder to get it. Their plan is made. They will carry bombs containing Lewisite, and efficient gas masks to protect themselves from the lethal effects. If any attempt is made to stop their operations, it will mean not only Sue McEwen's losing her life, but the death of scores of men in headquarters.

I am stating facts. Lewisite when properly spread in the air is one of the deadliest poison gasses known to chemical science. Only one part of it in ten million parts of air will render a man helpless in one minute. If he is exposed to its action for as long as two minutes, it means certain death. In warfare it is not regarded as highly as mustard gas, because rain completely destroys it by washing it out of the air, but tonight the crooks, if challenged, will use it inside a closed building. Kroth and Lorsh are determined to make use of their bombs at the slightest show of opposition. If they do, it will fill headquarters with corpses, and only the crooks will escape alive.

I urge you, McEwen, to make no attempt to stop them. Allow them to take their booty. You will have ample opportunity later to reclaim your daughter, find the loot, and capture the killers. Unless you do this—if you persist in your plan to trap them—it will mean an appalling tragedy.

M.M.

McEwen's teeth crackled in his cigar as he passed the letter to Steve Thatcher. Thatcher had no need to read it. He had written the warning, which only the Moon Man could raise, in the hope that it would conquer McEwen's determination. He realized, when he looked up into McEwen's gleaming eyes, that the attempt had failed.

"It's a trick!" the grizzled detective rasped. "The Moon Man knows the plan because he cooked it up himself. He's trying to bluff me into laying off. They won't dare fill this building with poison gas. I'm going ahead exactly as before."

Thatcher protested earnestly: "The Moon Man has never played you false, Gil. You've got to believe he's sincere—he means what he says. You can't go ahead now."

McEwen snarled: "My plan's all set."

Thatcher gestured desperately. "It's suicide, Gil. Their gas will kill Sue. It will be murder for everybody in the building—wholesale murder, exactly as the Moon Man says. Think of those men who'll be dropped by the gas—their families. Gil, you can't—"

"I can't stand by and permit a gang of cop-killers to invade headquarters!" McEwen roared. "I can't let 'em come in here and dig up two hundred grand in loot and get away with it! I'm a cop! Every man in this building is a cop. It's our job to try to stop 'em. You can't argue me out of it, Steve. I'm going through with it!"

Thatcher's shoulders sagged in despair.

"I've already appointed every man to a station. I thought of hiding a few in the furnaces, but that's too dangerous—they'd be trapped and killed without a chance of defending themselves. The whole furnace room is going to be cleared. Headquarters will apparently know nothing about what's going to happen, but every man will be ready to act when I give the signal. We're going to show those crooks the battle of their lives—and stop 'em!"

McEwen's teeth dug again into his cigar as his glare turned from Thatcher to Keanan and back. "We've got a special job, the three of us. The job of grabbing the Moon Man. Let him show himself! We'll shoot that glass mask off his head. We'll drop him on the spot. We'll collar that fancy crook so hard he'll never get away this time. If he comes into this building tonight, he'll be on his way to the chair!"

The hardened detective's shoulders drooped and a cloud of despair dimmed his eyes. "As for Sue—she's a cop's girl. She's got to face it with us. No matter if it costs her life, I can't let it stop us—I can't!"

THE TWO hours that passed, after Thatcher left McEwen in the chief's office, were an interminable period of torment.

In the small hours of the morning, a somnolent hush filled headquarters. Patrolmen played cards in the desk room while telephone calls flickered in and out of the switchboard. The men in the radio room twanged routine announcements to the squad cars prowling the city. The work of the police went drowsily on—while those in headquarters held themselves alertly ready for an alarm.

Steve Thatcher left his office and quietly descended two flights of stairs. The furnace room was dark and silent when he pushed into it. He peered up, at the two plugs of a sprinkler system in the ceiling, as he crossed to the outer door. When he opened it, a dark figure drifted from the alley. As a stocky, neckless man glided in, Thatcher closed the door.

"Okay, Boss," Dargan whispered.

A criminal for whom all the police of Great City were searching had slipped unseen into headquarters. Thatcher led him toward a row of furnaces. He opened one of the iron doors, intently studying Dargan's anxious face. He had telephoned Dargan during the evening, and mapped out the Angel's part in a desperate plan. Now he whispered:

"McEwen decided against putting any of his men in the furnaces, Angel—too dangerous. If you're spotted in there, you won't be able to get away from a bullet. It's almost suicide, but—"

"I'll chance it, Boss. All set!"

Thatcher helped Dargan crawl into the open door feet first. He crept far back into the firebox and squirmed around. Though he was invisible in the darkness, Thatcher pictured him facing the door gun in hand. He clicked the iron latch into place and opened the slide to give Dargan air. No hint of the Angel's presence remained as Thatcher climbed from the furnace room.

In the lower corridor he went to the door of the arsenal. It was stocked with cartridges, machine-guns, bullet-proof vests, rifles, tear-gas bombs. Thatcher took one of the rifles and left the door behind him. As he climbed to the second floor he heard McEwen's heels hammering again in the chief's office. He looked in, saw Keanan moving about nervously, and gestured. Keanan followed him back to the lower hall, to the entrance of the first-aid room near the street.

"Gil's still determined to go ahead, Steve," Keanan said in an anxious tone, "but I've got to admit I'm worried. The Moon Man wouldn't give us a false alarm. Hell, think what it'll mean if those killers throw their bombs!"

Thatcher nodded tensely. "We've got only one chance against the stuff, Mark. Rain washes it out of the air. In a closed building it will mean slaughter—unless we can start the sprinkler system operating. Take this rifle. Keep hidden in the first aid room. If the bombs break, aim at the sprinkler plugs on the ceiling—and hit every one!"

Keanan's eyes gleamed. "I've got it! But, Steve, you've given me an assignment! If the gas starts coming, and I fail to open the pipes, the stuff will kill everybody in the place!"

Thatcher said tightly: "You can't fail, Mark. No matter what happens, you've got to open those plugs."

He turned away. Pausing at the base of the stairs, he looked back to see that Keanan had gone into the first-aid room. It was dark and the door was standing slightly ajar. Assured that Keanan's position enabled him to survey the entire length of the lower corridor, Thatcher mounted to the chief's office.

McEwen's heels were still hammering. The slow-ticking clock on the wall indicated a few minutes past two. A subtle tension was tightening the air as the zero hour neared. Thatcher knew that all over headquarters, men were pretending to be casual and sleepy while in reality their nerves were snapping. Thatcher was filled with consuming anxiety as he watched the haggard McEwen tramp back and forth across the floor.

The tinkle of the telephone stopped McEwen short. He snatched up the instrument and hesitated with the receiver at his ear. He growled a hello and heard a whispering voice speak one ominous sentence: "Go down to the entrance now." He straightened, heart hammering, and thrust out the office.

THATCHER HURRIED at his side down the steps. Quick strides took them to the big street door. As McEwen gripped the handle, Thatcher glanced aside to make sure Keanan was still hidden in the darkness of the first-aid room. A quick pull and McEwen opened the way. With Thatcher at his side, he stared.

Two cars had drawn to the curb directly in front of the entrance. Six men and a girl had alighted from them—and all the men were masked with handkerchiefs. All were gripping automatics. Each was carrying a gas mask on a strap around his neck. One had a mongrel dog in his arms. They crowded at the door, the gloved hands of another holding the arms of Sue McEwen.

The girl's face shone white with terror in the light, but her chin was lifted, her eyes resolute. An automatic was pressed to her side. The man holding it had a finger snugly on the trigger. McEwen and Thatcher, gazing in cold dismay, knew that one quick jerk of the finger would send a bullet into Sue McEwen's body and instantly kill her. They stood frozen as a voice came from the mask below Tony Kroth's eyes.

"Take it easy, McEwen. Do exactly as I say. The instant you lift a finger against us, the girl dies."

Kroth stepped in. His five masked lieutenants entered behind him. Nate Lorsh, holding Sue McEwen's arm, kept his automatic thrust against her side. The glittering guns forced McEwen and Keanan back. Again the edged voice of Kroth sounded:

"More than that, McEwen, we're prepared to kill every man in headquarters if necessary. You see that our pockets are bulging. We're carrying dozens of bombs containing Lewisite, or Death Dew. In case you think we're bluffing, or if you doubt the power of the gas, you may witness a little demonstration that will prove we mean exactly what we say."

At Kroth's gesture, the one masked man lowered the mongrel. It ambled out the open door as another of Kroth's henchmen removed a small, gleaming glass sphere from his pocket. McEwen watched with furious fascination as the ball poised in midair and the dog trotted to the curb. Suddenly the bomb became a streak that ended in the gutter with a splattering sound. Cloudy fumes sprang up. The mongrel recoiled, tottered, then fell and lay still.

Kroth grated: "Instantly killed. That gas out there is being dissipated on the wind and will do no further harm—but it'll be quite different if we throw the bombs inside this building, McEwen. I intend to proceed at once with our plan. At the slightest interference, we'll use the bombs. You'll notice, too, that your daughter is not provided with a mask—nor will she be given any. Have I made myself perfectly clear?"

Sue McEwen, her eyes widened, whispered anxiously: "Don't let them stop you, dad."

McEwen straightened swiftly. His glare told Thatcher that now he realized the dread truth of the Moon Man's warning. He hesitated in a torment of consternation, trying to keep his aching eyes from Sue's white face. Thatcher saw his shoulders sag. He said in a low rasp:

"Go ahead!"

Kroth's eyes gleamed with evil triumph as he stepped back. He commanded his lieutenants: "To your places!" Immediately the masked men began a concerted move. The beating of their heels in the corridor brought blue-shirted patrolmen to the door of the desk room. They reached for their service gats, but subsided when McEwen snarled: "Let 'em alone!" McEwen went with Steve Thatcher along the hall, watching in outraged fascination the execution of a diabolical plan.

Nate Lorsh kept the automatic pressed to Sue McEwen's side and forced her toward the basement door. A man carrying two heavy picks went down behind them. Tony Kroth followed. Of the three who remained upstairs, one stationed himself directly in front of the arsenal door. Another stepped to the giant switchbox near the garage entrance and opened it, exposing the gleaming copper blades. A third climbed quickly to the second floor, and Thatcher saw him thrust into the radio room. A shot sounded, and a crash, before that man reappeared—and Thatcher knew the amplifying tube of the station was shattered, the antenna dead.

McEwen suppressed a snarl of rage as heavy, thumping sounds came up the basement stairs. Pick-points were already driving into the cement of the furnace room floor. A crackling noise meant that the hidden cavity containing the loot was being opened. The driving blows continued as McEwen stood rigid, his eyes gray ice.

The man at the switchbox drawled: "I wouldn't try going down there, McEwen. That'll start the bombs coming and put a bullet in your daughter's heart." His masked eyes shifted threateningly to Thatcher. "The same thing applies to you, and anybody else in headquarters. You haven't got a chance of stopping us. We'll walk out with the money over your dead bodies."

McEwen growled in a whisper that carried no farther than Thatcher's ears: "By damn, one shout'll bring every man in headquarters down on 'em! Every cop in the place is ready to rush 'em right now. I'm going to give 'em a chance to start out with the stuff. We'll try to get Sue clear, by damn—they can't scare me off!"

Thatcher looked intently along the corridor. The first-aid room was still dark. The door was still standing slightly ajar. Keanan was still inside with the rifle, waiting for the first spattering sound that would mean the breaking of a poison gas bomb. McEwen's grim whisper promised Thatcher that noise was certain to be heard—a tinkle of bursting glass that would bring clouding doom.

Thatcher's eyes turned on a masked man descending the stairs. His was the gun which had disabled the broadcasting equipment. His eyes shone with contemptuous triumph as he pushed through the door connecting with the garage. Thatcher exclaimed, "He's going to disable the cars!" The guns of the other two men in the corridor peered at him as he followed.

In a partitioned space in the far corner of the garage, a head-quarters mechanic was dozing in a chair. He did not stir as the masked man moved from car to car. Thatcher stood just inside the door, watching in dismay as Kroth's lieutenant opened the hoods of the police machines, snapped the covers off the distributor boxes, and dropped the distributor-arms into his pocket. He left each machine unable to function. He was working with cool efficiency near the broad street doors when Thatcher drifted quietly into the darkness at the rear.

Thatcher glided to the side of his roadster. He turned a key in the lock of the rumble compartment. He reached into the black hollow and removed a black bundle. During the evening he had ventured back to the empty store beside the old Shipper's Restaurant. He had found the robe and mask of the Moon Man still hidden beneath the wooden box. Now, clutching the precious regalia under his arm, he silently opened a rear door of the garage and slipped into the open space in back of it

Lights flashed in the furnace room as he shook the black robe over his shoulders. The sound of driving picks continued as he pulled on the black gloves. Loot which had lain hidden for eight years was being brought to the surface while he fitted the shining silver mask over his head. The Moon Man stole silently toward the rear entrance of the room where the girl he loved was held hostage, where lay two hundred thousand dollars that he had marked for his own.

THE MOON MAN'S globular head glittered in the flashing light shining through the door. He saw two masked men opening the cavity in the cement floor, pulling up the crusted bundle. He saw Tony Kroth straighten with it, eyes gleaming with triumph. Near the door, Nate Lorsh was still gripping Sue McEwen's arm, still pressing the automatic at her side.

Kroth ordered: "Start out!"

The Moon Man's thrust cracked the muzzle of his automatic through the pane of the furnace room door. The noise spun Kroth and jerked Lorsh's eyes. The shafts of their lights stabbed at the entrance. The Moon Man's black-sleeved arm reached inward as he took swift, careful aim.

Three times his gun fountained flame. Three slugs whined to their mark. Nate Lorsh staggered back with his arm spurting red. His automatic twirled from his paralyzed fingers as Kroth fired. The bullet cracked into the door while the Moon Man sprang in. His muffled voice commanded:

"Up, Sue! Quick!"

Kroth's light clattered down. His hand flashed to his coat pocket. The Moon Man whirled away from the beam of light on the broken floor as Kroth's gun splashed fire again. Then a softer sound—the musical tinkle of breaking glass. A shining ball spattered to bits on the cement and misty vapor clouded up.

At the first crack of the Moon Man's gun, the door of one of the furnaces had clicked open. Ned Dargan, lying prone, a revolver in one hand and a torch in the other, had thrust it open. He peered in terror at the swelling fog as another and another of the glass bombs burst. He aimed with grim certainty at a man he could scarcely see. He fired four times in rapid succession—and howled with wild joy.

Water sprayed from the bullet-broken sprinkler plugs. It spilled down the walls, spattered on the floor, rained on the men and the girl in the room. Drops trickled over the surface of the Moon Man's mask, confusing his vision in the uncertain light, as he sprang toward the furnace that concealed Dargan. Guns clashed again through the downpour as swift steps sounded on the iron stairs.

The Moon Man gasped: "Outside, Angel!" He sped through the lashing shower toward Sue McEwen.

"Up!" he commanded again. She hurried at his side toward the metal steps while crashing fire sounded above.

The muffled reports from the furnace room had signaled a desperate attack by Kroth's masked henchmen. At the same instant they had gone into action. The gloved hand of the guard at the switchbox pulled the master switch open. Darkness flooded the corridor, alleviated only by the faint glow from the street, as the other masked man at the arsenal door fired a slug at the lock to jam it. Blinding torches played through the blackness in the hands of the killers while gun-flame streaked at McEwen and the scattering patrolmen.

Spattering glass! Glass bombs flew through the gloom. Splintering fragments spilled from the walls and the floor. The streaking beams of the torches cut through rising clouds of fumes. A sharp pungency, promising swift doom, sprang into the air as Mark Keanan shouldered desperately out of the first-aid room. He raised the rifle and howled:

"Lights up! Lights on the ceiling!"

No headquarters man comprehended the command. The killers' torches swung across scattering patrolmen. The blue-shirted men sprang toward the exits with service gats gripped in their hands. The fog rapidly grew thicker. In the misty gleam, grotesque figures moved—men whose faces were fat and brown, with long, tubular noses. Kroth's lieutenants had affixed their masks. The lethal vapor mounted as Keanan, forced to depend on the crooks' own lights, frantically raised his rifle.

CRACKING REPORTS echoed through the sound of running feet. Bursting concussions shook the ceiling. A sprinkler plug flew to bits and water cascaded. Keanan fired again and a second outlet streamed. He was aiming for a third desperate shot when the torches of the masked men swung upon him. His rifle opened another plug as killer guns stabbed at him. He sagged, groaning, and dropped in a pelting rain.

McEwen's voice rasped: "Keep 'em in!"

His torch whipped toward the basement door. He was groping through the sluicing downpour, when a startling gleam of silver shone in his light. He peered dumbfounded at Sue McEwen running up the stairs. Behind her he glimpsed a black phantom figure with a globular head. His torch kept on the shining ball and he aimed with grim certainty as he blurted:

"The Moon Man!"

The crack of the Moon Man's gun preceded McEwen's by an instant. His bullet whined over Sue McEwen's shoulder. It drove straight to the glaring lens of her father's torch. The beam vanished when the Moon Man's slug tore the tube from McEwen's hand. A black-gloved fist smashed McEwen's face as a ghostly figure rushed past.

"The Moon Man! Stop the Moon Man! He's heading into the garage!"

A swinging beam flickered on the Moon Man's silver head as he thrust desperately through the connecting door. He vanished in darkness while McEwen plunged toward him. The downpour from the open valves was drenching the whole length of the corridor. Spitting gun-flames lighted the storm of water. It lashed in McEwen's eyes as he flung himself through the door into the black garage.

"Close him in! The Moon Man's here!"

McEwen's planned strategy had sent blue-shirted men running to cover every possible way out of headquarters. At the first fusillade, six of them had sprung into the garage. Three had closed the street doors and stationed themselves in front of it. Two others had hurried to the entrance at the rear. Another was guarding the exit McEwen sped through. No rain was falling inside the big room, an unearthly darkness filled it.

"Use your lights! Find the Moon Man!"

Dazzling shafts swung across the cars. Looming shadows twisted on the walls as McEwen raced between the lanes. He jerked a flashlight from one of the men at the street entrance and returned with its shaft slashing the gloom like a sword. He paused as a voice called out of the far corner:

"Okay, Gil! I'm closing in from this side!"

McEwen rushed on. Loping along the rear wall, he came face to face with Steve Thatcher. Thatcher whirled at the rear of McEwen's coupé and hurried along the inner wall. McEwen trotted back in the opposite direction. When he came to a stop in the cleared space in the center of the big room, Thatcher came toward him.

"He's not here, Gil!"

"He's got to be somewhere in here! I saw him come in! He couldn't possibly get out!" He howled at the men with the torches: "One cop at each door—that's enough! The rest of you look for him! I tell you, by damn, we've got him trapped!"

Steve Thatcher smiled wryly as the patrolmen scattered, and followed McEwen to the connecting door. When they pushed through, blinding light flooded the hallway. A patrolman had reached the switchbox and thrust the master control home. Bulbs gleamed in streaming water. Cascades still poured from the open sprinkler vents as McEwen and Thatcher hurried toward the girl standing in a paralysis of anxiety at the base of the stairs.

"You all right. Sue?" her father gasped.

She whispered: "I'm all right!" as she gazed with unbounded relief at Steve Thatcher. She flung herself into his arms with an irresistible impulse. He whispered, "All safe, darling—all safe." His gesture sent her up the stairs as he turned to hurry after McEwen.

The grizzled detective was hurrying toward the basement stairs. A blue-shirted man, wet to the skin, was hastening up to them with a torch. He stumbled to a stop and gasped at McEwen:

"They dug the stuff out of the floor! It's gone. One of 'em's got it!"

McEwen grimly turned back. Blue-shirted men were still stationed at the doors, water spilling over them, their guns leveled through the downpour. The ring of steel enclosed three criminals who cowered in the rain, two more who lay motionless on the floor while drops pelted over them. Tony Kroth had torn off his grotesque mask. His lips curled viciously as he snarled at McEwen:

"The Moon Man got that money!"

The glint of McEwen's eyes hardened as he turned toward the garage door. He was reaching for the knob when it opened. The patrolman who shouldered in stared as though at a ghost He said in a husky whisper:

"He's not in there, Gil—not the Moon Man! He melted away into thin air!"

McEWEN DREW up. He saw Mark Keanan braced against the wall near the first-aid room, blood soaking through his shirt, gripping a rifle, grinning wildly. He tramped to Keanan, quickly examined the painful flesh wound. Keanan sighed: "It worked, thanks to Steve! Am I glad I shot straight!" McEwen growled as he turned away and glared again at the captured crooks.

"Throw 'em into cells! Every one of those rats is going to the chair!"

The streams of water from the sprinkler vents diminished as someone spun the main valve. The patrolmen's shoes sloshed as they herded the living killers toward the cell tiers and carried the dead pair into the locker room. McEwen pushed through into the garage while Steve Thatcher gave commands that restored some degree of order to headquarters. After a few tight minutes McEwen tramped back, stopped, glared and snapped:

"By damn! By damn! I'm taking Sue home."

The girl's cold hand closed snugly on Steve Thatcher's arm as he took her into the garage. One of the patrolmen had reclaimed the distributor-arms from the pocket of the dead Novik. One was fitted into McEwen's coupé, another into Thatcher's roadster. Before McEwen took the wheel he snarled at the patrolmen who were still searching:

"Listen! The Moon Man came in here, and he couldn't get out. He grabbed a bundle containing two hundred thousand dollars, and he's either ditched it somewhere or keeping it with him. He's flesh and blood, and that loot's cold cash. Neither of 'em can melt into thin air. Keep on looking till you find that crook and that money!"

As he ducked to his daughter's side he growled: "They won't find a thing, by damn—not a thing!" Sue shivered in her wet dress while McEwen put his coat around her. His hands gripped the wheel tightly as he swung into the street. The girl, glancing back, saw Steve Thatcher's roadster following, and smiled softly.

"You hate the Moon Man, don't you dad—even though he kept me safe. You're just as determined as ever to get him—even though he made the capture of those men possible. Nothing will ever stop you."

"I've sworn to send the Moon Man to the chair," McEwen grated, "and by damn, some day I'm going to do it!"

McEwen and Sue were just hurrying into their house from the garage when Thatcher parked at the curb. Thatcher had stopped to call Dargan, was reassured that he'd gotten away unharmed while the prowl cars were helpless.

McEwen saw a strangely joyful smile on his daughter's lips. He stood frowning, baffled, as his daughter went into the arms of the man she was going to marry. She whispered a good-night and ran up the stairs. Thatcher, returning to the entrance, said quietly:

"Better stay with her, Gil. She's pretty upset. I'll go back to headquarters to help mop up."

"Steve," McEwen said gravely, "you saved a good many lives tonight. Keanan told me opening the sprinkler plugs was your idea. We've cracked us a case! Between the two of us and—"

"And the Moon Man," Thatcher said smiling. "All due credit to him, Gil."

McEwen exploded. "By damn! I'm stumped. It just isn't possible—but he did it. Whether he helped bag those crooks or not, the day's going to come when I'll nail him!"

Thatcher murmured: "I'm sure of it, Gil." He closed the door as he went out. In the gloom of the garage he twisted the handle of the luggage space at the rear of McEwen's coupé. Out of the darkness he brought two wet bundles.

Steve Thatcher drove from the relentless detective's home with a fortune in loot for the needy and the even more precious regalia of the Moon Man.

ROBE OF
BLOOD

CHAPTER I

FLAME TRAP

IN THE darkness a black figure moved with ghostly silence. It drifted along a hallway. It melted through a door. It glided across the luxurious library and paused in front of a bookcase. It stood in the faint glow filtering through the heavily draped windows—a dark-robed being whose head was a mottled sphere of silver—the Moon Man.

Somewhere below—in one of the rooms of the two lower floors—a clock gonged twelve. Midnight.

The black-gloved hands of the Moon Man gripped the section of shelf. He swung it outward on concealed hinges. His globular head glimmered as he stooped in front of an inset safe. He thrust at the handle and found the steel door locked, but a chuckle sounded inside his glass mask. Locks meant nothing to the Moon Man. He intended to open this safe with the magic of his fingers and escape as noiselessly as he had come—with thousands as his loot.

This was the huge, magnificent home of Andrew Latham—socialite, sportsman, financier.

The black fingers of the Moon Man carefully turned the combination dial. The spherical shell enclosing his head looked opaque as a mirror from the outside, but the notorious criminal could see through the Argus glass as clearly as though it did not exist. He intently watched the revolving circle of bright steel—until, suddenly, breath whizzing past the deflector inside his mask, automatic gripped, he jerked erect.

A muffled concussion had shocked through the house. While the Moon Man stood alert, silver head twinkling in the glow, the floor quaked and the walls trembled. The muted force had come from somewhere below, jarring doors in their frames, rattling the windows. It struck once, giving no hint of its nature—and silence followed.

Warily listening, his nerves drawn tight, the Moon Man turned back to the safe. He twisted the combination dial again, with the utmost care. As he worked he sensed a strange agitation in the air. When only one more revolution of the dial would open the safe he rose, heart pounding with dread. A strange fluttering sound, a faint crackling, whispered a warning of danger—and suddenly the Moon Man knew.

Fire!

His black robe rustled as he crossed the library. A gasp of dismay sighed inside his glass mask as his black-gloved hand drew the door open. The darkness of the hallway had disappeared. It was filled with a bright yellow flicker, a thickening mist of smoke. Flames were dancing on the stairs. The gleam shone on the silver head of the Moon Man as he poised—but suddenly he whirled back.

Consternation quickened his moves as he returned to the safe. His pulse pounding, he carefully gave the combination dial its last turn. The pungency of the smoke was penetrating the library when he gripped the steel handle. He thrust it down, swung the black slab wide open. His gloved hands reached into the safe—and stopped. He crouched motionless, staring through the sheen of his mask—at nothing.

The safe was empty.

A quick sound in the hallway jerked the Moon Man upright. He spun, automatic leveled, as footfalls hurried to the library door. The knob rattled—and his breath stopped. The door flashed open—and his automatic lifted. He stood in the wavering light of the flames, a black phantom figure without a face, peering at the man who came to a sharp standstill in the doorway.

Abruptly the lean silhouette leaped backward. The door stopped swinging within three inches of the latch while a claw hand groped inward. A metallic click echoed through the snarling of the flames before it slammed shut—then a clatter. Again, his robe flapping, the Moon Man moved swiftly. He sprang to the door, seized the knob—and froze.

It was locked.

In the fluttering glare and the suffocating smoke in the hall the emaciated man backed. His evil eyes gleamed when he saw that the rear stairway was impassable with gushing flame. He whirled to the front of the house, protecting his malicious face with his arms as he plunged through the billowing fumes. He stumbled down two flights and leaped through a wall of fire. He sped into a fogged room with a crazy laugh breaking from his ugly lips.

He snatched up the telephone and spun the dial to zero. He choked into the transmitter: "Police—connect me with the police!" Recoiling from the withering heat as the connection clicked through, he sputtered over the line:

"The Latham place is on fire! The Moon Man set it! He's in the library on the third floor now—locked in—trapped! The Moon Man!"

IN THE chief's office in police headquarters Gilbert McEwen, ace sleuth of the plainclothes division, relentless hunter of crooks and sworn nemesis of the Moon Man, was working late. Sue McEwen, his very personable daughter, was waiting patiently for him to complete his routine tasks so that she might drive him home. They looked up as fast footfalls beat toward the door.

Mark Keanan, detective sergeant, as doggedly determined to capture the Moon Man as McEwen, thrust in to blurt wide-eyed: "Grab that phone, Gil! Something about the Moon Man being trapped! Latham place burning—and he's in it!"

McEwen gripped the phone as Sue's eyes flashed alarm. She rose in consternation as a husky voice sounded in her father's ear. His hands went white on the instrument when he heard:

"He's the blaze bug you're lookin' for—the Moon Man! I saw him sneak onto the Latham place a little while ago. He set it on fire, but he's trapped himself. Third floor—he can't get down. You can grab him if you make it fast!"

McEwen sprang from the desk as the connection broke. Striding into the hall he rasped at Keanan: "Flash the prowl cars in Section G to surround the Latham place!" Sue hurried anxiously after him as he headed down the stairs. "The Moon Man's in that house!" He bounded with a rasping: "Orders to shoot him on sight if he tries to slip away!" Jaw clamped, fists clenched, he charged into the garage while Sue McEwen, face white with dismay, hastened with him.

She slipped into a police sedan while McEwen ducked under the wheel. "By damn, this time I'm grabbing that fancy crook!" Steely eyes gleaming, he whirled the car into the street. "He's gone too far this time—turning into a filthy fire-bug!" Hammering the horn-button, he jammed the accelerator all the way down. "I've sworn a thousand times to get the Moon Man—and this time I'm going to do it!"

The sky above the Latham place was red with the glare of flames. Sparks were fountaining high, misting over the surrounding estates. Yellowish smoke was clouding into the zenith. The blaze was flooding a garish gleam along the boulevard. McEwen shot his car into it while Sue McEwen, made speechless by a dread she could not utter, stared aghast at the flame-wrapped house.

McEwen's radio alarm had whipped the efficient police organization into swift action. Squad cars had turned off their peaceful tours of Section G to rush toward the Latham home with sirens screaming. Two were already standing empty at the gate while uniformed men, guns in hand, skirmished across the flame-lighted lawn. A third whirled into sight like a wailing banshee as McEwen slammed to a stop at the curb. Frozen with despair, the girl hurried onto the grounds with her father—gazing appalled at flames and fumes pouring from every window of the mansion.

"No sign of him yet, lieutenant!" one of the squadmen gasped to McEwen as he sped past. "If he was in that place when we caught the alarm, he's still there!"

"Watch every way out!" the grizzled veteran snarled. "He can't stay in there. He's got to show himself or get burned to death!"

Sue McEwen stood paralyzed, her red lips parted in anguish, her face deathly white, while the patrolmen scattered to strategic positions. She scarcely heard the shrieking and the clanging as the fire trucks sped into the drive. She gave no glance to the rubber-coated men who howled frantic commands as they whipped hoses into action. Her aching eyes remained fixed on the glaring windows of the third floor, and a name broke from her dry throat:

"Steve! Steve!"

The snaking hoses fattened. White water shot to the flaming walls. A deafening hiss mingled with the roaring of the fire as the plumes of spray waved in the glare. Steam mixed with the clouding fumes. Helmeted men desperately drove axes at locked doors. While the fire-fighters made an organized attack, and the prowl car men kept their post around the grounds, a florid-faced man hurried to McEwen to blurt:

"Moon Man in there? He hasn't got a chance, McEwen!" Chief Rankin's narrowed eyes noted the negligible effect of the thundering streams. "That house is going down to the foundations! We can't save it now!"

A howling voice carried through the rumble: "On the roof! Somebody on the roof!"

McEwen's sharp eyes had glimpsed the black flutter of movement above the dormer windows. He stood rigid, his leathery face a grim mask, watching. He saw something black whipping in the wind. He saw a bright spot, shining through the sheeting fumes—a round object with a glassy gleam. He snagged his service gat into his hand as he grated through the turmoil:

"That's his mask! That's the Moon Man on the roof!"

SUE McEWEN had come to her father's side. Her one trembling hand gripped his arm as her appalled gaze clung to the ghostly thing on the roof. The sight held her speechless with despair, but it urged Gil McEwen into a desperate run toward the flaming entrance of the house.

Chief Rankin spurted after McEwen. He clutched the grizzled veteran's arm. They stumbled to a stop in blasting heat, while the swinging hoses whipped rain over him. His voice scarcely audible in the bedlam, the fire chief roared:

"Hold on, McEwen! Where do you think you're going? The whole house is coming down!"

McEwen snarled: "I'm going up to the roof! I'm going to drag the Moon Man down."

"That's suicide!"

The gleam in McEwen's eyes belittled the warning. He snapped: "Listen, chief! For three years I've been trying to learn who the Moon Man is. If the fire gets him, I'll never find out. Nothing's going to cheat me now! I'm going up there!"

He twisted his arm from Rankin's grasp. He broke into a crazy run toward a door that was framed in flame. As he plunged into the blinding glare, shielding his face with his arms, the fire chief spun to bellow at the nearest hose crew: "Cover him! Shoot it through the door—up the stairs!"

McEwen flung himself into the vestibule and stumbled to a stop in the blasting heat. Then he staggered—lurched forward as the force of the hose struck him. The stream hissed around him, drenching him as it played up the smoking stairs. Brackish water came cascading down as McEwen started up. He drove himself like a madman into the heart of the inferno while Chief Rankin's howling orders gave him the only possible protection from a horrible death.

He passed from sight. A moan broke from Sue McEwen's lips at that moment. It was echoed by the despairing patrolmen at their stations, by the hose crews who shifted to beat the flames from McEwen's probable path as best they could. They played their streams blindly through the broken windows, over the stairs, into the halls, onto the roof. Storming water beat upon the doomed dwelling—but McEwen could not be seen.

The lashing spray blackened the area of the roof where the glassy gleam had been seen. A gust of wind tore away the curtain of flame and smoke. It revealed again the fluttering black robe and the shining sphere, but only for a moment. Then again the fire and the fumes leaped high with a savage roar—while smarting eyes watched for McEwen to reappear.

A sudden shout: "He's made it!"

"He's on the roof!"

Through the gusting steam McEwen's figure was dimly visible. He was crawling through a broken dormer window, perilously bracing himself against the gutter of the sloping roof. At Rankin's order, rubber-coated men rushed close with a spread net—but McEwen did not drop. He clung grimly and climbed. Gun in hand, he pulled himself toward the black robe fluttering in the hot wind—and again he disappeared.

Sue McEwen watched in torture while the fire-fighters played their hoses around the spot where McEwen had vanished. An eternity of agonized uncertainty passed while the flames rumbled and the water hissed. A hoarse shout greeted a new flicker of movement on the roof. Sue glimpsed her father climbing down—and the glassy thing was coming with him.

McEwen did not hear the urgent shouts of the firemen below—frantic entreaties to jump into the net. He fell in through the flaming window. The glare blotted him out—and again Sue McEwen waited in terror. Unconsciously she went closer, looking up the flaming stairs—and suddenly a hysterically glad cry broke from her lips. Chief Rankin's bellow once more turned the hoses above the entrance:

"He's coming out!"

McEwen stumbled into the open. He tottered to a stop with his clothing steaming, his burned hair matted, his eyebrows singed away, his skin shining a painful red—and under his arm a white spherical object gleamed. His eyes ran tears as he drew clean, cool air into his lungs. Men hastened to support him—and Sue McEwen, stunned, speechless, gazed dumbfounded at one of them.

McEwen gasped: "That wasn't the Moon Man on the roof! It's another of his tricks! He slipped out before we got here—and left this! *This* is what I thought was the Moon Man!"

It was the spherical globe of a ceiling light fixture.

The young man at McEwen's side urged anxiously: "Steady, Gil. You're all right. You got out again—that's more important than anything else."

Sue McEwen whispered: "Steve!"

In consternation and despair she gazed at the young man she was engaged to marry. For she knew-as her father did not—that her fiancé, Stephen Thatcher, detective sergeant and son of the chief of police, was the notorious criminal known as the Moon Man.

CHAPTER II

MOON MAN'S WARNING

GIL McEWEN'S eyes glittered dangerously as he tramped into the chief's office. His suit was charred and sodden, but he ignored the chill discomfort. His face was smeared with an unguent salve and his hands were bandaged, but he gave no thought to the stinging pain. He coughed as he spoke, but the fumes he had breathed did not impair the rasping determination of his voice:

"Get Andrew Latham on the wire, wherever he is!" His jabbing forefinger directed the command at Mark Keanan. "I'm going to grill hell out of him right here in this office. I'll get at the bottom of this thing, by damn—and the Moon Man's going to get the works!"

He growled a greeting to the kindly-faced old man seated at an ancient rolltop desk in the corner—Chief Peter Thatcher—and paced the office. His teeth crushed into an unlighted cigar. His squinting eyes shone with ferocious anger as the chief began: "You've got to take it easy, Gil. You ought to be in a hospital instead of back on the job. We've got the dragnet out, and if we pick up the Moon Man—"

"I'm on the job and I'm sticking, chief!" McEwen snapped. "The Moon Man has stooped to one of the most contemptible crimes on the books—arson. As long as I can stand on my feet, by damn, I'm going to do my best to grab him!"

Sue McEwen had returned to headquarters with her father. In the turmoil at the Latham estate she had had no opportu-

61

nity to speak to Steve Thatcher. He had taken command of the squad car men while McEwen abandoned the place. White-faced, a wild determination shining in her eyes, she watched McEwen jerk to a stop at the jangle of the telephone.

Chief Thatcher answered the call. His grave face hardened as he listened. The kindliness left his eyes as he made monosyllabic answers. When he broke the connection he told McEwen with a vehement rasp:

"Chief Rankin has found two bodies in the ruins of the Latham place—both women. They were probably asleep in bed when the fire broke out, and were trapped." He passed his blue-veined hand across his heavy-jowled face in a gesture of revulsion. "The Moon Man's gone too far this time, Gil. We've got to do everything possible to make him pay for that. The chair's too good for him."

To the ears of the horrified Sue McEwen, the chief was really saying: "We've got to do everything possible to make Steve Thatcher pay for that. The chair's too good for my only son." That's what he'd be saying had he known Steve was the Moon Man.

Gil McEwen was reaching for the telephone, grimly intent on reiterating his orders to the prowl cars that were searching the city for the Moon Man, when the bell again jangled. He snarled a "Hello?" into the transmitter—and paled. His bandaged hands clamped on the instrument as he heard a muffled voice speak calmly over the line:

"This is the Moon Man speaking, McEwen."

Instantly McEwen cupped the transmitter. His eyes gleamed like burnished metal at the connecting door as it opened. As Mark Keanan stepped in he growled: "Trace this call! Make it fast, Mark! It's the Moon Man!" Keanan, with a blurted exclamation, whirled back. Sue McEwen saw him reaching for another telephone before the door closed. She stood paralyzed with terror as McEwen said over the line, forcing his voice to seem casual:

"What's the name? I didn't quite get it."

"On the contrary, McEwen," the muffled voice answered, "you understood me distinctly. You are playing time in order to have this call traced. I don't mind telling you I'm using a downtown pay station. My message will be completed, and I will be well on my way, long before you can get your men here. I have important information, McEwen. Listen carefully."

McEwen's teeth drove deep into his cigar.

"I am aware you believe I set the Latham house afire tonight—that I'm the master mind of the gang of arsonists who are operating in the city. It's not true, McEwen. I have no connection with that pack of rats. Tonight, however, I saw one of the guilty men. He is the crook named Lenny Dickler. Arrest him, McEwen, sweat a confession out of him—and your arson case will be cracked. Please believe in my sincerity."

McEwen was listening to the voice of a man who had committed innumerable robberies in the city. He had, besides, presented evidence to the Grand Jury which had resulted in the Moon Man's being indicted for three kidnapings and a murder. In the entire nation McEwen believed there was no more infamous criminal than the man who was speaking to McEwen now.

Again and again the Moon Man had materialized in the dead of night, wearing his black robe and his globular mask, in daring defiance of the police. Month after month the relentless McEwen had trailed him—in vain. The Moon Man had repeatedly escaped McEwen's traps, until the very name of the crook had become anathema to the veteran detective. For the Moon Man McEwen held a consuming enmity which could never die.

He said tightly: "Listen, Mr. Moon Man. I don't trust a word you utter. You've become a sneaking, contemptible firebug, and you're attempting to shift your guilt onto an innocent man. I won't fall for that! You're the man I want—you're the man I'm going to get. I've promised it a thousand times, and I promise it again—I'm not going to stop, by damn, until I see you die in the electric chair!"

IN A telephone booth a few blocks from police headquarters, Steve Thatcher listened to McEwen's grim pronouncement of doom. A click on the line told him the connection was broken. A chill gathered around his heart as he shouldered out. He was filled with an urge to repeat his warning, but he knew McEwen would not answer, that to remain here would invite capture. He left the drug store hurriedly and strode grimly toward the turreted headquarters building.

When he climbed the worn wooden stairs he saw Sue McEwen entering his office. She turned upon him as he went in, a fierce light shining in her eyes that he had never seen before. She gazed at him silently, her small hands closed into fists, while he closed the door. He asked in dismay:

"You don't think I did it, Sue! You can't believe I set the Latham place afire. I was there when—"

"I don't think that, Steve." She spoke in a strained tone. "I know you didn't. But—nothing like that must ever happen again."

He said quietly: "You know why I've done it all, darling— you've known from the beginning."

She knew that Steve Thatcher had become the Moon Man in the cause of human mercy. She knew he had defied the law only in order to help those who must have assistance or perish. He had stolen only ill-gotten money, from the selfish and the profligate, and had distributed every cent of his loot among the poor. But she knew, too, that in the eyes of her father this could never make a difference—that someday the Moon Man must pay the penalty for his crimes.

"I didn't dream Gil would go into the building, Sue," Thatcher explained anxiously. "I put the globe and the robe on the roof only to give myself time to get clear before the dragnet closed in. Gil was already inside before I got back. I would have stopped him if—"

"He might—might never have come out." Sue's red lips trembled as her eyes challenged Thatcher's. "He's like that, Steve—nothing can stop him from trying to get the Moon Man. But that—that's only part of what I'm thinking of. I'm thinking of what it will do to all of us, if ever you're found out."

Steve Thatcher knew all too well it would mean tragedy. The revelation that his son was the Moon Man would break the heart of the kindly old chief. It would crush even the hard-shelled McEwen. It would destroy all the dreams of happiness Thatcher shared with the girl he loved. It would mean dis-honor—and death in the electric chair for a murder he had not committed.

Sue's hands closed hotly on Thatcher's. "It's not worth it, Steve! I can't let you keep on running such frightful risks. Tonight you were almost caught, and dad might have been killed. Darling—this has to be the end of the Moon Man."

Thatcher's lips pinched. "Sue, dear, you know there are hun-dreds of people who must have money in order to keep from starving—and the Moon Man is the only one who helps them. What will become of them if I stop? If it weren't that circum-stances force me to keep it up—"

The girl interrupted softly: "Aren't you thinking too much of them, Steve, and too little of—you and me?"

The anguish in Sue's eyes made Thatcher painfully silent. He studied her drawn face a long moment before he asked: "What do you want, Sue?"

"I want the Moon Man to disappear, and never be seen again, Steve." As he hesitated, her words rushed: "I know you'll give your promise, as you have before—and I know you'll sincerely try to keep it—but something will come up to force you to break it. It's because you're so unselfish and so loyal to those who look to you for help, but I can't let it destroy everything we have together, Steve. This time, instead, I—I'm going to make you a promise."

Thatcher asked gently: "Yes, Sue?"

"If you ever put on the robe and mask of the Moon Man again, Steve, I'll never marry you—never."

Tears glimmered in her eyes as she jerked the door open. A sob broke from her lips as she ran from the office. Steve Thatcher stood stricken, his haggard eyes following her, as she hurried down the stairs without a backward glance.

DETERMINATION THINNED Thatcher's lips as an earnest decision formed in his mind—a decision that the Moon Man had passed out of existence. He strode toward the stairs, intent on giving his assurance to the girl he loved but he paused at the sound of McEwen's rasping voice. The grim words that penetrated the chief's door and stopped him were:

"You paid the Moon Man to set your place afire, Latham! That's the truth, and by damn I'm going to get it out of you!"

Thatcher's lips quirked bitterly as he turned back. The chief's office was silent when he entered. McEwen, his teeth driven into an unlighted cigar, was standing with bandaged hands clenched. A tall man with an unruly shock of gray hair, whose face was working with anxiety, flinched before the detective's savage glare. Thatcher stood by quietly as Andrew Latham huskily answered:

"You're going too far, Lieutenant McEwen—charging me with—"

"All right!" McEwen's knuckles clicked on the desk. "I'm stating a fact when I say two women died in that fire tonight. It started so suddenly and went through the house so fast they didn't have a chance to save themselves. That fire wasn't an accident. It was deliberately set, and the man who set it is responsible for two deaths. Who were those women, Latham?"

Latham mumbled: "This is all a horrible surprise to me, lieutenant. I was at my club, you know, when it happened. I thought the house was empty. It was the servants' night off, but the two maids must have stayed there for some reason. I can't understand how they—"

"That means plenty!" McEwen snarled. "The fire happening when you thought nobody was in the place. You didn't count on that where you made your bargain with the arsonists, did you, Latham? You didn't think you were making yourself an accomplice to the crime of homicide."

Latham feebly attempted a protest. "Look here. I resent your tone. I'm a respectable citizen. You can't bully me—"

"Resent it all you please!" McEwen snapped. "You've been keeping up a front, Latham. Your business is all shot, but you've managed to cover that up. Your stable of racing horses has eaten into your reserve, but you haven't dared let them go because it would reflect on your financial and social standing. You've borrowed up to the limit. You've been living with your back to the wall. You took desperate measures tonight, didn't you, Latham?"

Latham swallowed hard.

"You hooked up with the arsonist gang—the same gang that's been setting fires in this city for weeks. A pack of filthy, sneaking vandals. You paid them to set your house afire so you can collect the heavy insurance. You thought it would give you a new start financially, but it's put you on the spot, Latham. You're going to answer for the deaths of those two women!"

Latham mumbled: "I've a right to call my lawyer. You can't question me like this without—"

"Call every lawyer in the city if you like!" McEwen raged. "I'm going to get you absolutely cold. Do you think a house can be fired like that without traces being left? Arson investigators are pretty damn clever! When they get through poking through the ashes, they'll be able to say exactly where that fire started, and how. There'll be enough evidence to send you to prison for life. I'll see you go there, Latham—unless you talk!"

Latham's eyes bulged.

"That gang of fire-bugs you hired—they're sneaking, contemptible cowards!" McEwen pressed on. "They've not only destroyed millions in property, but human lives. I'm out to get them and I'll never stop till I do. You've got one chance of beating the rap, Latham—just one. Talk! Tell me the truth! Give me a statement that the Moon Man is the head of that gang of arsonists!"

Steve Thatcher's throat went dry as he watched Latham. Latham's lips twisted painfully. He winced before the savage glare of McEwen. He made a gesture of utter despair and answered huskily:

"I—I was insane to think of such a thing, I guess. I didn't realize—" He straightened with an effort. "Very well, McEwen. I'll give you a written confession. I'll tell you everything I know."

McEwen began exultantly: "Start talking right now. By damn, and—"

A splintering report stopped his words. His surprised gaze jerked to the window. In the pane he saw a neat round hole, rimmed with white, that had not been there before. His wide eyes darted back to Latham, and he saw Latham looking bewildered. There was a growing spot of red just over Latham's heart. McEwen grabbed at his service gat and Steve Thatcher started forward in dismay at the same instant—and at that instant Latham fell.

A murdered man sprawled down in the office of the chief of police!

CHAPTER III

MURDER HUNT

McEWEN SLAMMED the window up. While Steve Thatcher stooped above the fallen man, McEwen ducked his head out. His Police Positive swung toward a flash of movement in a dark window across the street. It vanished as swiftly as he glimpsed it—but McEwen fired. The report was clattering up and down the startled thoroughfare as he whirled back to rasp:

"Come on, Steve!"

He charged out of the office, bounded down the stairs, shouldered past blue-shirted men who were crowding up. Thatcher sped after him out the entrance. Their commands rang sharply as amazed patrolmen hurried after them. McEwen raced directly to the door of the rooming house opposite the chief's office with Thatcher at his heels.

"Get around back! Watch the alley!"

McEwen's order sent his men sprinting around the corner with guns drawn. He glanced up, saw the open window was on the third floor, thrust into a musty hallway. His revolver pierced through the murky yellow light as he took the stairs four at a jump. Eyes gleaming slits, he strode straight to a closed door. His heel cracked against it. As it slapped open McEwen leaped through.

His swift glance caught a rifle lying on the floor near the open window. Except for a single chair, the room was empty. Crushed cigarette butts on the floor testified that a killer had waited long hours in this room while watching the chief's office. McEwen whirled to a connecting door, shouldered it open, tramped through another deserted room to another open window. He looked across the platform of a fire escape, into a bleak yard where patrolmen were skirmishing, and snapped:

"He's skipped! Steve, take that rifle across to the fingerprint room. If there are any impressions on it, get 'em out fast! If they match any prints in the file, radio a general alarm."

McEwen ducked out on the platform as Thatcher hurried out with the rifle. He snarled with rage at the men searching the alley and the yards. He knew when he turned back that they would find no murderer and no clue to his identity. His snapping orders ignored the bewildered questions of the patrolmen who crowded in and sent them scurrying out again. He glared across the street, into the office where the murdered man lay, and said coldly:

"They can't get away with that."

His determination urged him to a minute search of the rooms. When he jerked open the door of a closet, his eyes widened with a long, narrow wooden box leaning against the wall. Lifting it out carefully, he pried its lid up. The brackets inside told him that this was the container in which the rifle had been expressed from the factory, which a killer had used to conceal the weapon while bringing it to this room.

A smear of black paint on its side obscured the shipping notations and wiped across a glued label. The heavy pigment completely blotted away the name and address on the paper rectangle. McEwen's teeth ground into his cigar as he studied it. His mind working carefully, he carried the box to a washbowl in the corner. He brought out his pocket knife, cut through the paint at the edge of the label, and held the marked area under the streaming faucet.

McEwen paid no attention to the fruitless search through the house and the yards while he waited for the seeping water to soften the paper. With the utmost care, he pried it up, a fraction of an inch at a time. When, at last, the entire label peeled free, he tossed the box aside. Closely examining the bit of paper, he saw that the paint had stained through—but a trace of the name and address remained.

The keys of a typewriter had embossed each character faintly in the fibers. McEwen pieced the reversed letters into a name and snorted with rage. They read: *Gilbert McEwen!* His teeth crushed the cigar anew as he made out the address: *Winfield's Pier, Great City.* Eyes gleaming, he thrust the wet label into an old envelope and tucked it carefully into his pocket. He was striding toward the door when Steve Thatcher came to a breathless step on the sill.

"No luck, Gil," Thatcher reported. "No prints at all on that rifle."

"Sure not!" McEwen grated. "He used gloves—just as the Moon Man always does. By damn, Steve, the Moon Man knew I'd be able to get at him that way—through one of the property owners who hired his arsonist gang. That's why he camped here. That's why he killed Latham!"

Thatcher protested tightly: "It's not like the Moon Man, Gil—a cowardly thing like that."

McEwen didn't hear. "When the Moon Man first started working, he ordered his mask under my name. This time he pulled the same trick getting hold of that rifle, so we can't trace it, but he made a slip. He left a lead. I'm following it, Steve, for all it's worth—alone, because I'm taking no chances. The time's come when I'm going to nail that crook!"

Steve Thatcher stared in dismay, tortured by uncertainty, as McEwen tramped down the stairs. He followed to see McEwen striding into the headquarters garage. His mind drummed with a haunting dread—"This time—he left a lead!"—as McEwen sent a police car spurting into the street. With aching eyes he watched McEwen set out on a murder trail—alone.

McEWEN'S JAW-MUSCLES bulged as he sent the car humming across the city. When he swung onto the broad cement road that wound along the course of the river, he dimmed the headlamps and slowed. Every nerve tight, he slid off the pavement and rolled across an open, cindered plot. He eased from the wheel, gun in hand, peering at the hulking structure at the edge of the water which he knew to be Winfield's Pier.

Fog drifted on the wind as McEwen went closer. He kept in the shadows, the slight sounds of his movements covered by the lapping of the water. The sluggish stream flowed past a long row of wharf houses and coal sheds, turgid and lightless. So many corpses had been dragged from its evil depths that it had become known as Murder River. The mist was like a shroud mantling the bleak structure which McEwen cautiously approached.

He paused at a door, tossed his cigar away, listened alertly. Not the faintest light shone through the weathered cracks, but the vague rumbling of voices warned McEwen of hidden presences. He pressed against the boards to find a bar fastening the door. Soundless step after soundless step, he went along the wall. Once past the corner, he paused at a grimy window overlooking the river. A flicker of his torch showed him a fastened catch—and a broken pane.

Straining on tiptoes, McEwen angled his arm into the hole. Making a breathless effort, he reached the latch. He freed it, withdrew his arm, stood with gun leveled, listened again. He pried his fingertips into the crack beneath the sash and widened it carefully, inch by inch. Fog wreathed over him as he legged over the sill. He stood against the wall in dank darkness, while the water lapped, listening to muffled voices speaking above.

Groping, he sought his way to the rear of the black void. His outstretched hand found a flight of wooden steps. With his gun ready, risking a betraying creak at each move, he went up. He crouched near the top of the flight, beneath a closed trap. A fluttering gleam told him candles were burning in the room where men were talking.

A dominating voice reached down: "... better be sure you didn't leave anything behind you, Graven. Every cop in town is looking for you right now. If you're grabbed you'll go to the chair."

A second voice protested wildly: "I tell you he was goin' to talk! I could tell it by his face—I could read his lips. McEwen was forcin' him to blab. There wasn't any other way of shuttin' him up. That's why Klar put me there with the rifle, wasn't it, Dickler?"

Dickler! The name wrung a start from Gil McEwen as he huddled in the darkness on the stairs. He had heard that name once before tonight—spoken by the muffled voice of the Moon Man.

The first voice—Dickler's—answered gruffly: "You better tell that to Klar when he comes. If I was in your shoes I'd beat it down to the office and try to get him on the phone."

"I'm goin' to do that right now."

Fast footfalls pounding across the floor of the upper room chilled McEwen's blood. They came directly to the closed trap above his head as he twisted. He began a frantically quick descent as rusty hinges squealed. In dismay he twisted, yanking his gun upward—with candlelight showing him to the others. He crouched on the stairs as a shadow loomed and a blurted whisper sounded:

"McEwen!"

Flame lashed from McEwen's gat. The bullet splintered into the sloping roof at the instant the chunky man leaped. McEwen lunged aside desperately, jerking the trigger for another shot, but an arm hooked his neck. He lurched down, pulled by the heaving weight of the other man, groping blindly for support. His gun whipped out a wild bullet as he sprawled down with the arms of a killer pinioning his.

McEwen fought with silent ferocity, vaguely aware that the second man was leaping into the battle. He felt his gun gripped, his wrist cruelly twisted. A fist exploded in his face and the revolver was torn away. He kicked savagely in a desperate effort to tear free—but the butt of his own weapon cracked viciously on his skull.

McEwen felt his limp body lifted and dragged through dizzily spinning blackness. Fantastically leaping flames appeared before his aching eyes—the candles in the upper room. Stunned, he could not resist the ropes that drew painfully tight around his ankles and wrists. Giant figures loomed over him while a gag was stuffed into his mouth and tied in place. He forced his vision to clear, and saw two men facing him with leveled guns, their cold killer's eyes glittered threats.

McEwen blinked at the mean features of Lenny Dickler and choked out a burst of mirthless laughter. More painful than the tightness of his bonds and the burning cut on his scalp was the bitter realization that the Moon Man had told him the truth.

IN THE chief's office in police headquarters the old clock ticked with sonorous deliberation. Steve Thatcher's aching eyes turned to its scaled face again and again as he nervously moved about. Three hours had passed since Gil McEwen had taken up a murderer's trail, and now the gray-rose light of the dawn was blending through the bullet-punctured window. Three hours of growing anxiety, without word from the veteran detective.

Thatcher stepped into the connecting office. Mark Keanan was sitting at a table, coat off, sleeves rolled, tie askew, exhaustedly rubbing his bearded chin. Two other weary plainclothes men stood beside him, shoulders sagging with despair. Opposite them sat two men whom Keanan had called into the office in a grim attempt to find a new lead to the arsonist ring. Both were the owners of buildings which had mysteriously burned. Both had collected substantial insurance payments. Both were successfully withstanding Keanan's merciless grilling.

His fist slammed. "You can't get away with it! Chief Rankin bottled some smoke when your places were burning. He had it analyzed and found traces of gasoline. That proves both fires were arsonist jobs. We'll face you with that evidence in court!"

The suspects shrugged. One of them answered with a thick accent: "Maybe. It might be somebody had a grudge against me. Your evidence might be pretty good. But it don't prove I had anything to do with setting the fire—if it was set."

The other whined: "I don't know anything about a gang of firebugs. The fire in my place just started, that's all. Defective wiring or something. Who can say?"

Keanan snarled: "It's always defective wiring!"

Thatcher backed out. Another glance at the old clock strengthened the dread weighing on his heart. Suddenly he left the office and hurried from headquarters. Entering the little cigar store across the street, he shouldered into a telephone booth. The number he dialed was one known only to himself and two others. The voice that answered said quickly:

"Boss!"

"Any news, Angel?"

The man on the other end of the line was the ambassador extraordinary to the Moon Man. Since the night, years ago, when the Moon Man had rescued him from sickness and starvation, Ned Dargan, ex-pugilist, had served the notorious criminal loyally, distributing the loot to the poor, guarding Steve Thatcher's secret. His courageous devotion had made the Moon Man's crimes his own. He faced the same dread penalty if ever the relentless McEwen captured him—death in the electric chair.

"I've been on the job ever since you phoned me the first time, Boss," Dargan reported. "Checking up on Dickler, I've found out he's been seen around with 'Bones' Groven and Max Klar. They've got a hideout somewhere, but that's all I know so far. I'll try to spot it, Boss, but—"

"Keep after it, Angel," Thatcher directed. "It's doubly important now because McEwen's still missing. Those men are merciless killers—anything may have happened to him. When you get something, Angel, phone me at once."

"Trust me, Boss!"

Anxiety shone in Thatcher's eyes as he left the booth. When he climbed the headquarters stairs he saw that the office adjoining the chief's was open and empty. He found Keanan slumped in a chair near the chief's desk, face haggard, eyes despairing. Pulling himself up, Keanan rasped:

"I had to let 'em go. The whole force could work on those birds for a week, and they wouldn't open up. I thought we could get a new lead that way, Steve, but it's no go. I'll tell you something. If Gil McEwen doesn't walk into this office within a few minutes, I'll go crazy with worry."

Even as Keanan spoke footfalls sounded in the hall. He turned eagerly. Thatcher went anxiously to the door, reaching for the knob. It opened abruptly—and the expectant light went out of Thatcher's eyes, the sag returned to Keanan's shoulders. The man who entered was Detective Sergeant Wright, to whom Thatcher had given a special detail.

"You can be sure of one thing," he growled. "I've checked by radio, and I have turned almost every damn street in this city but I haven't found it. Wherever Gil McEwen went in that car, there's not the slightest sign of it."

Thatcher and Keanan read the dread in each other's eyes as Wright went out. Keanan went back to his chair. Thatcher looked intently at the bullet-pierced window. They knew the same thought was in both their minds—a premonition they could not shake. They were silent until Keanan jerked up, fists clenched, eyes blazing.

"Where'd he go? Why didn't he tell us? How do we know what's happened to him? How can we help him if we don't know where he headed? I don't want to see McEwen brought back dead—murdered by those sneaking killers!"

Steve Thatcher's eyes stung as he gazed past Keanan at the door. It had opened quietly. A white-faced, anxious-eyed girl had paused on the sill. She had heard every one of Keanan's uncontrollably rushing words. Thatcher pressed back a moan of despair as Sue McEwen stood frozen.

CHAPTER IV

DOUBLE CAPTURE

THATCHER STRODE from the office, firmly taking Sue's arm. He led her to his own desk and closed the door behind her. The pleading in her eyes stabbed him with pain as he faced her. She asked, almost afraid to utter the question:

"What's happened to dad, Steve?"

"He's missing. That's all we know."

She faltered: "I was afraid something was wrong. I couldn't get dad on the phone—I was worried—I had to come. You—you're afraid he's been—killed."

Thatcher's fingers tightened on Sue's arms. "Listen. Gil went out of here with a hot lead, but he didn't tell another soul about it. We've been trying our damndest to pick up something that might take us to him. We haven't found the slightest clue—the police haven't. Do you understand that, Sue?"

The girl anxiously searched his eyes.

"Mark Keanan and Steve Thatcher, have been making absolutely no headway," Thatcher went on grimly. "But Angel has. He's following a new trail right now. It might lead to McEwen and it might not. Whatever it's worth, headquarters knows nothing about it Angel can make his report to just one person, Sue—nobody else—the Moon Man."

Sue blurted: "You can't, Steve!"

"Give me a chance, Sue! It's the only way of finding out what's happened to Gil—the only way of reaching him. What if he needs help? What if his getting help is the difference between life and death? Think of that, Sue! Can you hold me back now—realizing that?"

Tears flickered in the girl's eyes. "Steve, darling, you know dad and you are my whole world. If something's happened to him now—it's too late. If you went after him as the Moon Man you might get caught. I—I wouldn't have anything left, Steve— nothing!"

Lips tightened, eyes blazing, he asked again: "Sue, are you going to hold me back now?"

She answered in a whisper: "I mean what I said, Steve."

He turned from her with pulse pounding. His hands worked into hard fists as he went down the worn stairs. He was aware that Sue's gaze was anxiously following him, but he did not look back. He strode out the entrance, along two blocks growing busy with the coming of the new day, and went into a drug store. Coldly determined, he spun the dial of a pay telephone to the number of police headquarters and asked for Keanan.

He stuffed a handkerchief into the transmitter horn to muffle his voice and, when Keanan answered, said deliberately:

"This is the Moon Man speaking."

Keanan blurted: "What! Listen! If you know where Gil McEwen is—if you've done anything to him, you—"

"Pay close attention, Keanan," Thatcher said in the voice of the Moon Man. "I don't know where McEwen is. I have infor- mation which may lead to your finding him. The men you want are Dickler and Groven and Klar. You've got to find them before it's too late, or McEwen may never again be seen alive. I beg of you to trust me, Keanan."

Keanan's answer was a snarl. "Why should I trust you? You're right in the middle of this arson gang. We're making it hotter for you than ever before and you're desperate to clear yourself. McEwen didn't believe you—why should I? You—"

"Go after those men!" the Moon Man pleaded. "Find them and sweat the truth out of them. I promise you, it's your chance of finding McEwen in time. If you don't—"

Steve Thatcher's voice trailed off in a whisper—for the connection was broken. At the other end of the wire Mark Keanan had slammed the receiver on the hook. Hopelessness shone in Thatcher's eyes as he sidled out of the booth. He walked quickly, thrust into headquarters, climbed the wooden stairs. He saw Sue still in his office. Going toward her with shoulders sagging, he heard Keanan's voice growling in the chief's office:

"Pick 'em up and bring 'em in—Dickler and Groven and Klar. I don't trust that tip a particle, but the least we can do is follow it down for Gil's sake. Let me know as soon as you've found 'em."

It brought scant hope to Thatcher's heart. He went to Sue's side and searched her clear eyes. Her face was drawn, but her lips were firmly set. He began anxiously:

"Sue, can't you understand? Won't you give me this last chance? It's the Moon Man's job to—"

She broke in, her voice trembling: "Not—not even if it means dad's life, Steve. I'll never marry you if you ever become the Moon Man again."

THATCHER STRAIGHTENED, the lines deepened around his mouth, his eyes pinched. He took Sue's arm firmly and went with her along the hall. She scanned his face wonderingly, but he did not speak while he took her to his roadster. She was sitting tensely beside him when he turned the car out of the garage, and as he drove he kept a bitter silence.

In a quiet neighborhood on the opposite side of the city he swung to the curb in front of a little house. While Sue watched anxiously he unlocked the rumble compartment of the roadster. Lifting out a small black case, he went with her to the front entrance. He saw that the garage at the rear was standing empty. It told him Ned Dargan was on the job—following the spider web trail of a trio of killers.

Thatcher's key admitted him to the hideaway of the Moon Man's secret emissary. Carrying the case, he escorted Sue into a comfortably furnished room. A table lamp glowed warmly in these quarters where a fugitive sheltered himself from the constantly searching police. His eyes shining bitterly, Thatcher placed the case on a table and opened it.

He lifted out the black robe which month after month had cloaked the Moon Man during his daring operations. He fingered the neat automatic which had repeatedly aided him to escape the shrewd traps laid by the relentless McEwen. He lifted the hinged halves of the fragile spherical mask, and wryly smiled. It had no duplicate in all the world—no other like it could ever exist. It had kept the secret that Steve Thatcher, detective sergeant, was the Moon Man—and now the Moon Man was done with it.

Thatcher carefully returned the regalia to the case and snapped the lid down. A deliriously happy light shone in Sue's eyes as he carried it to a cabinet built into one corner of the room. He opened the triangular space and placed the case inside. His eyes stung when he closed it in. And turned the key in the lock. He proffered the key to Sue.

"You'd better keep this," he said gently.

She blurted: "Steve! You know it's only because I love you so much I—" She flung her arms about his shoulders, pressed her cheek to his, and clung with a sob trembling on her lips. His fingers strayed into her hair while the bitter smile still curved his lips. She drew back to whisper:

"It's the only way, Steve."

A sound tightened Thatcher's nerves—the gritting of a car stopping in front of the house. He turned alertly to the entrance as footfalls crossed the porch. The young man who stepped in, eyes gleaming exultantly, was stocky and neckless. A cauliflower ear testified to Dargan's past encounters in the resined ring. He strode quickly to Thatcher and blurted:

"I'm glad you're here, Boss! It's swell seeing you again, Sue. I—"

"It's for the last time, Angel."

Dargan's smile faded as he asked quickly: "What's that, Boss?"

Thatcher answered tightly: "You're seeing us in the Moon Man's hideout for the last time. There isn't any more Moon Man, Angel. He has passed out of existence." He extended his hand. "You ought to be glad to hear that, oldtimer. It means we'll all be safe."

Dargan blurted: "I don't get this, Boss!"

"It's very simple, Angel," Thatcher said through an aching throat. "The Moon Man will never appear again. I'll bring you a railroad ticket tomorrow, and in a few days you'll be so far out of McEwen's reach, you'll never have to worry again about getting grabbed." As Dargan's hand clamped his he added: "You're the best friend I've ever had, Angel. I'll never forget you."

Dargan blinked. "Gosh, Boss, you know I think you're the swellest guy on earth. There's nothing I wouldn't do for you and Sue. I guess—I guess you're doing the right thing." His smile came back crookedly. "It's kind of funny, Boss. I came here to telephone you—to tell you I've spotted Klar's hide-out"

Thatcher asked sharply: "What?"

"Sure, Boss!" Now Dargan's words rushed. "After I phoned you last time, I began looking for those rats in earnest. I couldn't find Dickler and Groven at any of their hangouts, but I spotted Klar. I found him taking a phone call, and whatever he heard it was like throwing him into high gear. I followed him in the car—to Winfield's Pier."

"Is he there now, Angel?"

"He's there, Boss! With Dickler and Groven, I think. And maybe they've got McEwen! That's why I beat it back here to tell you—"

Steve Thatcher's eyes narrowed. He turned suddenly on Sue, and the very vehemence of his movement caused her to recoil. He told her, each word crackling:

"You heard that! All the cops are in to look for that place—and Angel found it! He's done a better job than the police—following the Moon Man's orders. Sue, listen. I've got to keep Angel covered—but there's nothing to stop me from going after those killers—without the robe and mask!"

He strode to the entrance with Dargan. His jaws clamped hard as he slammed out. Sue stood wide-eyed anxiously listening to them hurry to the car together—the accomplice of the Moon Man and Steve Thatcher, detective sergeant.

THATCHER SENT his roadster whirring along the broad cement pavement which twined along the bank of Murder River. His headlamps shafted into the shadows lurking around the wharves and sheds while Dargan sat tensely beside him. When they neared Winfield's Pier, Thatcher clicked off the switches and swung abruptly from the road. The car rolled into desolate darkness and stopped in the fog clouding off the brackish stream.

They eased side by side through the shadows. No car whirred over the boulevard, no boat chugged in the river while they stole to the side of Winfield's Pier. Tensing at the barred door, they turned to the wharf. At a window they paused. They could not know McEwen had slipped in through it; it was closed and latched. As they peered under broad doors hanging shut over the turgid water, Thatcher whispered:

"That boat."

He dropped to his knees, reached far under, gripped the rail of a motorboat that was made fast inside. It bobbed outward a foot. Bracing against the edge of the wharf and the door, he slid his legs onto it. He wriggled along and straightened in the misty gloom. He glided the boat forward again and waited until Dargan crouched at his side.

Looking up he whispered: "Listen!"

Through the boards of the ceiling voices were carrying. One, hushed and anxious, said:

"He knows enough to send us all to the chair if he ever gets back. Keepin' him tied up here while we skip is takin' too much of a chance. We can't get any more'n one dose of the hot-squat if we do him under."

The answer came in a cold, commanding tone: "It's handy enough here. Plenty of rope and a couple of anchors. All we have to do is drop him off the wharf. They'll be a long time trying to find McEwen after that."

"It's gettin' light. Maybe we better wait."

"Not much. Tie those weights on him right now—then carry him down."

Thatcher's eyes gleamed grimly as he pulled up. Dargan heaved to his side. Their guns snugly in hand, they groped through eye-baffling mist. The water lapped and footfalls sounded on the boards overhead. Each step a risk, Dargan and Thatcher ventured toward the rear wall. Thatcher stopped abruptly when a burst of breath broke from Dargan's lips.

The next instant—a crash!

Thatcher whirled back. Dargan jerked up breathless at his side. In dismay they peered down at a pair of oars. A slight touch of Dargan's shoulder, while they leaned unseen against a post, had toppled them down. The loud clatter brought startled exclamations out of the gloom.

"Somebody below!"

"Down and get 'em!"

Thatcher straightened in consternation as hinges creaked. Light flared from a trap opening in the ceiling. Two black figures sprang down on the stairs. Their guns glittered as they leaped off—then spat flame. A third man bounded down the flight, his automatic echoing a vicious blast. Bullets whistled past Thatcher and Dargan as they backed.

"Drop 'em!"

The swift attack in the darkness caught Dargan and Thatcher at a bewildering disadvantage. To them the gloom was a trap; to the three scattering killers, who knew every step, it gave shelter. Slugs ripped around them as they ducked. Thatcher, leaping back, struck the board wall. He groped blindly at a bar fastening a door as he fired. Splinters flew in his face while he realized that suddenly the wharf house had become a death-trap.

Clashing automatics flamed in the dark, outlining a staggering man. Dargan's scarred face, twisted with rage, marked with red, was an image that vanished instantly in the darkness. The impact of a falling body jarred the floorboards. Thatcher desperately wrenched the bar free as a husky call tore out of the gun-storm: "Get clear, Boss! Get clear!"

Three guns were turning upon Thatcher when he leaped back. Holes drilled the door as he slapped it shut and whirled away. He raced through a gray confusion of fog while slugs slashed through it. Skirting behind the next shed, he fired past the corner at the ghostly figures springing into the open.

His bullets stopped the killers' advance. They were ducking back when he spun. He sprinted to the roadster, slid behind the wheel, kicked the hot motor into action. Swerving to the pavement, he glanced back to see Winfield's Pier standing silent, apparently deserted, in the mist. He swung onto the pavement, pressing the accelerator down hard, stunned by a realization that struck him like a blow.

Ned Dargan, fugitive from justice, wanted for murder, was now a prisoner with the detective who had sworn to send him to the chair.

THATCHER'S MIND raced faster than his car as he followed the river road. Braking at a bend, he peered back again, tortured with wonder. Had the shots raised an alarm? Would the reports bring the district prowl cars speeding to the pier? And if they came—Thatcher thrust the dread thought from his mind. His breath returned after a tormenting minute of waiting. No *whirr* of tires, no singing of sirens, disturbed the sinister hush that brooded over the pier.

Thatcher spurted along the boulevard, braked abruptly when he neared a drug store. He forced his manner to be casual as he strode in and entered a telephone booth. He spun the number of police headquarters on the dial and asked the Phone Sergeant for Keanan. Keanan's voice was weary, despondent.

"Any word about Gil, Mark?" Thatcher asked anxiously. "Any new lead?"

"Not a thing, Steve," Keanan growled. "The chief's got every cop in town looking for him, but they're turning up absolutely nothing. No sign of Gil or his car. This thing is driving me crazy! If we don't find him damn' soon, it'll mean—"

"He's dead." Neither Thatcher nor Keanan uttered the words, but they shared that gnawing dread. And Thatcher was forced to keep silent because the Moon Man, and not he, knew the danger threatening McEwen.

Thatcher forced out: "I'm on the job, Mark," and shouldered from the booth. His jaw was squared with grim determination when he returned to the roadster. He drove rapidly, angling at corners, cursing the arrival of the new day because it robbed him of the cloak of darkness. It spelled a new menace—but Thatcher's purpose was indomitable when he braked in front of the hideaway of the Moon Man.

Thrusting open the door he called "Sue!" but the echo of his voice was the only answer. He strode into the empty living-room, stood with eyes narrowed at the corner cabinet. Prying at the door with his fingers, he found it firmly locked. He turned grimly, snatched a shoe-horn from the dresser, thrust it hard into the crack.

He levered with all his strength. His metal implement bent, the wood creaked. He persisted—until a sharp snap brought a wry smile to his lips. He flung the door wide, reached in—froze. The space inside was empty. The case was gone.

Thatcher spun, fists clenched. His heels hammered hard as he hurried out the door. Again behind the wheel of his roadster, he drove with cold purpose. He turned into a familiar residential district. He braked in front of the little house that was the home of Sue and Gil McEwen.

He thrust at the call button on the door, rapped his knuckles sharply. His eyes blazed at the sound of footfalls on the stairs. The hand of Sue McEwen drew the door open. She stood back, an alarmed light shining in her tired eyes, her lips parted in dismay at sight of the chill hardness in Steve Thatcher's face.

"What do you want, Steve?"

He stepped in. He took Sue's arms in his hands, his eyes searching hers. His voice was dry and husky when he said:

"You know what I want. You know I've come here because there's no other way. You've got to understand, Sue."

She shook her head frantically. She tore from Thatcher's hands, and hurried to the stairs. His quicker steps brought him to a grim standstill in front of her. The girl recoiled at the fierceness of his gaze. She had never before seen this savage light in Steve Thatcher's eyes. The lash of his tone made her wince as he said:

"I've come for the robe and the mask of the Moon Man."

CHAPTER V

SUICIDE SOLITAIRE

SUE McEWEN answered faintly: "I won't give it to you, Steve. I won't!" Thatcher's fists clenched. "Listen, Sue! I'm thinking of Gil and Dargan. I know where they are. I know they'll die together—in Murder River—if they're not taken out of the hands of those killers somehow. There's no time to argue about what might happen to me, to us, I've got to have the robe and mask."

The girl protested wildly: "It's work for the police—not the Moon Man!"

Thatcher made a swift gesture of impatience. "Don't you understand? The same crooks have got Gil and Dargan prisoners. They're being held together at Winfield's pier. I can't tell the police that. If they manage to save Gil, they'll capture the Angel. You know what that means for him. The chair—because he's the Moon Man's accomplice!"

Thatcher's fist smacked into his palm. "Dargan has worked at my side in spite of every danger. He's helped me in spite of the risk to himself. You heard me tell him tonight—he's the best friend I've got in the world. I meant that! I can't send the police to that place, even for Gil's sake, and have Dargan brought up for murder!"

Sue shook her head in protest.

"Steve Thatcher's hands are tied!" he went on savagely. "Nobody can keep Dargan out of the hands of the police but the Moon Man—if it isn't already too late. Sue, listen to me.

Listen to every word! I love you with all my heart—with all my heart I want to do as you ask, because I know you're right—but you can't force me to stand by and see Dargan go to the chair!"

The girl began huskily: "If you're caught, Steve—"

"Where are the robe and the mask?" he cut in angrily. "Where are they, Sue?"

She stepped back, her arms stiff at her sides, her chin lifted defiantly.

"I won't tell you, Steve. Nothing you can say will make me tell you that."

He turned away with a wrathful exclamation. The girl stood rigid, her anguished eyes following his moves, as he began a grim search of the lower floor. He opened closets, probed behind the books in the cases, even into the drawers of McEwen's desk. He straightened to demand:

"Tell me where they are, Sue!"

"No."

He thrust past her and ran up the stairs. Sue followed him wearily, her lips trembling, her eyes still adamant. Thatcher strode into her bedroom, slid open the drawers of her dressing table, slammed them shut. Turning, he gripped the knob of a closet door—and a hot burst of breath came from his lips.

"You put it in there," he said tightly. "You locked the case in that closet when you heard me knock because you thought I was coming back for it. Where is the key, Sue?"

"I won't give it to you, Steve."

Angrily he turned back to the dressing table. He fingered into Sue's jewel case vainly. Tortured by a growing urgency, he swung back to the girl. She was standing against the wall now, one arm thrust behind her back. He straightened stiffly, extending his hand.

"You've got it."

"I won't give it to you, Steve."

A driving anxiety possessed him. He took one swift step forward and seized Sue's arm. In spite of her resistance, he forced her arm up. Her fist was clenched white. While his blood pounded, he forced her fingers open. She tried desperately to tear away from him, but the power of his grip held her. He clutched the key she was holding and snatched it away.

Breath rushing, he said: "I'm sorry I had to do that, Sue."

Her face was deathly white as he turned to the closet. He thrust the key into place, twisted it. His eyes shone with exultation at the black case on the shelf. He snatched it down, swung it to the bed, clicked its lid up. Inside it the black robe of the Moon Man was wrapped around the fragile mask.

He swung it under his arm and started for the door. He heard Sue following him, and at the head of the stairs he stopped. "Wait, Steve," she had said very quietly. He looked back to see her coming with extended hand—the hand that had held the key. She added in the same, soft, hopeless tone:

"This—this is something you forgot."

She dropped it into his fingers and turned away stiffly. Suddenly she ran into the bedroom and closed the door. Steve Thatcher heard her sob as he gazed at the glittering thing on his palm. The sparkling of a diamond stung his eyes. It had come from Sue's finger—the engagement ring he had given her.

His hand closed on it. He went blindly down the stairs. The slam of the front entrance as he went out echoed loudly through the house. He strode to his roadster with the regalia of the Moon Man under his arm—and in his hot fist the solitaire symbol of the girl he had lost.

SUE McEWEN stood rigid, listening to the purr of a car in the street. Through the window she saw Steve Thatcher's roadster skirting from the curb. She did not move until the sound had blended away in the hush of the street. She forced the tears from her eyes as she went out of the room and down the stairs.

Her movements were automatic as she went to the garage and started her coupé. There was no sign of Steve Thatcher's roadster when she turned into the street. She scarcely saw the pavement ahead of her as she drove. She looked out of a void of grief to find herself passing the turreted headquarters building. Still dazed, she parked the car and pushed through the entrance.

Nervous footfalls were crossing the floor of the chief's office when Sue opened the door. Mark Keanan, bearded, eyes red-rimmed, stopped abruptly as he saw her. Chief Thatcher, rising from his padded swivel chair, went to her gently. She lowered her head exhaustedly against his shoulder, his stout arm around her, as she asked:

"Is there—any word about dad?"

"Nothing, Sue."

Keanan scowled. "We've done everything possible to find him, Sue. I even acted on a tip the Moon Man phoned in, and sent out a squad to pick up Dickler and Groven and Klar—the men he said are the arson ring. No good. They haven't been brought in. Believe me, if there was any other lead I'd go after it for all I'm worth!"

"I know you would, Mark."

Chief Thatcher said: "Don't you worry, honey. We're sure to find a new lead. With thousands of men hunting—they're sure to turn up something."

Keanan snarled: "They'd better do it damn fast!"

He half spun as footfalls came from the stairs to the chief's door. The patrolman who entered was one assigned to the radio detail. He wagged a salute, blinked, and began while Keanan stared hopefully:

"I don't know whether it means anything or not, but I'm reporting on it because maybe you can tell—"

"Out with it!" Keanan snapped, "What've you got?"

Patrolman Blakely shifted his feet uneasily. "Well, about an hour ago, when we were touring down by the bridge, I thought

I heard shots. We went along, hunting for something wrong, but everything looked all right. They seemed to come from one of the sheds along the river, so Murphy and I—"

Keanan raged: "Hell, get to the point!"

"Yes, sir. Murphy and I began looking around there until it was time to go off duty. The door of the wharf house was locked, but I found this on the ground near it. I don't know whether it's worth anything, but—Lieutenant McEwen smokes cigars, doesn't he—or chews 'em without lighting 'em?"

Keanan and the chief jerked tight as Blakely drew his hand from his pocket. Sue McEwen's eyes widened in dismay at the thing the patrolman displayed on his palm. It was a cigar—a cigar which had not been lighted—indented by many tooth marks. Keanan stared at it as Blakely mumbled on:

"If a man's got a cigar in his mouth, and starts doing something important, he's apt to put it aside or throw it away. That's why I thought maybe Lieutenant McEwen had been around there. Of course, thousands of men smoke cigars and I wasn't sure—"

"Thousands of men don't use this kind without lighting them!" Keanan snapped. "There's the band still on it. It's the make McEwen smokes! Blakely, you numbskull, you should have phoned this in the minute you found it! McEwen was there! I'll bet my last dollar on it. Come on! What's the rest?"

"It's the old Winfield Pier, sergeant. I didn't think—"

"You didn't think—and McEwen was probably within a few feet of you!" Keanan snarled: "Now it may be too late! You blinking nitwit, get out of here!" Keanan swung. "Listen, chief! McEwen means a hell of a lot to me. Give me the chance to handle this!"

Chief Thatcher said gravely: "It's your job, Mark. Play the chance for all it's worth."

Keanan snatched up the telephone. His rasping voice sped the connections. Words rushing, he ordered:

"Flash the prowl cars in Section R—in code. They're to ease up on Winfield's Pier. Radio the police boat to take a position right opposite it. Every man to use the utmost care—because if McEwen's still there the killers must be with him. All men to stand off until the chief and I take command. Get that out fast!"

Sue McEwen watched with caught breath as Keanan clashed the receiver down and snapped: "Come on, chief!"

Consternation speeded her heart while the two men hurried from the office. With their heels hammering the stairs, Keanan's voice echoed in her stunned mind: "Winfield's Pier!" It was the place Steve Thatcher had mentioned.

The anguished girl rushed from the office, after Keanan and the chief, driven by the realization that Winfield's Pier was the destination of the Moon Man.

A LOW, murky sky darkened the water of Murder River. The fog had thickened with the coming of the day. It billowed along the banks and clouded over the gaunt sheds, wreathing slowly in the windless air. It was a curtain that wafted around Steve Thatcher as he hurried from his roadster toward Winfield's Pier—carrying the black case that contained the regalia of the Moon Man.

The boulevard was a vague lane in the mist beyond the wharf house. Somewhere on the river a boat was chugging. Alert for every sound, for any flicker of movement, Thatcher came to a stop at the dewy board wall. At the spot where he paused, new bullet holes marked the wood. Listening, hearing no sound inside, he eased past the corner to the pier.

The fog shielded him as he poised at the nearest window. Peering around, he opened the case. He unrolled the black robe and shook it over his shoulders. He pulled the black gloves on his hands. He raised the precious glass mask and halved it together over his head. Transformed into a ghostly figure, he stood in the mist, gun in hand—the notorious criminal known as the Moon Man.

His black-gloved hand slipped a thin-edged steel tool from a split in the side of his cloak. He pried it into the crack of the window sash and bore down with the utmost care. Through the sheen of his mask he saw the screws of the latch tear out of the old wood. He opened the way, inch by inch, while the dank mist flowed around him.

Sliding over the sill, he found himself in a small partitioned office made gloomy by the heavy murk. Easing past a desk he noted a small safe in the corner, its partly open door revealing its emptiness. He glided out of the partitioned space, gun pointing the way toward the stairs at the far wall. When he paused his glittering head bowed over dark marks on the floor—bloodstains at the spot where Ned Dargan had fallen.

A rustle of movement sounded above him as the Moon Man stole towards the steps. He paused again, as his eyes became accustomed to the deeper gloom, sensing a pungency in the air. Near the wall he saw a drum labeled Gasoline, a limpid drop still clinging to its open spigot. Around the posts and the edge of the floor wet excelsior was piled. At the base of the flight the Moon Man stopped, realizing that a deadly firetrap had been set.

The chugging of a motor brought a chill to his heart. Through the grimy windows overlooking Murder River he saw the dim outlines of a boat drifting near the opposite bank. His silver head raised when quick steps sounded overhead, then stopped. His automatic peered at the closed trap while he crept upward. He crouched, one black-gloved hand raised to the hinged leaf, as a voice spoke in the upper room:

"I'm tellin' you it's true! There's a reason why a piece of canvas is hangin' down, coverin' up the name. That's the police boat! They've spotted us!"

The Moon Man huddled motionless, his chilled blood speeding, as a second man spoke huskily from a spot almost directly above him.

"There's a prowl car comin' down the road! I can tell it by the red headlights. It's swingin' off, gettin' out of sight. There's another one, comin' the other way! They've found out we're hidin' here—they've spotted us!"

With sharpening apprehension, the Moon Man heard an answer in a dominating tone:

"What're you mugs afraid of? We've got the fastest boat on the river. The Tommy gun will keep that police tub off—send it to the bottom. We'll be out of here before the prowl cars know what's happening."

A husky question: "What about those two guys, Klar?"

A chuckle. Then: "We didn't have a chance to chuck 'em in the river with those two cops prowling around, did we? That's why we put the stuff downstairs. This place will go up like it was made of celluloid. And they'll burn with it."

Another question snapped: "What're we waitin' for?"

"Nothing. Get into the boat right now. I'll set the stuff just as we push off. There won't be enough left of McEwen and this tough guy to tell anybody was in the place."

Again footfalls thumped on the board floor of the upper room. The keen ears of the Moon Man caught, beyond that rhythm, the whining of tires on the wet pavement and the bubbling of the boat in the river. His tensed muscles released like coordinated springs. With one swift thrust he burst the trap open and straightened into glimmering candlelight to face three evil-eyed men.

His muffled voice commanded: "One moment, gentlemen! You're not leaving quite yet. Stand just where you are!"

THE GLEAM of the Moon Man's automatic struck paralysis into the three. The magic suddenness of his appearance silenced the warning shouts on their curling lips. Like a phantom instantly materialized out of the gloom he stood before them, gun waving, silver head shining. And a muffled chuckle came from his shell of a mask.

"You may choose to disregard my orders, gentlemen. In that case I trust you are prepared to meet a speedy death. I will have no hesitation whatever in shooting you through the heart at the first indication of treachery. Step back—toward your prisoners."

The masked eyes of the Moon Man were probing into the gloom of the far corner. He saw Gil McEwen, bound hand and foot and gagged, straining up to stare. He saw Ned Dargan, likewise trussed with stout ropes, his forehead marked by an ugly bullet gash, braced against the board wall with pinched eyes gleaming. While Dickler and Grovan and Klar stood with gun hands frozen, his muffled voice sounded again:

"Before you begin carrying out my instructions, you will do well to rid yourself of your automatics. Make the move very carefully, gentlemen. Toss them down through the trap. Any delay, you know, will only allow the police ring to draw closer around you."

The three moved—carefully. Their hands drifted to their holstered guns. The automatic of the Moon Man covered them steadily while their malevolent eyes glittered impotent defiance. Dickler, then Grovan, then Klar tossed their weapons. Three thumps echoed from the darkness below. Chuckling again, the Moon Man took a rustling step forward—and the three retreated.

"Klar," he ordered, "you will liberate my good friend Dargan. Dickler, your task is to loosen McEwen's bonds. You are to free only his feet, leaving his hands bound behind him—a measure of precaution for my own sake, you understand. Move quickly, gentlemen!"

The Moon Man stood erect, silver head gleaming, while the three stooped to obey his commands. Their eyes stayed on him, narrowed, glinting. McEwen, growling behind his gag, glared as his feet came free. Ned Dargan, breathing fast, struggled up, rubbing his wrists, kicking the severed strands from his ankles, tearing the wadded cloth from his mouth. As he sprang from the corner, the Moon Man gestured him toward the trap.

The ghostly figure with the silver head retreated, gun still covering the men in the corner. In a whisper which could not carry to McEwen he warned:

"Go down now, Angel! Out through the office. Try to reach one of the other sheds. The fog may be thick enough to cover you. Slip out later, when the way's clear. It's your only chance."

Dargan protested breathlessly: "What about you, Boss? If the cops are closing in—"

"Make it fast, Angel!"

The Moon Man's imperative tone turned Dargan to the trap. While quick footfalls below marked his escape from the building, the Moon Man stood motionless, covering the men in the corner. McEwen glared with wrath as the sounds disappeared. The Moon Man, standing at the head of the wooden flight, raised a beckoning, black-gloved hand.

"You are quite free to go, Lieutenant McEwen. I trust you now believe I have no connection with the arson ring, that I offered you my information in the best of faith. Nearby you will find the police waiting to close in on this building. I hope you will not forget, while you order them to capture me, that the Moon Man holds you in the highest esteem, and is very glad to have been of service."

McEwen glared as he strode from the corner. His gag silenced him as he tried to pierce the baffling sheen of the Moon Man's mask, to learn the secret of the man who wore it. His leathery face hardened, McEwen tramped down the flight while the Moon Man backed. He descended until only his spherical head was visible above the trap, and his muffled voice came again:

"You will pardon me, I trust, gentlemen, for hoping that I have better luck than you in effecting an escape!"

He darted down into the deeper gloom as McEwen shouldered at the bar of the door. His black-gloved hand was drawing it aside to open the way when a crash spun him. Streaking shadows on the stairs marked the leap of two men through the trap. They dropped into darkness as McEwen, with a choking snarl, thrust out. The third was desperately springing down when flame stabbed from a killer's gun.

Flame—multiplied instantly a thousandfold!

The spark of the bullet created a lightning bolt that struck with a roar across the cavernous room. It split into a hundred forks that speared into the gasoline-soaked excelsior. The dark heaps magically became flaring red. The gloom of the wharf house vanished in a roaring glare. It blazed in front of the Moon Man as he crouched beside the open door—a door outside at which dogged police were stationed.

IN STUNNED dismay the Moon Man crushed against the wall to escape the flames that licked around him. From outside, through the rumble, he heard a chorus of shouts—the police charging. He could see nothing through the blinding glare, but he heard fast footfalls, then the snort of a starting motor. The sound warned him that the three gunmen had sped to the speedboat, were preparing to dart out into the river. He braced as the tongues licked closer around him—then leaped.

He whirled to a stop near the stairs, surrounded by walls sheeted with leaping red. In the blinding light he saw the boat skirting under the door. Three men crouching, turned guns upon him. He flung himself down as bullets slashed through the churning air. When he raised, a white wake marked the way the boat had gone—and uniformed men were hurrying past the open, flame-framed door.

McEwen's rasp carried through the tumult: "The Moon Man's in there! Watch the doors! The Moon Man!"

Keanan's order came: "Stop that boat!"

Guns barked into the bubble of the escaping craft as the Moon Man whirled. He saw two other exits barred by swelling fire. Through the windows, washed by flame, he glimpsed patrolmen scattering. Desperately seeking a way out of the roaring trap, he backed while the staccato burst of a machine gun sounded on the river. He was nearing the partitioned office when a crimson flare at his knees startled him.

His robe was blazing. The Moon Man's breath whistled inside his mask as he frantically ripped at the collar. He whipped the cloak down and kicked it free. It fell into the water as he spun again—a weird figure of a man with a spherical, silver head. Suffocating heat beat upon him as he poised to leap into the corner office—heat that threatened to crack the precious mask that never could be replaced.

He halved it off his head, gripped it under his arm—and sprang. Steve Thatcher flattened breathless against the wall inside the little office. He knew that to attempt to escape the building with the mask would mean discovery—that to leave it inside the blazing building would mean its destruction—but an exultant exclamation broke out from his lips as his gaze turned to the safe in the corner.

Gently, while the fire thundered around him, while the withering heat grew more intense, he placed the mask inside the safe. He thrust the slab home, spun the combination dial, tried the handle to make sure it was fastened. Choking in the smoke, he twisted to the window and stared out. While he raised the sash, determining to chance a desperate gamble, flame gusted in behind him and the whole structure quaked.

Patrolmen were skirmishing along the bank, firing at the boat that was swerving to skirt up-river. Men on the police patrol craft, stationed in the center of the stream, were driving it back with lashing bullets. Its machine-gun stuttered a lethal song as prowl cars sped to the upper banks to stop its advance with a leaden barricade.

While guns sparkled through the fog and the fumes of the burning wharf-house, Steve Thatcher spilled out of the window. Blinded by scalding tears, lungs filled with stinging smoke, he stumbled off the pier, onto gritty ground. Dragging up, he tottered past uniformed men who gave him scarcely a glance.

When he jerked to a stop, with the heat of the blaze still playing upon him, he was facing the hard-eyed McEwen.

"Steve!"

Thatcher blurted: "Just came from the front, Gil! Nobody can get out that way now. If the Moon Man—"

McEwen raced in savagely: "If the Moon Man didn't slip out some way, he's done!"

Thatcher turned to stare at the trembling structure. Its dry wood had swiftly carried the flames through its every inch. It was a white-hearted inferno threatening to collapse at any instant—yet patrolmen and plainclothesmen, guns in hands, were still grimly stationed around it. Watching the windows and the doors, fingers tight on the trigger for a quick shot, they were waiting for the Moon Man to show.

Another burst of shots turned Thatcher's aching eyes to the fog-banked river. Two men were crouching aboard the speedboat while a third, arms limp, slumped motionless over the rail. The machine gun rattled out a long fusillade that raked the water's edge. The men on the police craft, as it churned closer, whipped lead across the fugitive craft. Their telling attack spelled death.

Max Klar jerked up from the tripoded gun, stretched in agony, toppled stiff into the brackish stream. Dickler poised to dive—but instead fell, his head punctured. The unmanned craft circled crazily, its motor bellowing, until it drove with a crunch into the mud of the bank. Grim-faced men smiled as the police guns along the river went silent.

Mark Keanan ran to McEwen's side to gasp: "We got 'em, Gil!"

McEwen snarled: "Sure we got 'em—but what happened to the Moon Man? What about him?"

A sob turned Steve Thatcher. A girl was standing behind him. Her face was white, a wild light shone in her eyes. Sue McEwen came to Thatcher slowly, tears streaking her cheeks, a smile trembling on her lips. She said softly, "Steve!" and suddenly her arms were around him.

GIL McEWEN stood near the bank of Murder River and wryly eyed a heap of smouldering ashes. Fire engines had come screaming to the spot too late. Hissing hoses had been unable to quench the roaring flames. The wharf house had collapsed into a mound of glowing coals that now were black. Smoke still wisped up from the ruins of Winfield's Pier as McEwen gnawed on a fresh cigar—unlighted.

"Maybe the Moon Man was trapped in there, and maybe he wasn't. I won't believe he's done for, by damn, until he hasn't turned up for ten years!"

Keanan, standing at McEwen's side, wagged his head. "Whatever happened to the Moon Man, Gil, I don't give a damn this time. You're all right—that's what I'm thinking of!"

A patrolman came puffing to McEwen's side to report: "No sign of Dargan anywhere around here, lieutenant. We've been through all the sheds for a mile both ways. I guess he's skipped again."

"All right," McEwen sighed. "All right. I'm satisfied to be alive. I'd be nothing but ashes in that heap right now if it hadn't been for the Moon Man. I've got to admit, I owe him my life. But by damn! He's a crook. I'm a cop. I say again, the time's coming when I'm going to send him to the chair!"

Steve Thatcher heard that and bitterly smiled. He was looking into the smoking mound, at a blackened cube which sat askew in the steaming mud. It was the safe into which he had put the precious mask of the Moon Man.

Perhaps, in spite of the protection of the thick steel, the intense heat had cracked it. Certain it was that the safe could not be opened now without an acetylene torch. Thatcher planned—planned, as he turned away—to come back, to somehow carry the safe away, to open it and learn if a notorious criminal had lost the faithful keeper of his secret.

Sue McEwen smiled as he climbed wearily into the coupé. Her cool fingers curled into his as she said:

"You did the only possible thing, darling. I was thinking of you—wanting to keep you safe in spite of everything. I'd do it all over again—and so would you—but we can't let it change us, Steve. Believing it all as wholeheartedly as you did—if you hadn't taken the key, I would have hated you!" She raised her hand slowly. "A ring belongs on that finger—your ring. Please put it back."

He slipped it in place, and felt the soft warmth of her lips on his. Very softly he said:

"With the best wishes of the Moon Man, Sue."

THE
WHIS-
PERING
DEATH

CHAPTER I

MURDER FOR MILLIONS

IN THE hugest studio of the American Broadcasting Company building in Great City an audience of hundreds was eagerly witnessing the enactment of the most sensational radio program of the year.

The tom-tom rhythm of the famous dance orchestra playing on the stage was being echoed by millions of loudspeakers scattered from coast to coast. The multitude was waiting hopefully for the final announcement of the nationwide contest which was reaching its climax tonight. Fifty thousand dollars in cash prizes were ready to be awarded to the lucky winners.

Suddenly the brasses broke the swinging melody with a triumphant fanfare. An expectant hush followed as every eye turned to a pair of chromium doors at the rear of the auditorium. They had parted. Foremost among the men who had entered was one wearing aviators' coveralls. His face was greasy, his eyes rimmed with goggle marks, his lips curved in a tired, happy smile. As he strode toward the platform, David Crane, famous announcer, sprang breathlessly to the mike.

"Ladies and gentlemen! During the past ten hours the entire United States has been following the progress of the epoch-making air race from the Pacific Coast sponsored by the Emblem Oil Company. Three of the fastest planes ever built, their tanks fueled with the same Emblem Gasoline dispensed to your cars from our thousands of service stations, have been roaring across the zenith, each battling to reach this destination. The winner has just stepped into this studio!

"A few moments ago, by remote control, you heard the thrilling arrival of the winning plane at the Great City airport. Now the man who tonight hung up a new transcontinental record—the winner of the Emblem Speed Prize of twenty-five thousand dollars in cash—is here to claim his reward. Ladies and gentlemen, I present the ranking record-breaker in the world tonight—Phil Loring!"

Thunderous applause rocked the room and surged across the nation. Loring, a perfect picture of an air ace, bowed modestly from the stage. A short, squat man, white-headed, officious and of commanding presence, came forward to grip Loring's hand. He was one of the wealthiest industrialists in the country, a man whose name was known around the world, the backer of the widely acclaimed air race.

"Mr. Bennett Burlington, President of the Emblem Oil Company, is about to reward Phil Loring's achievement with the prize of twenty-five thousand dollars in cash!" the announcer zestfully continued. "Immediately afterward we will announce the winners of the nation-wide essay contest, the prizes of which total another twenty-five thousand dollars. The winners of the ten highest awards are present in the studio and will be called to the microphone in turn. First, a brief word from that ace of aces, Phil Loring!"

The excitement of the moment was shared, but not pleasantly, by a dozen plainclothesmen from police headquarters who were stationed about the studio. Their alert gazes centered on the neat stack of envelopes placed prominently on a table near the footlights—envelopes containing crisp new banknotes totaling a small fortune. The two men in charge of the protective detail stood near the platform, acutely conscious of the service gats in their holsters.

Gilbert McEwen, ace sleuth of the Great City force, a relentless hunter of wanted crooks, scowled his disapproval. "Fool

stunt!" he rasped. "All that cash lying around loose. It's getting
'em plenty of advertising publicity, but it may give us plenty of
headaches. I've got a feeling, Steve, something's going to
happen."

Stephen Thatcher, smartly tailored, erect and clean-cut, son
of the chief of Police and the fiancé of McEwen's personable
daughter Sue, smiled happily. "Perhaps you're right. Gil, but
I'm glad Phil's collecting the big prize. One of the best friends
I've ever had and one of the finest men living—he deserves a
break. He's been having a tough time of it, you know. Look at
that—twenty-five thousand being put into his hands right now.
It means a new lease on life for Phil and Mary."

McEwen growled: "I'm damn glad of that—but I wish they'd
used checks!"

The announcer was chattering: "Now, at last, ladies and
gentlemen, the moment we've been waiting for. It brings to
Phil Loring—"

Death.

A short, coughing sound broke into the announcer's words.
Something sped past his head with a swift, whispering sigh. A
soft, slapping noise came from behind him—the impact of
something hitting solid flesh. He jerked around. His eyes
widened wildly. Phil Loring was standing stiff, a startled expres-
sion on his face, the envelope containing $25,000 in his
hands—and to his right cheek a small tuft of red bristles was
clinging.

And suddenly—while millions listened to the thud of his
body—Loring dropped lifeless.

"THE WHISPER killers!"

The horrified gasp rose in unison from hundreds of throats.
Men and women jerked terrorized from their seats. The musicians on the platform stared aghast. Bennett Burlington took
a wary, recoiling step. The announcer attempted to blurt something into the microphone to cover the abrupt break in the
program, but he had no voice. It had happened with such mer-

ciless suddenness that a cold paralysis gripped the hundreds, after the first chorused gasp, until a command came from Gil McEwen:

"Cover the doors!"

Dismayed headquarters men sprang into action. Steve Thatcher and McEwen hurried grimly toward the platform. At the same instant five men among the audience leaped from their chairs. Unlike the scores who began a mad scramble toward the exits, they closed in on the platform. They were leveling strange weapons, like huge automatics, but with what appeared to be two parallel barrels. As they crowded to the table on which lay fifty thousand dollars in cash, they snapped ringing orders:

"Get back! Back!"

Three of them whipped toward Steve Thatcher and Gil McEwen. Their hard faces had a weird, expressionless quality, like masks, but their eyes gleamed with murderous determination. They aimed their grotesque weapons swiftly. Another coughing sound broke into the hubbub of the wildly scattering crowd, then another, then a third. Thatcher and McEwen flung themselves down, chilled by the breath of flying darts.

Frantically, because they knew the horrible deadliness of the crooks' weapons, they dropped for shelter behind the edge of the platform. Behind them a stifled scream sounded, a muttered gasp. They saw the colored tuft of a dart spotted against the soundproof wall. They saw a second clinging to the shoulder of a middle-aged woman who was collapsing. They saw a third protruding from the neck of a hoary-headed man who was sprawling down among the chairs—instantly killed.

Steve Thatcher desperately jerked up, risking the prick of a hissing dart that would mean certain, swift doom. The five armed crooks, their faces still uncannily impassive, had leaped to the table where the prize money was stacked. With one of the weird weapons leveled at him, Thatcher dared slip the muzzle of his service gun over the edge of the platform.

Bennett Burlington, the announcer, the musicians, were cowering before the crooks' air pistols, fearful of the lightning death that had sprawled Phil Loring on the stage at the moment of his triumph. One of the killers snatched the envelope from Loring's dead fingers. Another scooped the pile off the table. With fifty thousand in loot they whirled to rush from the studio.

Steve Thatcher's Police Positive blasted. His eyed widened in stunned amazement when he saw the effect of his bullet. A deep gash appeared across the cheek of one of the raiders. It gaped like an excruciating wound, yet the crook did not even wince—and not a drop of blood flowed. Held rigid by bewilderment at sight of that dry, clean cut, Thatcher heard the sneeze of an air pistol and felt the impact of a dart.

It drove into the padding of the shoulder of his coat—a red token of destruction. McEwen, crouching, heard it strike and gasped frantically: "Get down, Steve! Down!" They huddled below the platform as quick footfalls sounded—the killers rushing toward the swinging doors. Then, ducking up, they sprang with service gats ready. Moans of dismay broke from their lips as the milling crowd cut off their line of fire.

Pandemonium in the studio. Terrorized men and women, massing toward the exits, fell back at the killers' commands. Headquarters men, swept aside by the power of the mob, shouldered toward the doors. Air pistols coughed—again, again, swiftly. Darts hissed. Groans blended into shrieks as the whispering death struck. The doomed dropped—detectives, civilians, women—while the killers fled to elevators that were standing open.

The crazed crowd was a barrier Thatcher and McEwen had to fight. They shouldered their way desperately toward the door. Those who had fallen were being trampled by the mob—and each of the dead was marked by a clinging, colored dart. Three headquarters men lay sprawled in the corridor, tufted projectiles driven into their flesh. By the time Thatcher and McEwen battled their way to the elevators, the sliding doors were closed.

"Phone headquarters!" McEwen rasped. "Flash the prowl cars! Stop 'em before they get out of the building!"

But he knew—because this was the sixth time the crooks had struck ruthlessly and swiftly according to a diabolically shrewd plan—that the Whisper Killers were already escaping.

MILLIONS, SCATTERED from coast to coast, each listening in hope that his name would be called as the winner of a coveted prize, had heard instead the outbreak of terror in the studio. The hundreds who had witnessed the daring raid fled in horror into the streets—except the victims who lay dead, branded by the poisoned darts. The very radio system which had been attacked was the first agency to spread the startling news.

"Ladies and gentlemen! The nefarious gang of criminals called the Whisper Killers have vanished after executing, with crashing success, the most daring of their infamous coups, the robbery of fifty thousand dollars from the American Broadcasting Company building. Behind them they left eleven dead, four of the victims being women. Under the direction of Detective Lieutenant Gilbert McEwen, the police of Great City are whipping into action to capture the ruthless murderers."

Extra editions poured from the newspaper presses. "POLICE FAIL TO TRACE WHISPER KILLERS!" Wildfire rumors, spreading terror, penetrated every home. "The cops can't touch them. They kill without warning. Nobody's safe." Flash followed flash from the police headquarters radio room to the hundreds of squad roadsters scouring the city.

"Calling all cars—all cars! Continue hunt for black sedans seen leaving front of American Broadcasting building. License numbers unknown. Occupants five men wearing tuxedos, no other description. Stop all black sedans on suspicion—use caution. Calling all cars!"

While Gil McEwen had rushed to headquarters to command the searching army of police, Steve Thatcher had remained at the studio to make the preliminary investigation. The ghastly thing he had seen had haunted him—the bloodless gash that had appeared in the cheek of one of the killers.

On the platform he had found something that seemed to be clay, three inches long, ragged and curled, its one smooth surface covered with a flesh-colored pigment. Puzzling over it, leaving the investigation in charge of experts dispatched from headquarters, he had started grimly for headquarters.

He entered a drug store, sidled into a telephone booth, dialed a number known only to himself and two others. One of the other two was the man whose cautious voice answered. Ned Dargan was the quarry of a continual hunt by the police, the accomplice of the notorious Moon Man. He asked huskily:

"Boss?"

"Angel!" Thatcher exclaimed. "Have you any report?"

A moan came over the line. "Boss, I've been trying my damndest to find some lead to the Whisper Killers, but it's no go. I thought I could dig up any inside information you need, but this time I'm stumped. There's only one thing it can mean, Boss. These killers have no connection with the underworld."

"I thought so. Angel," Thatcher answered quietly, "but I have another big job for you. I got a look at the killers' faces tonight. They were all unfamiliar. I saw one of my bullets cut a gash in the cheek of one man, and it didn't draw blood. I've got the answer to that. They've used a special putty to change the contour of their faces. My bullet cut some of the stuff off the cheek of one of the men, but it didn't touch real flesh."

"Hell, Boss, they're slick!"

"That's a clue, Angel—the first real one we've got. The putty is used by the whole band. It can't be reused because of the skin-colored pigment they spread on it. That means they need a rather large amount. It isn't likely they brought a big supply with them when they came to the city. They must have bought some here and they probably took no pains to cover the purchases because it was a pretty remote possibility that anyone would discover they're using the stuff."

"That's right, Boss!"

"If they've bought some putty in town, it can be traced, Angel. There's no store specializing in theatrical make-up materials in the city. Some drug stores sell the stuff—not many. I want you to begin checking them right now. Find the one that sold some nose putty recently, and if possible get a description of the purchaser. When you've got it, ring me."

"I'm on the job, Boss!"

Thatcher added quietly: "I'm keeping this clue to myself, Angel, for a special reason. It's a job for the Moon Man, because the Whisper Killers are smart enough to be watching every move headquarters makes. I'm pledging myself to get hold of their loot and return it to the rightful owners. More than that, Angel, I saw Phil Loring killed by that gang tonight—a fine chap, one of my best friends. They're going to pay for it."

"I'm with you, Boss, all the way!" Dargan answered grimly. "Count on me to the limit."

Again, as he broke the connection, Steve Thatcher declared from the depths of his cold heart: "They'll pay."

CHAPTER II

RED HOT MONEY

GIL McEWEN'S voice was rasping in the chief's office when Thatcher climbed the worn wooden stairs. He paused as the door opened. The pretty young woman who hurried anxiously toward him was Sue McEwen, the girl Steve Thatcher was engaged to marry. A suggestion of tears shone in her eyes as she impulsively took his hands.

"Steve, dear," she asked quietly, "is it true Phil is—dead?"

Thatcher answered tightly: "They brought him down with one of their darts, without giving him a ghost of a chance. They robbed him of the money he risked his life to win. Sue, listen. You know how tough it'll be on Mary. She hasn't anything now. I'm going to get that money back."

The girl answered tensely. "Yes, Steve—but oh, please be careful!"

Thatcher wryly smiled. "I know. Gil's turning all guns on the Whisper Killers now, but he hasn't forgotten the Moon Man. Nothing can ever make him let down on that. Sue, you'd better see Mary. I'm starting a job tonight I can't quit until it's finished. 'Finished' means the end of the Whisper Killers."

He pressed his lips to hers; she lifted her chin resolutely as she turned away. Thatcher went quietly into the chief's office. His father, the white-headed Peter Thatcher, was huddled in a padded swivel chair behind the ancient roll-top desk in the corner. He worriedly rubbed his loose-jowled face with a blue-veined hand as McEwen jabbed a stubby forefinger at him.

"The toughest case we've ever tried to crack, by damn!" the steely-eyed veteran was declaring. "The slickest crooks we've ever been up against. Everything shows it. We haven't a single lead to 'em—not one. Hundreds of prowl cars on the job, the whole force going over the city with a microscope, and nothing turns up!"

Chief Thatcher said gravely: "Gil, every hour those crooks run loose means the danger of horrible death to innocent people."

McEwen growled: "Haven't I tried in every possible way to trace the pop-guns they use? Air pistols can be bought any-where without a license, chief. None of 'em are registered. They probably were purchased in other towns, anyway. The darts are made for target practice—trying to identify 'em has led to ab-solutely nothing. Even tracing the poison came to a dead end. Every one of those crooks is as smart as the Moon Man!"

Suppressing a bitter smile, Steve Thatcher recalled a recent report of the city toxicologist. Chemical analysis had identified the poison on the Whisper Killers' darts as curare. Originating in the South American jungles, where it was concocted from secret lethal ingredients by tribal medicine men, curare had recently come into use as a medical treatment for certain dis-eases of the nervous system. Sterilized and greatly diluted, it was obtainable in ampules for intramuscular injection. By evaporating the amber liquid down to its original jellylike con-sistency, poison of appalling potency could be obtained.

"When one of those air pistols lets go at you," McEwen raged, "you're done for. It's impossible to be merely wounded by one of the darts. You might get a lead bullet in the leg or arm and go on fighting, but not when one of those darts hits you. No matter where it touches you, if it so much as breaks the skin—if it's no worse than the prick of a needle you're dead on the spot. By damn, it's plain murder to send cops out against that gang!"

Chief Thatcher insisted earnestly, "We've got to get out of these blind alleys, Gil. We've got to stop them—and soon."

"How?" McEwen challenged. "It's my job—it's up to me—but we don't know anything more about the Whisper Killers now than when they started—except, just as you said, every time they operate, by damn, it means innocent people getting murdered."

Steve Thatcher put in quietly: "Perhaps we do, after all, Gil. There are certain important facts about them right in front of our noses—facts we can and must use. I think we can definitely expect the Whisper Killers to pull another of their jobs night after next."

McEWEN STARED and asked: "What? What're you talking about, Steve?"

Steve Thatcher drew a folded paper from his inner pocket. "Let's map it out from the beginning, Gil. We know the gang came from out of town. The city underworld knows no more about them than we do. Our stool pigeons have been useless. We've hunted for them in the usual dives, but that's turned up nothing because they're probably staying like respectable guests at one of our best hotels. The gang is working with scientific efficiency."

McEwen nodded. "Sure."

"The usual crook," Thatcher went on, "maps out a job, pulls it, lays low for a while, then later repeats the process. Not this gang. They have actually planned a campaign of crime—an entire series of jobs. They don't lay low between times, but click off one coup on the heels of another. The secret of their success is perfect planning, quiet operation and, above all, speed."

McEwen grated: "Right!"

"I believe," Thatcher continued, "tonight's job, their seventh, was arranged down to the last detail before they put their first one into operation. The contest awards and the air race had been announced—they knew all about it. They'd obtained tickets to the studio. They fired the first dart at the precise instant it would catch everyone most off guard. Some of their men had guns on the elevator attendants even then, and their escape went off like clockwork. It was mapped out like an army attack."

McEwen nodded.

"They use air pistols because there are no loud reports to attract attention. They grab their loot and they're off in most cases before anyone else knows what's happening. The use of poison on the darts not only shows they're absolutely ruthless, but it has spread so much terror that almost no one dares to stop their getaway. Everything is minutely schemed out—each job in the whole series, before the first is done—that's what has thrown us into confusion but, also, that's the weak point we can attack."

McEwen demanded: "How?"

Thatcher flattened the sheet of paper on the desk. "Look at that. It's a list of their crimes. The first was committed on the night of the eleventh. The second was on the thirteenth. The fourth was the fifteenth, and so on through the rest—one every other night. Tonight the seventh came along as it should, according to the schedule, on the twenty-third. On the twenty-fifth, two nights from now, the next one is due. That's how we can strike back at them, Gil!"

McEwen glared at the tabulation. "Good work, Steve!" His knuckles rattled on the desk. "You're absolutely right! The gang's had me so busy running around in circles I didn't see it myself."

His eyes shone like burnished metal as he turned to a map of the city tacked on the wall. "I'm going to mark every location in the city where there's possible loot for the Whisper Killers' banks, everything. Night after next I'm going to have prowl cars stationed around every one of them. At each place I'll have men watching. No matter how fast the gang works next time, we'll be able to match their speed. One radio flash will surround 'em before they have a chance to get away. Thanks to you, Steve, we'll grab 'em!"

His eyes narrowed. "But where will they strike? I'm as positive as you are, Steve, they'll operate on schedule night after next, but *where?*"

That, Steve Thatcher told himself with a tight smile, was what he was going to attempt to learn—quite apart from the usual routine of police duty.

BRINGING ALL his crime-busting ingenuity into play, Gil McEwen spent the next day quietly perfecting his counter-strategy against the Whisper Killers. Newspapers bannered the failure of the police to trace the gang. Radio dispatches reiterated that no clues to the identities of the killers had been found. The mayor, the president of the police board, scores of influential citizens demanded that the gang be apprehended at once. And McEwen, saying nothing, allowing the unknown crooks to consider themselves safe, schemed with the wiliness of a fox to trap them.

The furor aroused by the daring radio raid still electrified the air of the entire metropolis when, next night, shortly after eleven, Detective Sergeant Steve Thatcher entered the drugstore located in the Manhattan Building in the midst of the downtown section of Great City. A secret report to headquarters had summoned him here. As he approached the row of telephone booths, he glimpsed the man who had called. Ned Dargan, emissary of the notorious criminal known as the Moon Man, his face shaded by a low-pulled hat, was waiting.

Only Thatcher saw the gesture that signaled him into one of the booths. Dargan shouldered into another. A moment later Thatcher's instrument rang. Dargan's voice came over the wire.

"All safe, Angel," Thatcher said quietly. "What have you got?"

"Boss, this is the store that sold the putty," Dargan answered. "The clerk remembered the man who bought it—name's Frankl. Frankl has an office on the tenth floor of this building—1001. He's apparently a business man, running an outfit called the Statistical Survey Company. I saw him go up a minute ago—he's there now."

"Good work, Angel!" Thatcher watched the store while he talked. "It's a thousand to one Frankl's surveys have to do with crime planning. His statistics are concerned with large amounts of loot. It bears out my suspicion the gang is running their program of crimes like an efficient business. Anything else?"

"I've seen five men go in and out of the office, Boss. They must be the brains of the outfit, with the rest of the gang set up in another place. I managed to check up the date when the Statistical Survey Company moved in, and it was about a month before the first Whisper Killers' crime. Hell, Boss! Look out the window! That's Frankl passing now!"

Thatcher quickly scrutinized the man who paused at the corner. "That's him, Boss—waiting to cross!" Dargan cued. In cold amazement Thatcher saw that Frankl was trimly, modestly garbed, like a successful conservative business man. His face now had none of the menacing masklike hardness that had characterized the Whisper Killers in the studio raid. The entirely different cast of his features made Thatcher realize the effectiveness of the pigmented putty as a disguise. He remained tensely silent until Frankl vanished through the traffic.

"He was the only one up there, Boss," Dargan's voice came again. "What're we going to do?"

Thatcher answered with a click: "We're going up."

He shouldered out of the booth, carrying with him a small black case that he had brought from his roadster. At the entrance of the Manhattan Building he waited until he was sure Dargan was following. He stepped into a waiting elevator. Dargan ambled after him. They neither spoke nor even glanced at each other as the cab glided upward. When it slid to a stop at the tenth floor, Dargan got off alone. Thatcher stepped out at the twelfth.

HE ANGLED in the corridor, paused at the door of the firestairs. He went through and down four flights to the tenth level. Dargan was waiting there, holding slightly ajar the door which could not be opened from the stair side. Quietly Thatcher lifted the lid of the black case.

He took up a voluminous black robe and shook it over his shoulders. He pulled black gloves on his hands. He lifted the hinged halves of a fragile sphere of silvered glass and fitted them together over his head. He transformed himself, in a moment, from Steve Thatcher, detective sergeant and son of the chief of police, into an infamous criminal… the Moon Man.

His muffled voice sounded: "Wait here, Angel."

The Moon Man was wanted for innumerable robberies. It was of no moment to Gil McEwen, his avowed foe, that he had stolen only ill-gotten wealth and had distributed every cent of his loot to the sick and needy who must have it or perish—every patrolman and detective in Great City had standing orders to shoot the Moon Man on sight, to capture him at all costs.

He whispered to Dargan: "Keep the door open for a quick retreat."

He was wanted for three kidnapings—one of the girl he loved, another of the jurist before whom he must come to trial if ever he was imprisoned. He was wanted for a murder—a murder of which he could not hope to prove his innocence—and the Moon Man at each appearance faced the risk of paying the supreme penalty. His apprehension must inevitably mean his death in the electric chair.

"Boss!" Dargan exclaimed in alarm. "Watch yourself, Boss!"

The Moon Man glided into the deserted corridor. His black robe rustled as he approached the door lettered *1001 Statistical Survey Corp.* His silver head twinkled as he listened. Lights were burning inside. A radio was playing softly. It warned the Moon Man that Frankl had stepped out only for a moment and would soon return. The evident danger gave the Moon Man only the briefest pause. He brought a pack of master keys from a pocket inside his robe and quickly began his daring work.

Locks meant nothing to the Moon Man. The bolt drew back at the second try. The ghostly figure melted through the door. The Argus glass of his mask seemed opaque as a mirror from the outside, but through it the Moon Man, seeing as clearly as though it did not exist, surveyed a suite of rooms equipped with the desks, files and appurtenances of a well-organized office. The gleaming black front of a safe drew him close.

His skill was equal to the intricate mechanism. He worked with quick precision, sensing the proper sequence of the right numerals on the steel circle. When he thrust at the handle it yielded. The Moon Man swung the steel slab wide.

The safe was empty.

CHAPTER III

SUICIDE BARGAIN

A **SOUND STARTLED** the Moon Man. It was the clicking of a key in the lock. He straightened with a gasp. He brought his automatic into his hand. As the entrance began to open, he swung the safe door shut, nudged the dial, and sprang into shelter behind a row of filing cabinets. The bolt snapped. Footfalls sounded. Voices spoke.

"Then the next deal is all clear. After that we're finished. We've had rather a successful season, don't you think, Beith?"

A chuckle answered. "Efficiency pays, doesn't it? Our competitors aren't accustomed to such smooth work. Yes, I think we can consider the next project closed and—"

Beith broke off because the Moon Man had swiftly straightened. His globular head flashed a silver signal of danger as he stepped alertly into the open. His automatic leveled, he studied the two amazed men who were peering at him. Frankl, as before, seemed a respectable, conservative business executive, and Beith appeared to be of the same stamp—except for their eyes. Their gazes gleamed with a sinister coldness while a soft laugh sounded inside the Moon Man's spherical mask.

"Good evening, gentlemen."

"The Moon Man!" Frankl blurted. He steadied himself at once. "Are we to consider ourselves honored by your visit? You'll find nothing of value here."

"I agree, gentlemen," the Moon Man answered firmly, "you have carefully hidden the fifty thousand dollars stolen from the

American Broadcasting building last night. I came here because I have a plan—one in which, I know, you'll be most interested."

The two men tried in vain to probe the glitter of the Moon Man's mask. Then they exchanged a glance of understanding that said the Moon Man had identified them beyond all doubt. It was Frankl who asked, with tense calmness:

"What do you want?"

"A proposition, gentlemen," the Moon Man answered. "It is that I join your business organization as an executive. I have information which is of the utmost value to you, and in return I shall expect a generous share of the—ah—profits. My bargain is based on the fact that you are not nearly so safe as you imagine—in fact, you will certainly meet with failure when you attempt your next deal—and I am the only one who can circumvent for you that very grave danger."

Frankl countered: "What're you talking about?"

"Let me see," the Moon Man murmured, his automatic still leveled, "your next deal is planned for tomorrow night, is it not?"

"How did you know that?" Beith blurted. "How the devil *could* you know—"

"I have many ways of learning pertinent information, gentlemen," the Moon Man interrupted smoothly. "If you are acquainted with my unfortunate reputation, you are aware that I know my way about Police headquarters rather well. I know, for instance, that Lieutenant McEwen has evolved a plan which will certainly be your undoing—a trap you cannot possibly escape—unless, gentlemen, you benefit by my advice. I am the only man living who can save you all from a very rapid trip to the death house."

Frankl and Beith stared aghast. Chuckling again, steadying his automatic, moving to the nearest desk, the Moon Man added: "I don't expect you to make your decision on such short notice, of course." He transferred his weapon to his left hand, tugged off his right glove, opened the cover of an ink pad. "This is to assure you I actually am the Moon Man."

He pressed his thumb on the pad, left a clear imprint on the blotter, wriggled his hand back into the glove. "If you attempt to betray me, of course, I can counter by destroying you. I hope we may trust each other, as business partners should. Suppose, gentlemen, you take a few hours to think it over. I will call you soon on the telephone."

Still the pair of master crooks stood silent. The Moon Man's robe rustled as he backed to the entrance. Again his muffled voice came from his shell mask: "My indispensable advice, gentlemen, in exchange for a quarter share of the proceeds on your next deal. Please wait for my message. Good night."

Suddenly the Moon Man was gone.

THE TELEPHONE zinged. Two men stared at it while the shrill sound penetrated the silence of the Statistical Survey offices. At the Moon Man's disappearance they had hurried into the corridor, but they had found not the slightest sign of him. During the three hours that had passed since his startling visit, they had earnestly consulted with their "partners in the business." The trilling of the bell told them the Moon Man was ready to receive their decision.

Frankl smiled slowly as he reached for the instrument. "If he makes one move against us, he'll go to the chair himself. I think we've provided for every exigency, haven't we, Beith? We've got the Moon Man exactly where we want him."

"Exactly," Beith agreed as Frankl lifted the receiver.

A ghostly voice came over the wire: "This is the Moon Man calling, gentlemen. Have we reached an agreement?"

Frankl answered: "We have. We will accept your proposition. One quarter share in the profits of the next deal in return for your information. This is not, of course, a matter in which we can draw up a written contract. We will be obliged to honor each other's oral promises."

"Precisely," the Moon Man answered. "One provision I must insist upon, gentlemen. You must give me your word not to attempt to unmask me. I will work with you only upon the assurance that you will make no attempt to see my face. That must be agreed now."

"We accept the condition explicitly," Frankl answered with a slow smile. "Now, as to the next step—?"

"A conference," the Moon Man suggested. "I find your office location is too prominent for such a purpose. I propose that you come to a place I have prepared. It is the house at Eighty Bridge Street. I will meet you there, gentlemen, in just thirty minutes. Again, good night."

Not far from the house at 80 Bridge Street, Detective Sergeant Steve Thatcher pronged his receiver. He lifted it again, called the number of police headquarters. Stuffing a handkerchief into the transmitter to muffle his voice he asked for Gil McEwen. He tightened when McEwen's rasp answered and said softly:

"Listen carefully, lieutenant, and please hear me through. This is the Moon Man calling."

"The Moon Man!" McEwen snarled. "By damn, I'm going to—"

"Wait!" Steve Thatcher urged earnestly. "Don't attempt to have this call traced, lieutenant. I beg of you to believe I'm sincere. I have found strong evidence pointing to the identity of the Whisper Killers. If you'll promise me a moment's immunity I'll tell you exactly how you can capture the gang before they have a chance—"

"I'll promise you nothing!" McEwen grated. "I'm out to get you, Mr. Moon Man! I've promised a thousand times to send you to the chair, and I'm going to keep my word! I wouldn't trust you to—"

"Listen!" Thatcher pleaded. "I want to see the killers brought to justice as badly as you do—for a special personal reason. Unless you heed what I say—"

He broke off abruptly. Fragmentary syllables carrying over the wire warned Thatcher that McEwen was ordering someone to another phone in an effort to trace the call. With anxiety burning at his nerves, he broke the connection. Dismayed by McEwen's refusal to listen, he made the only move remaining possible. He sidled from the telephone booth, left the cheap restaurant, and walked quickly to the house at 80 Bridge Street.

It was lightless, apparently deserted. He entered by a back door, went to a front room, paused at a blinded window. A whisper came out of the gloom:

"All set, Boss?"

"Yes, Angel." Thatcher was opening the black case he had left in the corner. "They're coming." He shook the black robe over his body. "I'm forced to take the step, Angel." He drew the black gloves on his hands. "I have two purposes—and both of them are of the highest importance. Neither of them can be achieved in any other way."

"But, boss," Dargan blurted, "I don't trust those killers! You're putting yourself into a trap. All they have to do is get you cornered, tip off McEwen, and then—"

Dargan choked off, but the thought completed itself in Steve Thatcher's mind. He realized full well the tragic consequences if ever the secret were revealed that the son of the chief of police was the Moon Man. It would break old Peter Thatcher's heart—the shock would surely kill him. It would crush even the tough McEwen. It would destroy forever the happiness Steve Thatcher and the girl he loved dreamed of together. It would mean disgrace, dishonor, death in the electric chair.

"McEwen's plan," Thatcher said quietly as he lifted the silver mask, "can go into operation only after the Whisper Killers have struck again. It can capture those cold-blooded murderers only after more innocent people have died by those damnable darts. I've got to prevent that, Angel, if it's humanly possible. There's only one way I can do it—by learning, somehow, beforehand, exactly where the crooks are going to strike tomorrow night."

"But if they don't come across with that, Boss?"

If they did not, Steve Thatcher grimly told himself, the Moon Man must face the most dangerous task of his career—a dilemma that might mean his doom.

DARK SILENCE filled the musty house. The Moon Man stood in the unfurnished room, a silver-headed ghost. In a closet, with the door standing slightly ajar, Ned Dargan huddled, gun in hand. Tonight the Moon Man was able to safeguard his secret against any treachery of the Whisper Killers but later, he realized as he waited, he could not. Dark silence—tense minutes passing—and at last a sound.

"They're here, boss!"

Quiet footfalls crossed the porch. The Moon Man's black robe flapped as he strode to the entrance. He opened it wide, standing back, automatic in hand. Frankl and Beith came in slowly, eyes narrowed. The Moon Man started as he glimpsed gleaming weapons in their hands—huge, grotesque guns leveled steadily at his body.

They were air pistols, loaded with darts tipped with deadly curare, ready at the slightest touch of the trigger to spit out death.

A chuckle echoed inside the Moon Man's globular mask. "I quite understand, gentlemen," he said quietly. "You have a natural distrust of me. By the same token, I hope you will pardon my keeping covered. I believe, as the situation stands, you enjoy a decided advantage. Shall we step into the next room and discuss our proposition?"

The guns were a mutual challenge—the two lethal air pistols pointing at the Moon Man, the Moon Man's automatic aimed at Frankl and Beith—as they moved through the darkness. They paused in silence, the two ruthless master criminals intently studying the silver-headed figure. Frankl spoke quietly:

"This is a business matter. We have decided to play ball with you because we stand to gain by it. If we work together in harmony, you will also be the richer. Any further deals we make with you must depend upon the success of this one. At the same time, because of the serious consequences we face in case of failure, we've got to protect ourselves. Is that understood?"

"Perfectly," the Moon Man murmured. He realized full well that at the first indication of treachery on his part, the Whisper Killers would swiftly destroy him. He knew he was stepping into a trap which might spring at any instant, that by allying himself with the murderous band he was placing himself between two fires. Yet, grimly determined to achieve his double purpose, the Moon Man accepted the danger with a muffled "Perfectly."

He went on: "You are here to learn the details of Lieutenant McEwen's counter-plan. I will give them to you. I desire, in turn, as an executive of our organization, to become fully acquainted with your next strategy. In exchange for my information, you will divulge to me the location of your next operation. Is that agreed, gentlemen?"

"Agreed," Frankl answered.

"Agreed," Beith nodded.

"Then, gentlemen," the Moon Man's voice sighed inside his silver mask, "let's get down to business."

CHAPTER IV

BLACK PROMISE

FRANKL AND Beith, their air pistols still leveled at the black figure, listened intently to the muffled voice speaking in the darkness.

"McEwen has discovered the key to your campaign of crime. He is prepared for our move planned for tomorrow night He does not know where we will strike, but he has mapped the location of every possible source of loot in the city. Around each point he will have men watching. He will be ready for swift action. No matter where we operate he will be able to surround us before we can make a getaway. That, gentlemen, is the danger we face—a tremendously serious one."

Frankl and Beith exchanged dismayed glances. Beith blurted: "Is that straight?" Frankl rasped: "Go on!"

"I assure you," the Moon Man continued, "it is the absolute truth. But note the weak spot in McEwen's plan. Its success depends upon both the telephone system and the headquarters radio station. That is, McEwen cannot act until word is flashed to him that we are already operating—flashed by wire. Then, in order to direct his forces against us, McEwen must reach the right spot with his orders—by radio. If those two lines of communication are cut off, McEwen will be absolutely helpless."

"Cut them off?" Frankl countered, his consternation mounting. "How the devil can we do it?"

"That, gentlemen," the Moon Man resumed, "constitutes my plan—the plan which is the basis of our bargain and a matter of life and death to you. As you realize, I am quite familiar with police headquarters. I know, for instance, that the telephone cable enters the building through a conduit which connects with a man-hole in the street, near the corner. I know the location of the radio room, and the precise spot in the broadcasting equipment which is most vulnerable. Listen carefully."

Frankl and Beith hung on every muffled word.

"Just before our operations start tomorrow night, the police telephone switchboard will go out of commission. The source of the trouble will be the man-hole. One stick of dynamite dropped into it will break the cable, or a few gallons of burning gasoline will destroy the insulation of the wires and cause a short circuit. Once the line is destroyed, McEwen will be unable to receive any report from the field."

Eyes gleaming, Frankl urged: "Go on!"

"But we must make doubly sure. On the rear wall of the broadcasting room, the two amplifying tubes are contained in screen cages. One is in use while the other stands ready, at the throw of a switch, for emergency use in case the first breaks down. We, gentlemen, will cause them both to cease operating, and very simply. Across the street from headquarters and down the block is a building from the roof of which the two amplifiers can be seen through the radio room window. Only two bullets from an accurately aimed rifle are necessary.

"Once the tubes are smashed, headquarters will have no voice, and McEwen will be totally unable to flash an alarm to any of the waiting squad cars."

Frankl smiled slowly. "Mr. Moon Man, I give you credit. Your plan is positively fool-proof. We'll not only be able to cripple the whole force and checkmate McEwen, but the two men who do the job will certainly make a quick getaway. We'll do it exactly as you've outlined."

A chuckle came from the Moon Man's mask. "Very well, gentlemen. I leave the details to you. Now, your part of our bargain revolves upon you. I'm ready to receive your information."

"That is—?"

"*Where* will we operate tonight?"

The Moon Man waited tensely for the answer. Through the sheen of his mask he watched Frankl straighten, a sly smile thinning Frankl's slips. The response came in a low, grating tone.

"We intend to keep our word to tell you that, Mr. Moon Man, but our bargain didn't stipulate when. We made no promise to tell you that detail tonight We must, you know, protect ourselves. Secrecy is absolutely necessary until the last moment. Just before we go into action tomorrow night, we will inform you."

In sudden anxiety the Moon Man protested: "Gentlemen! As one of your partners, I must know now—"

"Tomorrow night," Frankl interrupted dryly, "telephone our office. Call at precisely eleven o'clock. You will receive instructions over the wire. Tonight's conference, Mr. Moon Man, is concluded."

The Moon Man stared in chilled dismay as Frankl and Beith backed to the entrance. Their air pistols remained leveled at the phantom figure—weapons capable of killing instantly with no sound to raise an alarm. The silver-masked criminal stood silent, stunned because he was certain argument was futile. The two master minds of the Whisper Killers stepped out the entrance, into thick darkness.

Fast footfalls, and they were gone. The Moon Man's black-gloved hand grimly gripped the knob as he closed the door. He turned back to see Dargan coming out of the closet, eyes glittering with consternation. The Moon Man parted the hinged halves of his mask, lifted it away. The face of Steve Thatcher shone white as he blurted:

"They're keeping me trapped, Angel! They're forcing me to go through with it! My scheme didn't work—"

"We've got to stop 'em, Boss!" Dargan exclaimed. "Somehow we've got to stop 'em!"

Steve Thatcher echoed huskily: "Somehow...."

A POLICE car turned into the driveway of the modest home located far across the city from the deserted dwelling in which the Moon Man had held a secret rendezvous with the Whisper Killers. Two men alighted from it and trudged into the house. They were Gil McEwen and Detective Sergeant Mark Keanan—a sleuth as doggedly determined as the grizzled veteran to capture the Moon Man.

Sue McEwen greeted her leather-faced father with a hug, Keanan with a warm smile. They were not in a mood for pleasantries. They slumped into chairs, faces grim, while the girl anxiously watched them. His teeth grinding into an unlighted cigar, McEwen growled:

"By damn, how the papers are squawking! 'Break up the Whisper Killers'! We're getting it in the neck from all quarters, by damn! We're doing our best, aren't we? I'm all set to crack down on that gang when they pull their job tomorrow night—and mark my words, Keanan, the Moon Man is mixed up in this."

Sue's cheeks paled. A ring at the door took her away from her chair, though she continued to listen. As she opened the entrance, McEwen rasped on:

"Maybe he tried to give me a good tip, but I don't trust that fancy crook. He knows more about the Whisper Killers than we do—but that's all the more reason for going after him. I'd give my last cent to come face to face with the Moon Man tonight!"

The words rang mockingly in Sue McEwen's mind as she stood shocked rigid with consternation, staring out the door—for she was looking at the Moon Man.

He was a spectral figure standing just beyond the sill, a leveled automatic in his gloved hand, his silver head twinkling. The whiteness of the girl's face became stark as under her breath she said: "Steve!"

Without a word, the Moon Man strode past her.

McEwen jerked up, cigar angling down in dismay. Keanan sprang to his feet, muttering an incredulous exclamation. At the same instant their hands jerked toward their hip-pocket holsters, but a muffled command froze them: "Steady, gentlemen!" While the glittering automatic covered them, they stared at the silver-headed apparition the Moon Man in the home of the detective who was sworn to send him to the electric chair!

"Please pardon," the Moon Man said, "my rude intrusion. You must realize, lieutenant, that only the most pressing necessity would bring me here. I have come to implore your cooperation as a matter of life and death for those who might otherwise become victims of the Whisper Killers tomorrow night. I beseech you to believe in my sincerity. First, gentlemen, your guns."

McEwen began in a rage: "No you don't, I'll—"

"Put them on the table, gentlemen. I will take charge of them, of course. After I leave, you'll find them in the garden." His automatic enforcing his orders, he chuckled when the two detectives obeyed. "Miss McEwen, of course, will conduct herself discreetly while we talk." His black-gloved hand took up the two Police Positives and slipped them out of sight through a slit in the side of his robe. "This time, McEwen, you must listen to me."

McEwen straightened, grimly silent. Keanan glared. The girl stood chilled, her lips trembling with anguish because she knew, as her father did not, that the face concealed within the fragile glass sphere was Steve Thatcher's. She had loyally shared his secret while praying it would never be discovered. Now, dismay in her eyes, she watched the Moon Man step back and place his free hand on the telephone.

"You do not know, lieutenant," the Moon Man said quietly, "where the Whisper Killers will strike tomorrow night. Nor do I. But we both realize that once they go into action, it will mean a wanton slaughter of human lives. You have a plan for closing in on the gang, but it cannot operate until the death toll has already been taken. If it is humanly possible, we must prevent such a tragedy. Before the plan of the Whisper Killers gets fully under way, we must know where they will operate. I beg of you to trust me, McEwen, because I am the only man who can give you that vital information."

McEwen challenged: "If you've got the dope on 'em, and you mean what you say, tell me now!"

"It would be useless for me to reveal their identities now, lieutenant," the Moon Man answered, "because they are clever enough to have destroyed all evidence connecting them with their previous crimes. They cannot be convicted unless they are caught red-handed during their next job. I cannot tell you where it will be pulled, because I don't yet know. I will learn the secret tomorrow night, just before their new plan starts working at eleven o'clock."

"Well?" McEwen grated.

"I am here, gentlemen, to ask for a truce. Grant me a day's immunity. Give me your word of honor that you will make no attempt to unmask me or capture me until midnight tomorrow. For my part, I pledge you I will do my utmost to help destroy the Whisper Killers. Well, gentlemen? What is your answer?"

SILENCE FILLED the room. The Moon Man, one hand still on the telephone, stood with bowed head gleaming, automatic glinting. Sue McEwen gazed at him breathlessly. Mark Keanan squinted while his sharp mind worked. Anger lumped Gil McEwen's jaw muscles. His harsh voice broke the hush:

"Here's your answer—I don't bargain with crooks!"

The Moon Man spoke urgently. "I admire your integrity, lieutenant, but you're forgetting a higher demand resting upon you—the responsibility for safeguarding those who might otherwise die horribly poisoned. Unless you promise me a truce, you will have their deaths on your soul."

Sue McEwen said quietly: "He's right, dad. It's—it's your duty to meet his terms."

Keanan said wryly: "I agree with that. The district attorney grants crooks immunity, and the courts are lenient, if they aid the law—why shouldn't we? I'm out to get the Moon Man same as you, Gil—I don't want any murders on my conscience!"

The Moon Man added: "I ask it only until twelve tomorrow night, lieutenant. Once midnight strikes again, our bargain will be completed. Your promise will no longer hold—you will be utterly free once more to bend every effort toward capturing me. But in the meantime I hope that we, working together, will be able to destroy the Whisper Killers."

McEwen's eyes narrowed. "All right," he said. "You've got your truce. We'll keep our hands strictly off the Moon Man case until midnight tomorrow."

"Your word of honor, lieutenant?"

"My word of honor."

The Moon Man chuckled. Deliberately he lowered his automatic. As the weapon disappeared inside the black robe, McEwen jerked with an impulse to leap upon the notorious criminal, but he held himself back. Keanan eased. Sue McEwen, a sob of relief on her lips, watched the Moon Man lift the telephone.

"One more man must enter our agreement, lieutenant," he said as he spun the dial. "I will call him here, and you will explain the matter to him. I have special instructions for you all." And, holding the transmitter close to his shell mask, he said over the line: "Police headquarters? Connect me with Detective Sergeant Stephen Thatcher."

The Moon Man alertly studied McEwen's hard face. He heard an answer to his call: "Sergeant Thatcher is not in headquarters now," and the connection broke. Making sure McEwen had not heard the voice in the receiver, he pretended to converse—with himself. "Sergeant Thatcher? This is the Moon Man calling. An important matter demands that you come to Lieutenant McEwen's home at once. That's all. Good night."

He replaced the dead instrument, turned to confront the two detectives. "Because the information I have now is so meager," he said, "I cannot suggest a definite plan. We must be prepared, for any development. I am in the ticklish position of having to keep on the alert against the gang while leading them to believe I am working with them. One slip, and I am a doomed man.

"Therefore, lieutenant, you and Sergeant Keanan are to hold yourselves ready at police headquarters at eleven tomorrow night. As an extra precaution, in case your telephone should not be working at that time, be prepared to receive a call from me in the little cigar store on the opposite corner. At the same time, Sergeant Thatcher must wait for another call at his home. You will all have special instructions, I think, in time.

"That is all for the moment, gentlemen. I bid you good night. If you will, a handshake to seal our agreement."

Sue McEwen gazed in amazement at the spectacle of her father, then Keanan, gripping the black-gloved hand of the Moon Man. The robed figure turned swiftly. He glimpsed anxiety in the girl's eyes as he hurried to the entrance. His silver head twinkled away in the gloom. In the house a breathy exclamation burst:

"By damn!"

The Moon Man tossed two Police Positives into the garden as he sped out the gate. He paused in deep shadow, near a parked car. Gently he lifted the spherical mask off his head. He whipped out of the robe, pulled off the gloves, tucked the regalia in a black case. In the darkness the Moon Man vanished and Steve Thatcher appeared.

With the case locked in the rumble compartment of the roadster, his eyes shining with profound concern, Thatcher turned back to the McEwen home—to hear, as himself, the details of an amazing plan which he, as the Moon Man, already knew.

CHAPTER V

SECRET ORDERS

THE TIME lacked one minute of eleven o'clock. The date was the twenty-fifth. It was the night of the last daring coup planned by the Whisper Killers, the hour when the Moon Man hoped to receive vital information.

In a telephone booth in a downtown drug store, Steve Thatcher spun the dial to the number of the Statistical Survey Company. Clicking connections brought a voice over the line—Frankl's. Through a handkerchief stuffed into the transmitter to muffle his words, Thatcher said quietly:

"This is the Moon Man calling."

The clipped answer came: "Go immediately to office Number Twenty-Six-Thirteen in the Apex building. In accordance with our promise not to try to see your face, you will not be observed by any of us. You will find no one in the room. You will have just five minutes to mask yourself before I come in. You'll receive further information there."

"But—"

"That's all."

Thatcher's lips pressed hard as he listened over the voiceless line. Dismay chilled his heart as he shouldered out of the booth. When he strode from the door, Ned Dargan turned from a window and fell into step with him. Dargan's face was shaded; he was carrying the black case containing the Moon Man's regalia. A few blocks away the tallest skyscraper in the metropolis reared—Thatcher's destination, the Apex building.

"They're still keeping it back, Angel," he said tightly. "I can't call McEwen yet. They can't make a move until I know definitely where the job's going to be pulled. In the Apex building? I'm not sure. Stick with me, Angel—it's a chance, but there's no other way."

Eyes alert, they entered the spacious foyer of the white spire. An elevator cab lifted them to the twenty-sixth floor. At the door of 2613 Thatcher and Dargan paused to listen. A turn of the knob revealed it to be unlocked. They entered a small room furnished only with a chair and a table on which a telephone sat. Dargan's eyes shone with alarm as the door closed.

"Boss, you're taking an awful chance! They might be planning to hold you here and turn you over to the cops for the rewards after they've pulled their job!"

"A chance, Angel," Thatcher agreed, "that can't possibly be avoided. I'm forced to see it through. Listen at the door and mask yourself. At the first hint, we've got to flash the information to McEwen somehow."

Opening the black suit case, Thatcher quickly covered himself with the robe. He pulled the black gloves on his hands, fitted the silver hemisphere over his head. He angled his wrist to read the time indicated by his wrist-watch and saw that the five minutes had almost elapsed. When he turned to the door, at the sound of a step in the corridor, Dargan's face was covered with a handkerchief.

"He's coming, Boss!"

The man who stepped briskly into the office had Frankl's build, but his face was uncannily changed. The Moon Man saw that its contour had been cleverly altered by applied plastic, pigmented to look like natural skin. The disguise warned the Moon Man that the moment of the Whisper Killers' new coup was near. Frankl paused abruptly, narrowed eyes glittering at Dargan.

"My assistant," the Moon Man said gently. "He is implicitly under my orders. Now—?"

Frankl accepted Dargan's presence without a word—a move which chilled the Moon Man with the conviction that the Whisper Killers were guarding themselves shrewdly against a possible counter-move. Frankl opened the door. Two men, their faces also cunningly distorted with plastic, entered silently. They paused; their hands flashed. Suddenly two air pistols were covering the Moon Man.

"There is no cause for alarm," Frankl said gratingly, "if you're playing square with us. I noticed, when we first talked terms in my office, you were wearing an expensive wrist-watch. We merely want to take a closer look at it."

The dart guns covered the robed figure and Dargan as Frankl stepped forward. The Moon Man could not resist Frankl's deft removal of the wrist-watch. Filled with a deep presentiment of danger, he watched Frankl expertly open the gold case. Frankl drew a sheet of paper from his pocket, wrote briefly on it, closed the case, then smilingly returned the watch to the Moon Man.

At that moment the notorious silver-masked criminal felt an icy conviction that his doom was sealed.

FRANKL SLIPPED the page into a blank envelope. He handed it to one of the men at the door. That man went out while the other lowered his air pistol with a slow smile. Frankl sat at the table, spun the dial of the telephone. When the connection was completed he said, eying the Moon Man:

"Hello. Frankl calling. I have just sent a messenger over with a sealed envelope. Get these instructions exactly right. You are not to open the envelope in any case. If I call for it personally before one o'clock tonight, you are to return it to me. If I do not appear, you are to take the envelope directly to the chief of police—at once. Understand? That's all—"

Frankl briskly rose. "Mr. Moon Man," he said quietly, "no doubt you recognize this is a precaution. Your watch, you know, being an excellent one, is guaranteed, and its serial number is recorded at the store which sold it, with the date and the name of the purchaser. The number is now written into a letter which explains that the store's record is conclusive evidence—coupled with your thumbprint—of the identity of the Moon Man. The letter will be placed in the hands of the chief of police shortly after one o'clock tonight if you have attempted in any way to betray us."

In the hands of the chief of police! The words mocked Steve Thatcher. In the hands of the father of the Moon Man!

Frankl went on: "The letter is now being taken to my attorney. He will obey my instructions implicitly. If our plan carries through tonight, the job will be completed before one o'clock. I solemnly promise to reclaim the letter from my attorney, destroy it, and make no attempt to trace the number if, Mr. Moon Man, there has been no occasion to justify the letter being delivered to the chief of police. I must, of course, withhold the name of my attorney.

"In the meantime," Frankl said, moving to the door, "remain here. Since you are to share in our profits, you are also to share our risk. We will go into action soon. Final instructions will reach you by telephone, with the information you have been so anxious to learn. That's all for the moment."

Frankl and his henchman stepped out. When the door closed a moan broke from the Moon Man's globular mask. Dargan stared at him in abject dismay.

"They've got you, Boss! You don't dare make a move against 'em! If you do, it's your finish!"

"In that case," the muffled voice answered grimly, "the Moon Man has come to the end of his criminal career."

His silver head bowed as he lifted the telephone. Dargan stared speechless with consternation while the dial spun. The Moon Man's muted words were: " Police headquarters? Connect me with Lieutenant McEwen." He straightened, his hot breath whizzing rapidly past the deflector inside his mask. McEwen's biting rasp answered.

"Lieutenant," the Moon Man reported, "I am still unable to give you definite information. I'm reasonably certain, however, that the Whisper Killers are planning their attack somewhere in or very near the Apex building. I expect to have the exact particulars in a few minutes. Your only move is to come to the Apex building at once, and to wait in the drug store on the ground floor for further word from me. I will phone you, as soon as possible, at one of the pay telephones."

McEwen answered tartly: "I'm taking you at your word, Mr. Moon Man—but I'm reminding you, too, by damn, that it's getting pretty close to midnight!"

"I'm aware of that, lieutenant," the Moon Man answered bitterly. "Lose no time. You had best—hello!"

A sharp click echoed along the wire at the instant In the office in the Apex spire, the Moon Man heard it. Bent over the chief's desk in police headquarters, McEwen heard it. And McEwen heard far more. Simultaneously a jarring concussion shook the air around him.

He spun to the window, still gripping the instrument, and peered into the street. The explosion had roared in the very center of the pavement flanking headquarters. Flames were geysering up from an open man-hole. Its heavy iron lid, twirling through smoke-laden air, clattered down a hundred feet away. The roar rolled a deafening din along buildings from which broken window panes dropped jagged glass. Following the blast came a stunned hush.

"By damn!" McEwen grated. "Hello! *Hello!*"

The telephone line was dead. The first step of the Whisper Killers to cripple headquarters had been taken—as planned by the Moon Man. The second swiftly followed.

IN THE radio room on the third floor of the building, blue-shirted men looked around curiously as the rumble of the explosion faded. Suddenly new, sharp sounds startled them. Somewhere in the night a report spat. A white-rimmed hole appeared in the pane near the microphone. A louder, shattering noise brought dismayed exclamations from the men at the charts. The amplifying tube was dropping in fragments!

It sputtered out as water cascaded from its broken jacket. A rip in the protecting screen betrayed that a bullet had destroyed it. Quickly an astounded engineer leaped to the knife switch which could cut the emergency tube into the circuit and revive the dead antenna. Before he could touch it a second crack sounded, a second round hole appeared in the window pane— and the second tube spilled down, shattered.

Gil McEwen was charging out of the chief's office, his teeth driving into a cigar, when the announcer and the engineer loped into the hallway.

"We're off the air! Both tubes broken! The station's dead! We can't get any orders out until we install new tubes—tomorrow at the earliest!"

McEwen bounded down the stairs with Mark Keanan at his heels. "Every man on the job!" They hurried to the garage door. "Head for the Apex building!" Patrolmen and detectives began running from the desk room, the locker room, the recreation room, pulling into tunics, slapping helmets on their heads. "Go at it easy—keep out of sight when you get there—but *move!*"

In the garage starters snarled. Motors sang. Gears clashed. Police cars began to spurt into the street. At the wheel of the first, pushing the engine to the limit now, but prepared to make a cautious approach to the Apex building, was the determined McEwen….

At the entrance of the Apex tower, at that moment, other cars had already arrived. They lined up at the curb. Half a score of men alighted from them. Their faces were strangely impassive in the dim street light. Some of them were wearing topcoats with collars turned up, the cuffs of light gray uniform trousers showing beneath. They strode briskly to the elevators in the foyer.

One car was waiting open. A man with mask-like face stepped into it with one who was wearing a topcoat. Without warning he thrust the muzzle of an air pistol against the startled attendant's side. He commanded: "Go down!" The grille closed and, a few moments later, reopened. The building attendant had vanished. He was lying bound and gagged in the basement. The uniformed man at the cab controls had a strangely shaped face, weirdly expressionless.

Huge banks of elevators serviced the Apex spire during the working day, and even at night half a dozen remained in operation to serve the many night workers scattered up and down the ninety floors. One after another the efficient criminal army took command of the cabs. With the regular attendants overpowered and safely concealed in the catacombs below the ground level, the Whisper Killers achieved complete control of the passenger system.

Another vehicle drew to a stop near the entrance of the foyer. It was a green armored truck. Its uniformed driver remained at the wheel, his guard kept the front compartment bolted. Two more guards, in duplicate uniforms, opened the rear doors. They kept their posts though the steel-walled truck was empty, as if waiting to receive a precious cargo. They were armed, but their holsters sheathed automatics, unusually formidable, each with a cocking bar, above its barrel. And their faces had an unnatural placidity.

In the foyer men in civilian clothing, their features similarly impassive, entered the elevators. The grilles closed, the cabs ascended. None of the Whisper Killers who remained in the lobby betrayed the slightest uneasiness. Their supreme, evil confidence would not have been shaken even had they known that hidden police eyes were watching....

IN THE small office on the twenty-sixth floor of the tower, the telephone jangled. The Moon Man's black-gloved hand darted to it. He had been waiting torturously for this summons, while the zero hour of midnight inexorably ticked nearer. The damning watch on his wrist warned him time was perilously short. Over the line he asked breathlessly: "Yes?"

"Go up to the fifty-eighth floor," the voice of Frankl directed quickly. "The elevator operator is one of us. You will appear, ready for action, in exactly two minutes."

The Moon Man straightened as the connection broke. "Fifty-eighth floor!" he exclaimed. "It's the offices of the Emblem Oil Company, Angel!" He thumbed rapidly through the directory. "I went there the day of the last raid to ask them to use checks instead of cash for the contest awards." His black finger rapidly spun the dial.

A girl's voice responded: "Emblem Oil Com—"

"Who's in the office tonight?" the Moon Man demanded. "Is your safe open? If it is, close it! Bolt the doors! Answer me! Who is there and what—?"

"I don't understand," the girl said. "This is the Emblem Oil—"

"Yes! Listen! Connect me with someone in authority—anyone—hurry it! You've got to realize—"

"There is a very important directors' meeting being held now, and I can't interrupt," came the answer. "If you'll leave your number—"

The Moon Man had jerked up. "Directors' meeting! Is Bennett Burlington there? If he is—"

"Yes, sir, he's here, but I couldn't disturb him. If it's important, I'll give him your number and—"

The Moon Man broke the connection in frenzied haste. During his trying wait he had ascertained from information the number of a pay telephone in the pharmacy located on the street level of the Apex. Now he called it. The distant bell rang four times, while his nerves flamed, before a rasping voice answered—McEwen's.

"Lieutenant!" the Moon Man rushed out. "The Whisper Killers are invading the Emblem Oil offices now! It's a thousand to one they intend to snatch Bennett Burlington. Surround the building and close in on them! Look out for the elevators—their men are in charge. You've got to act fast, but it's our chance!"

"Right, by damn!" McEwen snarled back. "I've got 'em spotted! It's our chance—and also it's damn' near midnight, Mr. Moon Man!"

Heart frozen, the Moon Man whirled to the door. "Angel, find the freight elevator. Take charge of it at any cost. Look out for one of the killers with a dart gun, but take control of that car. Send it up to the fifty-eighth floor. Ignore the buzzer and open only for a signal rap—five times, fast. On your way, Angel!"

The Moon Man's black-gloved hand gestured danger as he opened the door. A passenger elevator stood open directly across the corridor. A man with a masklike face was waiting for him. With Dargan staying back until the way was clear, the Moon Man strode, robe flapping, into the cab. Immediately the grille closed and wind soughed past—while the Moon Man noted the bulge of an air pistol under the attendant's tunic.

The car slid to a stop. The Moon Man stepped out into a luxuriously furnished foyer. A corps of men with waxlike faces were stationed at a dozen doors opening in the offices beyond. One of them was directing a dart gun through a glassless window at a terrified telephone girl. Frankl was waiting. The Moon Man paused, confronting him.

"Let us proceed," Frankl said.

The Moon Man strode with him along a corridor. Men with air guns followed. Frankl gripped the knob of a door labeled *Directors* and opened it swiftly. His men crowded in behind him as he stepped, with the Moon Man, directly to the head of the great mahogany table around which fifteen men were staring aghast. The directors of the world-wide Emblem Oil Company started up, stunned exclamations punctuating dismayed gestures—but sinister weapons kept them at their places. Surrounded by killers with ghastly inhuman faces, overpowered by sheer surprise, they sat transfixed as Frankl addressed them.

"Gentlemen, a highly important matter must be presented to this board. I will outline it as briefly as possible. Mr. Bennett Burlington will in a moment leave this building with us and will disappear. He will return unhurt promptly upon your payment of the sum of two hundred and fifty thousand dollars. I trust none of you will be so unwise as to vote nay on this proposition, gentlemen. I should dislike very much the necessity of ordering my men to kill you where you sit."

CHAPTER VI

DOOM NUMBER

THE MOON MAN stood, heart chilled, at the side of Bennett Burlington. The face of the noted industrialist was white as death. His fellow executives gazed appalled at Frankl. The leader of the Whisper Killers smiled faintly as he leveled the weapon of horrible destruction. Briskly he continued:

"The sum of a quarter million dollars may seem excessive to you, gentlemen. Let me remind you that though a worldwide embargo is in effect, Emblem Oil is not affected. You are selling your fuel to all nations on the globe, to the extent of many millions of dollars. You cannot, of course, close any major contract without the signature of your president and chairman of the board, Mr. Burlington. A quarter million is a small sum to pay for his safe and prompt return."

Silence—while the Moon Man listened tensely for the first sound that would signal McEwen's attack. Silence while the seconds ticked toward the zero hour when his truce must end—midnight.

"Take your vote on this matter promptly, gentlemen," Frankl added. "A delay will cost you fortunes. When you are ready, merely insert a small personal ad in the Record saying 'Terms satisfactory' and sign it with the initials of the company. I will then communicate with you. That, I believe, is all. Mr. Burlington, kindly step into the reception room. Resistance will force us to take drastic measures."

The tight hush returned as Burlington stared. The men with air pistols retreated from the conference room, aiming at the directors still sitting transfixed around the table. Frankl, standing just inside, made an imperative gesture. The Moon Man's robe rustled as he stationed himself at the opposite side of the door. His hand gripped his automatic inside his robe. Bennett Burlington, whose word commanded a corporation that circled the globe, rose in abject obedience to a killer's order.

Suddenly elevator panels slid open in the reception room. A score of plainclothesmen burst through. Police positives glittered an ominous threat as the weird-faced criminals spun, jerking up their air pistols. Three swift, metallic coughs sounded before McEwen's rasping command rang:

"Drop those guns! Any man with a pistol in his hand gets a bullet in the heart, by damn!"

Frankl jerked back in dismay. The reception room was suddenly filled with the turmoil of a battling mob—dart pistols spitting, revolvers cracking, partitions quaking against a weighty charge. The Moon Man twisted across the connecting door— and McEwen glimpsed him. He slapped it shut, shot the bolt— and spun as Frankl's air pistol glittered up.

A sneezing report! The Moon Man ducking, felt the tick of a tufted dart against his fragile mask. For one paralyzed instant he poised, expecting the fragments of the irreplaceable glass shell to fall away from his face. Time stood still while the chill fear gripped him that Frankl and the fifteen directors of Emblem Oil would see his identity revealed. But the mask did not break. The dart drove into the wall behind the Moon Man an instant before he leaped at Frankl.

His desperate attack was another threat of destruction to the silver globe. Frankl swung his air pistol desperately in an attempt to crash it against the silver sphere, but a black-gloved hand gripped his wrist. The Moon Man's automatic prodded into Frankl's throat. He jerked up, tearing the killer's weapon away. Gun leveled, breath hissing inside his globular mask, he chuckled.

"You haven't the advantage of surprise this time, Frankl—and your gun is not a repeater!"

The air pistol spun from the Moon Man's fingers. It cracked through a window-pane, twirled out into the night. A harmless thing now, fated for destruction.

IN THE reception room a Police Positive blasted—the last shot of a desperate encounter. The bullet splintered into the arm of a man gripping an air pistol. The weapon coughed out a dart that drove into the floor. Gil McEwen spun away, teeth clenched with rage, seeing his men forcing mask-faced killers against every wall.

"We've got 'em, by damn!"

The suddenness of the police attack, the close quarters, the fact that air pistols must be reloaded after every shot, had brought McEwen a swift victory—but the deadly darts had taken their toll. McEwen had seen two men drop during their fight for the elevators. He saw three more here, huddled on the floor marked by evil colored tufts. He charged at a door, his eyes fierce.

"Some of 'em had to take it—some of 'em had to, by damn! Keep 'em covered, Mark! The Moon Man's in there. It's two minutes past twelve!"

Keanan gasped, as McEwen's fist pounded the panels: "Gil, are you going after him now—after this?"

"I've sworn to send that crook to the chair, and I'm going to keep my word!" McEwen's hand slammed. "Open up!"

A bolt clicked. McEwen shouldered through with gat leveled. He stopped short, glaring at the white faces of fourteen frenzied men. One blurted:

"Where is Mr. Burlington? He was here—but where did he go? They've got him! They've slipped out with him somehow. They'll kill him unless—"

McEwen barked: "Where's the Moon Man? I saw him in this room!"

Breathless silence answered. McEwen peered down at a man lying on the floor, sprawled out, unconscious. To McEwen's startled eyes that man's face seemed to be mauled out of all semblance to human shape. He saw the dent of a gun butt on the furrowed forehead—a wound that was not bleeding. While Frankl lay senseless, dropped in his desperate struggle with the Moon Man, McEwen demanded again:

"Where's the Moon Man?"

A quavering voice answered: "He went—out that door."

McEwen rushed through it. It gave into another corridor that angled back to the rear of the office layout. It was lined with doors. McEwen thrust at every one of them. His gun peered into office after office—each empty. When he reached one, at the end of the hall, which resisted his push, he grated: "He's in there!"

He crashed his shoulder against the panel. With all the strength he could summon he fought the bolt. The door shook in its socket at each blow. He stumbled in suddenly, brought himself to a tight-muscled standstill. He leveled his gat at a black-robed, silver-headed figure which lay motionless on the floor and he snapped:

"Mr. Moon Man, you're got!"

Men hurried into the office behind him as he stooped above his cloaked captive. He saw, without understanding it, that his prisoner's wrists were tied. He put his hands on the fragile glass sphere and halved it. Straightening, he peered speechless at the revealed face.

A voice beside him said quickly: "Gil—are you okay? I just got up. The Moon Man's orders had me stationed in the basement. Once you got on the job, I had a devil of a time climbing this high. We've lost men—it was inevitable—but the gang's cut to pieces. Every one of them will go to the chair."

It was Steve Thatcher's voice.

"By damn!" McEwen exploded again.

He was still staring at the face of the man who lay breathless on the floor—the man in the black robe, whose head had been concealed by the silver globe. It was Bennett Burlington.

NEWSBOYS SHRIEKED on every corner. "WHISPER KILLERS CAPTURED!" They howled along every street, selling papers faster than they could collect the coins. "GANG BROKEN UP!" The entire city resounded as if with a triumphal fanfare. "MOON MAN TRAPS KILLERS!"

Countless radios in the city blared into the morning hours with flash after flash.

"Lieutenant McEwen has exacted confessions from the ringleaders of the Whisper Killers. Frankl has disclosed the hiding place of the fifty thousand dollars in cash stolen at the cost of eleven lives. Mrs. Loring, wife of the aviator who flew to victory and death in the cross-country race, is assured of receiving the prize money he won. Lieutenant McEwen and the Moon Man, his criminal enemy, share honors for destroying the murderous gang—for it the Whisper Killers will inevitably march to the electric chair."

The chair. It was still a grim promise of dishonored destiny for the Moon Man. His dread secret was threatened with exposure. The time was a few minutes past one o'clock.

A coupé drew to the curb near the headquarters entrance. A puzzled but determined man left its wheel. He was Raoul Waterson, one of the most promising attorneys in Great City, a man of immaculate reputation. He was distressed by the discovery that his apparently conservative client Frankl was in reality a ruthless murderer. He was grimly intent upon carrying out Frankl's last instructions, because he believed it might establish a complete confession. His purpose now was to deliver to the chief of police the sealed envelope which had been entrusted to him.

He stepped toward the headquarters entrance—but abruptly stopped. A short, stocky man had materialized out of the small-hour gloom. Stepping close, a cauliflower ear showing faintly beneath the brim of his low-pulled hat, he pushed a revolver against Waterson's side. As the lawyer gasped, Ned Dargan said:

"This is as far as you're going. I'll take the envelope."

Waterson blurted: "What—what! Is this a hold-up? You can't get away with this! You can't intimidate me!"

Dargan's voice rang. "My instructions are to get the envelope. I was ordered not to hurt you, but I'll murder you on the spot if you force me to it. If they ever grab me I'll go to the chair anyway, so what's the difference? It's—it's the Boss's life if you deliver that letter. Hand it over!"

The snout of the revolver was pressing hard to Waterson's side. His fury faded. He fumbled the sealed envelope out of his inside pocket. Ned Dargan snatched it away. He backed into the shadow of the car. Suddenly running footfalls echoed across the street. A fleeting figure was dimly visible an instant. Then, swiftly, it was gone. Waterson strode through the headquarters entrance. He could not know that, even while he climbed the stairs, Ned Dargan was sheltered by the gloom of the alley behind the building, ripping a sheet of paper to shreds. Destiny had determined that the letter damning Steve Thatcher as the Moon Man should never be read when Waterson thrust into the chief's office.

He ignored the babble of voices, the excited milling of men. He strode straight to the desk of Peter Thatcher. He rapped his knuckles as he glared at the old chief, at McEwen. Steve Thatcher, standing near, listened with a tart tightening of the lips to Waterson's complaint.

"Held up! Held up right at the door of headquarters! An important letter—heaven knows how important—taken from me at the point of a gun. I demand that that criminal be apprehended!"

Steve Thatcher said quietly: "I quite agree, Mr. Waterson. It's an outrage. I suggest you tell me the full details. I assure you I'll give the matter my closest personal attention."

Gil McEwen put a fresh cigar in his teeth. "I've got a better idea," he said, grinning slyly. "It'll get results quicker. Just turn the case over to the Moon Man!"

CORPSE'S PLUNDER

CHAPTER I

GHOUL'S LOOT

THE FUNERAL procession turned with stately solemnity toward the great iron gate of the Sanctuary Cemetery. Following the majestic hearse came an impressive parade of cars carrying a reverent cortege which included most of the prominent personages of Great City. They were paying their final devout homage to one who had been a friend and leader—a sad and newsworthy occasion.

Mrs. Ashworth Pendleton, czarina of the social world, benefactress to thousands, beloved of all who had known her, was being escorted to her last resting place.

With her, into her grave, the dead woman was taking a strand of precious jewels as celebrated as herself—the famed Pendleton necklace.

The sedan rolling directly behind the wreath-banked hearse contained two men who were not mourners. They were hard-faced, sharp-eyed, alert. One was Mark Keanan, a stocky, hard-boiled plain-clothes man from headquarters. His companion was Detective Sergeant Tryce. Both had been detailed to this unusual duty by Detective Lieutenant Gilbert McEwen, commander of the Great City police department. Neither liked it.

"I'll be glad," Keanan growled, "when she's planted. Guarding a stiff gives me the jitters, especially when she's wearing two hundred thousand dollars worth of ice. Think of it, man—a fifth of a million in diamonds never to be seen again, locked in a tomb with a corpse."

Tryce asked: "Why not? Mrs. Pendleton gave most of her fortune to charity during her lifetime. She was entitled to indulge a sentimental whim. The necklace meant more to her than anything else in the world because her husband gave it to her as a wedding present. She wanted to keep it for herself forever. Her will said it's to be buried with her—and the wishes of the dead must be respected."

Keanan shrugged. "I suppose so. Just the same, I'll be glad when she's inside that special door with all the locks fastened. Then I'll want a drink."

DEEP WITHIN the hushed cemetery, a city of the silent within a city of the living, the Pendleton crypt was waiting to receive its dead. The hearse made its last turn to the ponderous gate through which its fare would never return. It was swinging into the solemn retreat when an unwonted interruption stopped the funeral.

No one in the procession had noticed the powerful sedan which had joined it on the lonely road leading to the sanctuary. Its driver and his companion looked like weird creatures from another planet. Their heads were encased in grotesque gas masks from which long snout like coils dangled to aspirators strapped to their chests. Through their owlish goggles they had cunningly watched the bloom-decked head of the black parade, tensing as the moment for the last turn neared.

Suddenly, with the accelerator jammed down, the sedan lurched out of line and roared past the mourners toward the ebon carrier of the dead.

At the same time another car was approaching from the opposite direction. It was an old, disreputable-looking vehicle, but it swooped to the gate with startling speed. Its hard-clamped brakes wreathed smoke as it bucked to a stop. Shot directly across the graveled path, it blocked the entrance to the cemetery. The hearse paused. A devastating attack struck it.

Keanan and Tryce, jerking up in the police machine witnessed the daring maneuver. Next they saw the pulsing sedan, which had sped from the rear of the funeral line swerve along-side the hearse. Two gas-masked men leaped out of it. A third sprang from the decrepit car which was crammed across the gate. Gripping automatics, the three acted in swift concert. Keanan and Tryce, desperately pushing out into the road, were challenged by blazing bullets.

Slugs slammed against the doors which Keanan and Tryce had partly opened. Dented metal clanged, and cracked glass went white. In spite of the danger the two plainclothes men thrust out. Leaping for shelter behind the car, they glimpsed glittering objects hurtling at them through the sunlight. Hollow, coughing sounds followed. Thick, white vapor spewed up from bursting tear-gas bombs. Keanan and Tryce found themselves in a blinding storm of choking fog cut by whistling lead.

The two detectives sprang away from their car to escape the scalding punishment of the fumes. The popping explosions, like mocking laughter, continued rapidly. The hearse was thickly clouded. Even when they found clearer air, Keanan and Tryce felt their eyes streaming hotly. They fired wildly at phantom figures in the steam. Goggle-faced killers returned their fire mercilessly.

Keanan gasped, jolted back by the power of the slug that slammed into his gun-arm. He pawed the thickened air, dove off the pavement, groped blindly for his lost gun while he vainly strove to see. Tryce groaned, doubling with agony, melting to his knees. Torturous pain filled his lungs, acid tears robbed him of sight. Both men, rendered helpless by their wounds, trapped by the strangling mist, sensed the swift movements of the masked attackers.

The cracking automatics, the whining bullets, the exploding bombs, had wrung shouts of dismay and screams of terror from the mourners. They had crowded out of their cars, outraged, fearful, stunned. Fumes flooded over them. As they scattered, the throbbing roar of a powerful motor broke through the mist.

The gas-masked raiders were escaping.

IN A modest residential district near the outskirts of the city, a police roadster was winding its way toward headquarters. The clean-cut, trimly garbed young man at the wheel was Stephen Thatcher, detective sergeant and son of the chief of police. The grizzled leather-faced veteran of the department who sat at Thatcher's side was Gil McEwen, dogged enemy of all crooks in general, the relentless hunter, in particular, of the notorious criminal known as the Moon Man.

McEwen gnawed angrily on his unlighted cigar. His choleric temperament had kept him in a mood of seething fury all day. He growled with wrath as the roadster turned a corner where a shrill-voiced newsboy was shouting:

"Moon Man's Mask Disappears From Headquarters! Evidence Against Moon Man Mysteriously Disappears! Daring Criminal Robs Chief's Safe!"

McEwen snarled: "By damn! That fancy crook's gone too far. He can't pull a stunt like that and get away with it. His luck can't hold out forever. The time's coming when I'm going to nail the Moon Man, and keep him nailed. I've sworn a thousand times to send him to the chair, and I'm going to keep my word, by damn!"

Steve Thatcher observed quietly: "You will, Gil. You'll corner the Moon Man someday—perhaps soon. You'll never stop until you see him fry."

"Never!" McEwen swore.

But the notorious criminal had succeeded, so far, in outwitting the inexorable McEwen again and again. Repeatedly the Moon Man appeared by night, in daring defiance of the police, clad in his black robe and silver mask, to perpetrate his amazing coups. Repeatedly McEwen had driven him into a corner from which escape seemed impossible, yet always, the Moon Man had eluded the trap as though with some black-magic power. Each time the Moon Man escaped his net, McEwen's indomitable determination to capture him became an even stronger drive.

Weeks ago McEwen had triumphantly seized the Moon Man's mask and robe. He had stored them in the safe in Chief Thatcher's office at headquarters, grimly confident that without them the uncanny crook would be unable to operate. This morning he had discovered the robe and mask missing. Somehow, with that bewildering resource which characterized him, the Moon Man had reclaimed his regalia.

"I'll sure get him for that," McEwen vowed vehemently, "if it's the last thing—"

Abruptly a nasal voice issued from the radio beneath the dash. It was tuned to the headquarters wavelength. The twanging alarm came breathlessly:

"Calling cars Fifteen, Twenty-One, Thirty, Forty-Two! Signal Thirty! Proceed at once to entrance of Sanctuary Cemetery. Block Cedar Road and stop all cars leaving vicinity. Look for sedan carrying three armed men. Use caution—they are dangerous. Calling cars...."

McEwen snapped: "Step on it, Steve!"

But Thatcher had already toed the pedal down hard. The roadster swung sharply at a corner, turning into a through street which would lead to the focus of the alarm. "By damn!" McEwen ground out. "It hooks up with the Pendleton funeral." Repeated cryptic signals rattled from the radio as the roadster sped. When it swerved on whining tires into Cedar Road, McEwen saw at one swift, grim glance that he was right.

Mingled with the costly automobiles of the funeral procession, strung out along the pavement, were two green prowl cars. Scores of startled men and frightened women were scattered around them, coughing, their widened eyes streaming stinging tears. A white, pungent mist was still weighting the air. On the bloodspotted tar around the halted hearse a crowd had gathered. Steve Thatcher, hammering the horn button, skirted toward it while McEwen, cigar clamped, hung out an open door.

The tough-skinned veteran sprang away, shouldered and growled into the crowd. Frock-coated men and veiled women fell back before him. He gave one glaring glance at Mark Keanan, who was sagging against the side of the hearse and nursing a red-dripping arm. He shot another at Tryce, who was standing one-legged, painfully sparing his punctured thigh. He climbed into the black vehicle and hunched, glowering at the bronze casket.

The bolts of its head section had been loosened. The hinged part had been lifted. Exposed against its pillow of white satin was the placid, waxen face of Mrs. Ashworth Pendleton. She lay clad in the ancient brocade of her wedding gown—but now no strand of precious stones glittered on her still chest.

Two hundred thousand dollars worth of diamonds had been snatched from this aristocrat of corpses.

ALARMS CONTINUED to flash from the headquarters broadcasting antenna. Prowl cars skittered back and forth along Cedar Road, plunged along every branch, scouted every byway. Posted patrolmen formed a circle around the Sanctuary Cemetery while half a score of detectives scoured the road for clues. News of the daring crime horrified the city.

Thousands of radios reproduced the breathless announcement: "The criminals who ruthlessly desecrated the body of the beloved Mrs. Pendleton succeeded in their inhuman purpose at the cost of two lives. The driver of the hearse, Louis Blake, and the mortician, Anderson Smythe, were both shot down when they attempted to balk the robbery. Detectives Keanan and Tryce were wounded. They, with twenty mourners, suffering from exposure to tear gas, have been rushed to Mercy Hospital.

"The police dragnet, thrown out by Detective Lieutenant McEwen, has so far failed to bag the crooks. The entire police force is concentrating on the case under McEwen's direction, but so far there have been no encouraging results."

McEwen and Steve Thatcher had sped back to headquarters. The hard-headed veteran's orders had whipped the entire force into action. Reports flashed back to him as he tramped the office of Chief Thatcher. Each brought a hotter flush to his face, a grimmer glint to his metallic eyes.

He pounded his fist on the top of the chief's ancient rolltop desk as he said: "They're lying low, right now, but they won't dare stay in town, by damn! That necklace is the hottest piece of jewelry in the world. They know I'm going over this city with a fine-tooth comb, and they can't risk being caught with it. They'll have to take the chance of ducking out, and they'll have to take it soon. When they do, by damn, they'll get hooked!"

Chief Thatcher's hoary head wagged. He palmed his loose-jowled face with a blue-veined hand. His position was almost an honorary one—the relentless work of crime-fighting lay mostly in McEwen's hands—but his orders, when he gave them, were still the supreme commandments of the department. "We can't let 'em get away with it, Gil," he said quietly. "We're going to concentrate on this case until we crack it—and we're going to crack it fast."

"I'm doing everything possible, chief," McEwen asserted. "This town is closed up tight. Nobody's going to get out of Great City with that necklace. But, by damn, it's a waiting game. We've got to wait until they try it."

Steve Thatcher had been working intensely at McEwen's side, organizing the police counter-attack. While McEwen fumed, he remained collected and thoughtful. He suggested: "Gil, these crooks are devilishly slick. They're working according to a shrewd plan. They must have counted on our throwing out the dragnet plenty fast, and if so they've planned a way of beating it. Suppose, instead of trying to sneak the necklace out, they—"

McEwen snapped: "A mouse couldn't get out of this town right now without being spotted. Any crook trying to slip away with that necklace is committing suicide. Yet they can't stay under cover. I'm turning this city upside down. I'm using every stool pigeon for leads, much as I hate to. Either way, whether the crooks stay or whether they skip—it's only a matter of time until they get grabbed, by damn!"

Thatcher agreed: "The crooks we want must have underworld connections, but I believe they're shrewd enough to have taken every possible precaution. With a necklace that valuable, that famous, that hot, they must have thought out beforehand a clever way of getting rid of it. I've got a hunch—"

"So've I!" McEwen cut in. "Within a few hours the three of 'em will be here in headquarters, with the necklace, getting hell whaled out of 'em. I tell you, by damn, all we have to do is wait."

Thatcher realized McEwen's ire, first aroused by the mysterious disappearance of the Moon Man's regalia from the chief's safe, intensified to a consuming wrath by the daring corpse robbery, was too overwhelming to permit cool thinking. With an understanding smile, Thatcher stepped from the office. Eyes glittering, mind humming, he went to his own desk and opened a file of recent letters. His routine duties had brought to his hand a communication from Scotland Yard.

It read in part:

> Conversant with our mutual arrangement, the following information is submitted. For two months, during his stay in London, we have had under surveillance one Stanislaw Dawst, diamond merchant, of Paris, France, whose description is appended. Though evidence is lacking, Dawst is suspected of being a member of an international ring of brokers who deal in stolen gems. He has today embarked aboard the *S.S. Ultima* and will arrive in your city on the 23rd inst. Any information you may submit concerning his activities while in your city will be of considerable moment to us.

Thatcher hurried down the worn wooden stairs, crossed from headquarters to the little cigar store on the opposite corner, shouldered into a telephone booth. The number he called was known only to himself and two others in the world. The ring of the distant bell brought a husky response:

"Boss?"

"Angel," Thatcher said quietly, "I have important instructions. They must be carried out quickly and carefully. The Moon Man is intensely interested in the Pendleton necklace."

CHAPTER II

COVER-UP TACTICS

SURPRISED SILENCE held the wire a moment. Then, the cautious whisper of the Angel came: "You mean you want to get the diamonds back, boss?"

"That's a comparatively unimportant part of it Angel," Thatcher explained. "I'm more interested in the crooks—most interested of all in the big money involved. I believe McEwen's using the wrong tactics, but he's too worked up to listen. I'm playing a long gamble, purely for charitable purposes."

"I don't quite get you, boss."

"The crooks who pulled the job," Thatcher went on, "are all set to make a clean-up. The necklace is worth a king's ransom. There's a far better use for the proceeds than lining the pockets of three killers. Hundreds of worthy families in the city need money for the bare necessities of life. We're going to try to give them the help they need, Angel."

"Count on me, boss. But what's the lead?"

"Several days ago, Angel," Thatcher continued, "I gave you the job of tailing one Stanislaw Dawst."

"I've been keeping an eye on him, boss, but he's behaved himself so far."

"I warned you at the time that headquarters is also interested in him."

"I've spotted two plainclothes men checking up on him, but they haven't stuck very close."

"I also told you Dawst might have something up his sleeve, but I didn't know what it might be. I'll wager the robbery this afternoon is the answer. He's your man, Angel."

"Gosh, boss! Maybe it's a hot lead, maybe it's no good at all, but it seems to connect. I'll find him and phone you a report."

"Be careful, Angel," Thatcher continued. "McEwen's too hot under the collar right now to think straight, but it won't be long before he remembers Dawst. We'll have to get to him before McEwen does. Work fast!"

"I'm on my way!"

Thatcher sidled out of the telephone booth. His nerves were tight with the urgency of his plan when he re-entered headquarters. Climbing the stairs to the second floor, he heard the beat of McEwen's heels in the chief's office. McEwen's rasp carried out:

"Slick—plenty slick, by damn! Look at that report, chief. A check on the old car they left in the cemetery gate. No registration—forged plates. No fingerprints worth a damn. No lead whatever. Well, I'm sure of one thing. Those killers are cold-blooded, experienced crooks. Something ties up with 'em, and before you know it, we'll have 'em!"

Thatcher went quietly toward his office. McEwen's heels kept pounding. His growl came again:

"What a day! First the Moon Man's mask and robe disappearing out of this safe. Then this corpse robbery. One more thing will make it complete—the Moon Man pulling another job tonight!"

Under his breath Steve Thatcher murmured: "I think I can promise you, Gil—he will."

Closing the door of his office, he smiled bitterly. McEwen knew the Moon Man stole only ill-gotten gains or undeserved wealth, but that did not lessen his determination to track the crook down. McEwen knew the Moon Man distributed all his loot to the needy, never keeping a cent for himself, but that did not alter his inflexible pledge to doom the notorious criminal to the electric chair. McEwen did not know, and would never believe, that the Moon Man was guiltless of the murder which made the supreme penalty his inevitable fate. McEwen did not dream that his quarry was Detective Sergeant Stephen Thatcher, son of the chief of police, his closest friend, the fiancé of his only daughter.

Alone in his office, Thatcher waited anxiously for a report from Ned Dargan, ex-pug, the secret emissary of the Moon Man.

THE TELEPHONE purred. Instantly Thatcher brought the receiver to his ear. The message he heard, in Dargan's cautious voice, was brief and cryptic: "Eldorado 5-5632. Waiting."

Thatcher rose immediately. The connection broke. Opening the door, he stopped short. He smiled warmly at the pretty, personable girl who was hurrying toward him from the stairs, but a glitter of anxiety remained in his eyes. Sue McEwen went at once into Thatcher's arms. She found his lips tense and dry; she drew back in alarm.

"What is it, Steve?"

He said quietly: "I'm sorry, Sue—we can't have dinner together this evening, as we planned. Gil's tearing the town wide open, and I have a special job of my own to do. Please forgive me. Perhaps I'll be free later."

Sue McEwen stepped into the office, with color fading from her face. Her coat fell open, disclosing her smart dinner dress. Its vivid hue contrasted sharply with the whiteness of her smooth skin. She took Thatcher's hands searching his eyes anxiously.

"What are you going to do, Steve?"

He smiled tautly. In all the world only Sue and Ned Dargan knew that Steve Thatcher was the Moon Man. She had guarded his secret loyally, had shared with him the danger he faced. She realized as keenly as he the tragedy which must surely follow if ever he were unmasked. It would mean heartbreak for the kindly old chief, even for the tough-skinned McEwen. It would destroy all the dreams of happiness which she and the man she loved cherished together. Thatcher thought of it as he looked into her eyes—dishonor, death in the chair....

"What is it, Steve?" Sue persisted. "And are you sure it's worth the risk, darling?"

Thatcher urged: "Stand by me, Sue. I know it's a crazy gamble, but there's no other way. Please trust me—and wait for me. Perhaps I won't be long."

He turned from her quickly. Her worried gaze followed him as he ran down the stairs. Again he crossed the street to the little cigar store, and shouldered into a telephone booth. He spun the dial to the number which Dargan had given him. Dargan immediately responded—speaking, Thatcher knew, from a pay-station.

"Boss! I'm in the lobby of the Grand Palace Hotel. I checked on Dawst right away and found he's in his room. It's 1541. A few minutes ago three men called his room and went up. They're still there."

"Three!" Thatcher exclaimed. "The trail's hot, Angel. What did they look like?"

"Fancy dressers, boss. If they're crooks, they're high class. One of 'em walks with a slight limp—wears a special high-heeled shoe. The second had a queer look in one eye—might be glass. The third—"

"Has a deep cleft in the chin," Thatcher quickly supplied, "with one temple gray, though the other isn't."

"Right, boss! You know 'em! Who are they?"

"Crooks as clever as we've ever been up against, Angel," Thatcher answered. "Their names are Govett, Englar and Forbs. Headquarters knows them well, but we've never been able to reach them. A week ago they came back from Florida, probably after a very profitable season. They're specialists in extortion, deluxe robbery and gambling, though no one's ever been able to pin anything on them. I think we've got it, Angel. I'm sure now that McEwen is on the wrong track."

"Why, boss?"

"They've made no attempt to skip town. They're not keeping under cover. They know they'll be picked up, sooner or later, for questioning about the necklace, so they're making a bold move to get rid of it immediately. That makes it doubly necessary for us to work fast. Orders, Angel!"

"Okay, boss!"

"Engage a room in the Grand Palace, on the fifteenth floor, as close to Dawst's as you can get it. Use the name of Hammerwell. Keep an eye on that trio. Wait for me, Angel. I'm coming."

Steve Thatcher quickly left the telephone booth, crossed to his parked roadster. Glancing upward as he started off, he saw that the window of his office was lighted, and knew that Sue McEwen was still there. He angled rapidly into the most fashionable hotel and apartment district of the city. He drew to the curb near the glittering marquee of the Grand Palace.

He unlocked the rumble compartment of his roadster, lifted out a small black case. It contained the robe and the mask of the Moon Man. Thatcher had obtained them from the safe in the chief's office, in the dead of night, by the simple expedient of using the combination. The case had remained hidden in Thatcher's car since then—while, all unsuspecting, Gil McEwen had ridden at his side. Now, boldly carrying the regalia of the most notorious criminal ever to operate in the metropolis, Thatcher strode into the hotel.

STEVE THATCHER left the elevator at the fifteenth floor. The ritual of inquiring for Mr. Hammerwell and being directed to the proper room had required only a moment. Its number was 1544, only a few steps from Dawst's across the hall. Striding briskly along the thickly carpeted corridor, Thatcher saw it open quickly and Dargan's square face appear.

Dargan stepped back at once. Thatcher, closing the door behind him, found Dargan breathless. All the police of Great City were looking for this stocky, neckless ex-pugilist, as an accessory to the Moon Man's crimes. Since the day Steve Thatcher had saved him, from torturing illness and starvation, Dargan had served the Moon Man loyally. His careful disguise could not eradicate one feature which marked him—his cauliflower ear. His fate, if he were recognized and captured, must lead him inevitably through the little green door of the death-house—yet he had obeyed instructions without question.

"They're gone, boss—the three of 'em!" he exclaimed. "Just a second ago. They must have been going down while you were coming up. I was just starting out to tail 'em."

Thatcher urged: "Go to it, Angel. Find out where they're bound. Phone me at headquarters. On your way!"

Dargan slipped out. Thatcher remained at the door, gazing through a crack, until Dargan disappeared into an elevator cab. He eased out, crossed the hall silently. He listened at the door of 1541, but there was no sound. Quietly he returned to 1544. He drew the blinds, shot the bolt. Then, quickly he opened the black case.

He unrolled a long black robe and shook it over his shoulders. He pulled black gloves on his hands. He inspected his automatic, slipped it through a slit in the side of his cloak. Last he lifted from the case the fragile glass mask which had kept the secret of his identity. He fitted the hinged hemispheres together over his face.

Detective Sergeant Stephen Thatcher vanished. In his place stood the Moon Man, a phantom figure garbed in midnight black whose head was a gleaming, faceless sphere of silver.

The Moon Man picked up the telephone. His voice sounded muffled as he asked for connection to Room 1541. After a moment a tense answer came: "Yes? Yes?" In his ghostly tones the Moon Man said:

"Mr. Dawst, you are about to receive a caller. His purpose is to discuss a highly important matter. He will be at your door within ten seconds."

The connection broke on a bewildered question. The Moon Man's robe rustled as he strode to the door. He listened along the deserted corridor, bowed head twinkling. He glided, with a faint fluttering sound, to the entrance of Room 1541. His black-gloved hand rapped gently. Since sending his message, ten seconds had not passed.

A bolt clicked back. A crack opened. An eye appeared—an eye which widened with dismay. The Moon Man's automatic leveled directly at it. He stepped forward alertly, tempered muscles pushing the door open. The occupant of 1541 staggered back. Quickly the Moon Man closed the door. His muffled voice steady as the glittering gun, he said:

"Perhaps, even in Paris, m'sieu, you have heard of my unfortunate reputation."

"The Moon Man!"

Stanislaw Dawst blurted the name with a thick inflection. He stood with hands raised abjectly, his vandyked chin fallen, his mustached upper lip trembling, his monocle slipping from his bulging eye. He took a deep, broken breath, making a gesture of despair. His mouth worked, but the same fear that put a haunted look in his eyes kept him silent.

"You have, I see," the Moon Man said quietly, "heard of me."

Dawst demanded: "I do not understand. Is this—what you call—a practical joke? Have you come to rob me? What do you want?"

The Moon Man's lowered tone became brittle. "You will soon learn I am completely in earnest. It will give me genuine pleasure to return the necklace of the late Mrs. Pendleton, but I have another purpose of greater importance. I want information, M'sieu Dawst."

Dawst gulped: "Necklace? What is it you say?"

The Moon Man stepped forward—a rustling move, briskly threatening. "You are what we call a fence, with international connections, M'sieu Dawst," he declared as the pudgy man recoiled. "You have just bought the stolen Pendleton diamonds at, I would estimate, twenty cents on the dollar. As a crook you're successful enough so that you needn't hurry about disposing of them. You intend to spirit them out of the country, recut the largest stones and market them in Europe. That's true—isn't it?"

"Non, non!" Dawst blurted.

"A question, then," the Moon Man parried, "which will soon be decided. I wish, as I said, information. What is the next move planned by the three men who just visited you—Govett and Englar and Forbs? Where do they intend to hide the money you paid them? Let's waste no time about it! You have one chance, here and now, to answer my questions!"

Dawst's fat tongue crept over his hairy lips. He wheezed through a constricted throat. Stark terror glittered in his eyes. He forced out his answer with a wrenching effort:

"I know nothing!"

"Very well."

The Moon Man turned briskly to the telephone sitting on a small table beside the bed. He lifted it, his automatic still leveled at Dawst's heart. To the hotel operator he said: "Connect me with police headquarters." When the voice of Phone Sergeant Doyle responded, he added: "Connect me with Lieutenant McEwen." When the sharp rasp of McEwen's voice ground over the line, he uttered a muffled chuckle.

"This is your old friend calling, lieutenant," he said softly. "The Moon Man."

CHAPTER III

KILLERS' RACE

DAWST STOOD paralyzed. His chubby hands hung limp. His perfectly barbered chin sagged. No breath passed his parted lips as he stared at the phantom figure of the Moon Man. In his eyes shone the dull hopelessness of a man facing certain doom.

Over the telephone line, echoing within the shell mask of the Moon Man, two grating words rang: "By damn!"

The Moon Man spoke quickly. "As usual, when I communicate with you, lieutenant, you will immediately try to have my call traced. This time it is quite unnecessary. I am telephoning you from Room 1541 of the Grand Palace Hotel."

McEwen gasped: "What!"

"Quite true, lieutenant," the Moon Man affirmed with an added chuckle. "I realize you will have half a dozen squad-car men charging into the place within two minutes. I have no desire to go to the electric chair, as you have so often promised would be my lot; so I must talk quickly. I am calling to inform you where you can find the Pendleton diamonds."

"*What!*"

"Precisely. You already have information concerning Stanislaw Dawst. He received the diamonds from the killers only a few minutes ago. You will find them, I'm sure, concealed somewhere in his room. I'm afraid, lieutenant, I cannot risk giving you any further information. I heard you a moment ago when you snapped orders to someone to flash the radio alarm. Good-night."

The Moon Man's breath whizzed rapidly inside his shell as he broke the connection. He strode briskly to Dawst, stopped only when the muzzle of his automatic pressed Dawst's chest. The pudgy crook was too terrorized now even to retreat. The hollow voice of the Moon Man rushed on:

"M'sieu, you are acquainted with the operation of our radio patrol system? At this very moment armed men are rushing toward this hotel, to capture you. Within a few seconds you will be placed under arrest, unless you agree to my bargain. I will attempt to keep you out of the hands of the police if you will tell me the plan of those three men. If you do not, m'sieu, your goose will be speedily cooked."

Dawst blurted: "I do not know—I swear!"

The Moon Man grimly straightened. "If you cannot tell me, you cannot tell the police. In that case I will be delighted to see them give you what we call the works. As an accessory to a contemptible robbery and two murders, you deserve the chair."

A strangled exclamation of terror broke from Dawst's parched throat. He stumbled blindly from the Moon Man. Too beside himself even to heed the danger of the robed criminal's automatic, he lurched to an inner door. The Moon Man took long, flapping steps to stop him, but Dawst squeezed through, frantically shut the way. He had closed himself in a crowded closet.

The Moon Man took a backward step. Beyond the door there was a sound of frenzied fumbling. An order rose to the lips of the cloaked crook, but he did not speak. A sudden, blasting report jolted the closet door. While the Moon Man stood frozen, a groan strained out—then a crunching thud.

A new sound penetrated the room to chill the Moon Man's nerves. It shrilled through the window from the street—the banshee whine of a siren. By the second it grew sharper, louder. It meant that the Moon Man's alarm was bringing a swift response. His information to headquarters was closing a trap around Dawst—and around himself.

The Moon Man's black-gloved hand gripped the closet knob. With the opening of the door the limp body of Dawst slumped out over the sill. The pudgy man rolled face up, his lax right hand losing a smoking automatic of foreign make. His temple dribbled blood as he stared at the ceiling with glazing eyes.

Stanislaw Dawst, the Moon Man realized at his first dismayed glance, was dead.

THE MOON MAN whipped around to the outer door. He paused a torturous second while someone passed along the corridor. In the street the wailing of the sirens had ceased. The silence indicated that already armed patrolmen were rushing up to 1541. Each second was tightening the self-made trap around the Moon Man. His moves desperately quick, he slipped out.

Long strides took him into 1544. Deftly he halved the silver mask and lowered it into the case. He jerked off the black gloves, snatched the black robe over his shoulder. Clasping the case lid, he slid it under the bed. The corridor was still empty when he stepped out. Hurrying past an angle, he heard the elevator grille slide open. The heavy tramp of headquarters men dogged Steve Thatcher as he sidled into the service stairway.

Thatcher hurried down until voices warned him someone was at work on a lower platform. He glimpsed overalled men lugging a divan out of the freight lift. He went into a corridor exactly like that of the fifteenth floor. At the elevator panels he pressed the up button. The cab which opened to receive him was already carrying six passengers. He murmured: "Wrong floor—fifteen, please." Stepping out, he saw the door of 1541 standing open, heard gruff voices mingling excitedly.

An assistant manager was standing just inside, looking horrified. A prowlcar man was opening the drawers of the bureau. Another was slipping a leather holster out of the pocket of a top-coat hanging in the closet. Two more were bending curiously over the body of Stanislaw Dawst. Five pairs of eyes turned immediately to Thatcher.

"Heard the alarm," he announced. "Found anything?"

"Nothing yet, sergeant."

Thatcher went to work. He searched, in rapid succession, a suitcase, a small steamer trunk, a traveling toilet kit, the clothing in the closet, the contents of the bureau. Nothing of interest came to light. He took up a portable typewriter case, looked in it, and was about to replace it when he noticed something odd. The leather-covered board to which the machine was fastened seemed unusually thick. Thatcher's eyes shone.

With his pen-knife he unscrewed the four bolts threaded into the feet of the typewriter. A rectangular section, marked by four neatly fitting edges, ordinarily hidden by the machine, was disclosed. Thatcher pried his blade into it, lifted a thin leaf. Clean cotton padding filled the cavity. Diamonds sparkled in the light.

Thatcher observed wryly: "There it is. Now she may be buried as she wished. Hold that for Lieutenant McEwen. I've got a lead to follow."

"By damn!"

Thatcher turned to see McEwen in the doorway. The grizzled veteran had lost no time driving across city to the hotel. He strode in, sinking his teeth into a fresh cigar, glaring at the diamonds, the corpse, at Thatcher. "All right, all right," he growled. "But what about the Moon Man? He phoned me from this room—a straight tip, by damn! Where is he now?"

Thatcher answered: "No sign of him when I arrived, Gil."

One of the prowl-car men reported: "We took a quick look around the floor, but he wasn't here, lieutenant. Two of the boys took the stairs. Another one's in the lobby and still another's in the service entrance. If the Moon Man's still in this building he'll have to do a slick job of getting out."

McEwen leveled his cigar grimly. "Let me tell you something. When a slick job of getting out of some place has to be done, the Moon Man can do it. I hate that fancy crook's guts, but I give him credit. He's probably 'way the hell and gone by now. What I want to know, how did he find out about Dawst, and what's the rest of it? Dawst didn't figure in the robbery."

Thatcher said urgently: "Dawst was the fence. He must have planned to wait until the dragnet went down, then fade. The real crooks sold out fast in order to break the trail. They've already got the money. You'll have a tough job using it to pin the robbery on them—*if* we find it, Gil. You're in charge here now. I'm following a hunch."

McEwen scooped two hundred thousand dollars worth of diamonds into his crusty hand. "I've got a hunch myself. The Moon Man's right in the middle of this case. He's done enough already to make himself an accessory, tip or no tip. As far as that goes, how do I know he didn't shoot Dawst—and can he prove he didn't? That's one more reason why I'm going to see that fancy crook burn."

A chill pierced Thatcher's heart as he strode out. He glanced anxiously at 1544 as he passed it—the room in which the Moon Man's regalia was hidden. The squad-car men stationed at the street entrances were searching every passing face, but they greeted Thatcher with smart salutes. The motor of his roadster sang a high note as he angled back to headquarters.

Climbing the stairs he heard the familiar peel of his telephone. The purring stopped when he opened the door. Sue McEwen was still at the desk. She had answered the call. The whiteness of her cheeks warned Thatcher that she had recognized the voice at the distant end of the line—Dargan's. She turned quickly from the instrument, eyes pleading, hands closing tensely on Thatcher's.

"Please, darling," she said softly.

Thatcher answered tensely: "I can't stop now, Sue. Not now!"

SUE UNWILLINGLY yielded the telephone. The intense light in Steve Thatcher's eyes warned her that argument would be futile. He spoke one tight word into the transmitter: "Okay."

Dargan's hushed tone responded: "Want a number, boss?"

Thatcher hesitated, thinking of the phone sergeant, downstairs in the desk room, who might be listening in, that he decided to play the gamble. "There's no time to waste, Angel. Let's have it."

Dargan's report came rapidly: "I picked 'em up outside the place, boss—understand? One of 'em was carrying a package. Money, maybe. They hopped a taxi, circled, changed to another, circled some more, then went to the Imperial. They asked for a key at the desk—they've got rooms—2010 and 2011. Still there, boss, and right next door to the first place!"

Thatcher's mind accelerated. "They didn't make any move to get rid of the package, Angel—they were only trying to shake off anyone who might be tailing them?"

"That's right, boss!"

"Listen, Angel. They must know that before long they'll be picked up and questioned. It's closer than ever now, because McEwen will soon have their descriptions as visitors to Dawst's room. In any case, they must be planning to get the money under cover—and in a hurry."

"How can they do it, boss?"

"There's one best bet for them, Angel—a safe-deposit box in a bank. Once they have the money locked in a vault drawer, nobody else will be able to reach it except on a court order. Even then it will be worth practically nothing as evidence. It doesn't connect with the murders and it probably can't be traced to Dawst. Even if McEwen should collar them, he'd have no case."

"That's the answer, boss. They're going to sink the money in a bank somewhere."

"But they've got to move fast," Thatcher followed through. "Waiting is too dangerous, even waiting until tomorrow. This is Saturday night. Every bank in town is closed, and will stay closed until nine Monday morning—except one. The Day and Night National is open now. It's the crooks' only bet. And there's one more reason why they would logically pick the Day and Night National."

"You're getting it, boss!"

"After they've laid low a long while, until the excitement has died down, if then they decide to make a quick getaway on short notice, they can get the money out of that bank at any hour of the day or night—Angel!"

"Sure, boss?"

"Once the money is locked in the vault, it will be beyond my reach for all time. We've got to beat them to it. It's a gamble, Angel, but we're going to play it both ways. Keep tailing those three men. Watch every move they make. I'm going to the Day and Night right now, on the chance they'll head for it in a hurry, especially when they hear that Dawst is dead."

"Okay, boss!"

"If they make a different move, you can reach me there by phone. If they don't, I'll be waiting for them. In case they go into the Day and Night, Angel, wait in the roadster in the alley beside the bank. Hold ready to move fast, on short notice. All set?"

"I'm on my way, boss—but Lord, you're running a terrific risk!"

Thatcher answered quietly: "The good that money will do— the satisfaction of collaring those three killers—it'll be worth it, Angel, if the play wins. If it doesn't—well, then McEwen will be making his promise good. On your way!"

Thatcher's muscles ached with tension as he turned from the telephone. Quickly Sue took his hands. Her red lips were trembling with protests, her eyes were a plea. He gave her a quick, wry smile.

"Please, Steve," she whispered. "Don't."

He answered: "I don't want to force all this worry on you, darling, but there's only one thing I can do now—go through with it. Gil is plugging at the angle of proving the Moon Man is an accomplice to the funeral killings. According to the letter of the law, he's right. I've got to vindicate myself."

"Steve!"

"The real crooks are two jumps ahead of him, Sue. They'll be in the clear tonight, perhaps in only a few minutes, if the Moon Man doesn't block their play. I can't do it, Sue—not as Steve Thatcher—because I haven't any more of a lead than Gil has. It's the Moon Man's job—nobody else's."

Sue's hands tightened desperately. "I can't let you, Steve! I can't!"

Thatcher answered firmly: "Stiff upper lip, Sue. I'm on my way."

He strode from the office, ran down the stairs. Sue McEwen stood rigid, anxious tears welling into her eyes. She heard the headquarters entrance close—a sound that cut her off from Thatcher while he hurried on a reckless mission. Suddenly, lips crushing with strengthened purpose, she hurried after him.

When she ran out the headquarters entrance, she found Steve Thatcher already gone.

CHAPTER IV

SEALED EVIDENCE

THATCHER BROUGHT his roadster to a stop near the Grand Palace Hotel. He stood a moment on the curb, hesitant with thought, striving to control a growing urgency. With quick decision he opened the rumble compartment.

He brought out a bound suit box. That afternoon it had been delivered to him at headquarters by his tailor. He opened it, removed the neatly folded garments, slipped them deep into the rumble compartment. When he strode into the hotel lobby he was carrying an empty box.

The corridor on the fifteenth floor was quiet. Opposite 1541, Thatcher heard gruff voices. Several headquarters men were in the suicide room, continuing the investigation. Quietly Thatcher opened 1544. He found the black case where he had placed it, under the bed. Transferring the regalia of the Moon Man from it to the suit box took only a few moments.

Thatcher was prepared to justify his presence if any headquarters man should accost him, but 1541 did not open. With a wag of his hand he passed the patrolmen still on duty in the foyer. Again in his car, he drove directly to the Day and Night National Bank.

Its golden-lettered windows shone brightly in an otherwise dark street. Several cash messengers, making deposits for firms doing a late business, were at the cashiers' corbels. The men in the cage were working with quiet efficiency. Thatcher strode directly to the bronze grille at the rear which fenced off the vault section.

"Detective Sergeant Thatcher," he identified himself to the girl who approached. An electric lock clicked, and he stepped through. "I'd like to see either Mr. Cartley or Mr. Babcock." He placed the suitbox on a table as Babcock approached—a fussy, bald man, cashier of the bank—and drew from his pocket a letter which he did not open.

"A routine duty," he said quietly. "You've been kind enough to assist me like this before. I should like to check this list I have against the names of your safe-deposit box holders."

Babcock murmured, "Certainly—always glad to cooperate with the police," and went into an adjoining office. Thatcher carried the suit box into one of the line of booths provided so that clients might conduct their business privately. Babcock brought him several typewritten pages. Thatcher briskly voiced his thanks, sat at the booth table, and made a quick check.

The bank's list did not include Govett or Englar or Forbs. It meant only that they might be using false names.

Thatcher, absorbed, heard Babcock's voice: "Certainly, Miss McEwen." His glance flashed with consternation. Sue was standing outside the gate of the heavy grille. Babcock, leaning over a desk near the huge circular entrance of the vault, pressed a button which tripped an electric lock. Sue hurried through, came to Thatcher anxiously. The firmness of her eyes was a challenge.

"Sue, you shouldn't have—"

"Steve"—her voice was strained and hushed—"I beg you not to do it."

He answered with gentle inflexibility: "Darling, I know you're right—it's an insane risk to run—but believe me, it's—" He broke off. A movement at the street entrance had drawn his gaze. His nerves grew tenser as he watched three men enter.

"Steve!" the girl exclaimed, alarmed at the sudden thinning of his lips. "What is it?"

"They're here," he said quietly. "Please, Sue—go back. Anything may happen now—and there's no way of stopping it. For your own sake—"

"I'm not going, Steve," Sue answered defiantly. "I'm not."

The trio who had just stepped into the foyer were Govett, Englar and Forbs—and Govett was carrying a small, neatly wrapped package.

They were approaching the grille gate. Thatcher quickly turned his back, his hand closing commandingly on Sue's arm. He guided her into the adjoining booth. "Stay out of sight, Sue!" Her staunch eyes did not flinch at his warning. Quickly he stepped back to the closeted table where he had left the suit box.

He closed the door to a crack. He saw Govett limping in through the bronze gate. Englar followed, one of his eyes shifting, his other staring straight ahead. Forbs, whose one temple was grayed though the other was not, remained in the lobby. Govett spoke to the young woman attendant, stepped inside the vault. Thatcher closed the door.

Quickly he removed the black robe from the suit box and dropped it over his shoulders. He raised the fragile, hinged hemispheres of silvered glass. He removed his hat, placed it on the table, fitted the globular mask over his head. Within the confines of the booth, Detective Sergeant Stephen Thatcher transformed himself into the Moon Man.

THE MOON MAN'S eyeless head twinkled as he glanced quickly through a slit of the door. A drowsy quiet filled the bank. He straightened, reaching into the box for his black gloves. He found one, drew it on. His breath came faster as he realized the other was missing.

Pressing time urged the Moon Man to abandon his search for it. "Once the money is locked in the vault," he had told Dargan, "it will be beyond my reach for all time." Every passing second was a chance that already the package of crooked money might be stored behind bolted steel. The Moon Man's gloved hand gripped the knob of the booth door. His bare one tightened on his automatic.

He peered out a crack, making a swift survey of the scene. In their cages the tellers were busy with routine checking. Bookkeepers were punching adding machines in the offices beyond. Forbs was moving about outside the grille. A girl operator was reading a magazine at a telephone switchboard set against the far wall. The attendant was still inside the vault with Englar and Govett. Babcock was standing at the huge, circular slab of steel which was swung out at an angle. He was performing a task which held the Moon Man's attention.

The cashier had unfastened a square, hinged leaf of glass set into the gleaming mechanism of the vault door. It exposed a row of three dials connected with small timepieces without cases. With a key Babcock had wound one, setting its disk to a predetermined number, the watchworks behind it ticking busily. Babcock, winding the second of the three devices, would in a moment set the third. It was the time-clock mechanism of the vault.

The closing time of the Day and Night National was near. It was nearly midnight, the deadline of the only period during the week when the vault was closed. Once the time-clock was adjusted, the slab swung home, and the combination scattered, the huge steel tomb would remain sealed until Monday morning.

The Moon Man stepped alertly from the booth. His robe rustled as he strode directly to the glittering entrance of the vault. The brighter light shafting from it gleamed on his silver head. Inside it, at a mosaic wall of lock-boxes, Govett and Englar were standing. One of the steel panels was open. Govett was in the act of sliding a long, black metal drawer into it—a drawer now containing the loot of the killer trio. The Moon Man's automatic turned upon him.

His gliding move from the booth had been so swift, so soundless, that none of the workers in the bank had noticed him. Even Babcock, whose back was turned as he twisted the third time-lock dial, had not suspected his presence. Suddenly the Moon Man's muffled command turned amazed eyes upon him:

"Wait, Govett!"

An electrical hush filled the bank. Inside the vault, Govett stood paralyzed, still holding the metal drawer. Babcock, twisting around, leaving the key in the dial socket, took a long, soughing breath. In their cages the tellers stared. Outside the grille, Forbs' hand tightened to reach inside his coat. At the telephone switchboard the red-headed operator slowly let go of her magazine.

"Ladies and gentlemen," the Moon Man said commandingly, "I hope none of you will make it necessary for me to shoot you. If any of you touches an alarm button, I shall have to resort to drastic tactics. The young lady at the board will regret it exceedingly if she attempts to make or answer any call. If you conduct yourselves discreetly, you will not be harmed; you will soon be rid of me. I am not here to rob the bank, but to relieve three contemptible killers of their swag. Your cooperation, if you please, ladies and gentlemen."

THE GALVANIC tension increased. During that charged moment there was only one movement in the hush. It came from the row of booths.

Sue McEwen had seen the Moon Man dart to the entrance of the vault. She was chilled by the realization that he had dared appear within a space bounded by stone walls, a steel cavity, a bronze grille reaching ceiling-high. Overwhelming concern for him had turned her toward the booth from which he had emerged. She had torn her stinging eyes from the ghostly figure with the silver head, to peer past the open door. Beyond it she had glimpsed evidence which, she feared, would prove Steve Thatcher to be the Moon Man if ever it came into the hands of the police.

On the floor, beneath the table, a single black glove. Beside the open box, a hat. She stepped inside quickly, closing the door. She snatched up the glove—remembering that fingerprint experts had recently learned to develop impressions on any fabric. She picked up the hat—and saw two golden initials stamped on its band: S. T. She saw on the cover of the box, beneath the printed name of the tailor, a written line: For Sergeant Stephen Thatcher.

Breathlessly Sue McEwen crushed the hat into the box, left the glove with it, closed the lid, clamped it under her arm. She sidled out, heart pounding, determined that this evidence must never be used to prove that her fiancé was the Moon Man.

Standing boldly in the light shafting from the vault, leveling his automatic through its circular mouth, the Moon Man asserted with a chuckle:

"Once I have seized their loot, ladies and gentlemen, I will be quite content to leave these three murderers to the police. Bring it out, Govett!"

At the same instant three desperate crooks dared challenge the Moon Man's command. Govett whipped a hand from the black drawer, slipped it inside his coat. Englar made the same swift move. Forbs, straddling outside the grille, accomplished it even faster. His automatic, darting out first, blazed.

The sheen of the Moon Man's mask hid the direction of his gaze. No one facing him could determine whether or not he was the object of the notorious crook's scrutiny. He had had his gun on Govett, his eyes on Forbs. The warning glint of gun metal turned his weapon on Forbs. He back-stepped as he fired. Forbs' slug slammed into the vault; the Moon Man's ripped through Forbs' hat.

The shots signaled a battle. Forbs fired swiftly, three times more. The lead slapping into the vault wrung shouts of dismay from Govett and Englar. The bullets caromed wildly, spattering stinging fragments. Terrorized first by the Moon Man's threat of capture, next by the rattling of bouncing slugs, they dived for the mouth of the vault. They whirled, backing, automatics seeking the phantom figure of the Moon Man.

The Moon Man played a swift gamble against the outnumbering guns. While Forbs blasted at him, he had sprung back to the shelter of Babcock's desk. His automatic cracked rapidly—not at the three crooks, but at the light fixtures overhead. In swift succession his bullets transformed four bowls into showering glass bits. Alleviated only by the shaded desk lamps in the tellers' cages and by the shaft streaming from the vault, gloom closed down.

Suddenly a deafening clamor broke out—the baleful clanging of a brazen bell, a din that overwhelmed the quiet of the street with a bedlam of warning. One of the men in the cages, defying the Moon Man's orders, had touched an alarm button.

The noise stirred swift movements in the semi-darkness. The Moon Man heard a rasping sound, then a rapid clicking. The first came from the door of the vault, the second from the electric lock of the grille gate. The gate swung open. A ghostly figure sped through, then a second. Quickly the light beaming from the vault faded. Thicker darkness enveloped a third hastening figure.

The killers' guns kept cracking. Overwhelmed by the savagery of the attack, chilled by the fear that a flying slug might burst his fragile mask, the Moon Man crouched behind the desk. Govett was slamming bullets at him. Splinters were flying; the desk was jolting with the impacts.

The onslaught gave way to swift footfalls. The three crooks had slipped fresh clips from their vest pockets into their gun-butts. They retreated to the street entrance, smashing slugs at the cowering employees. A whistling fusillade crashed into the tellers' desk lamps. The last bulb popped—glass chips rained in deep darkness.

The Moon Man looked up to see three shadows springing out into the street, blurring away past the gold-lettered windows.

The Moon Man darted toward the vault. He remembered that Govett had abandoned the metal drawer for a gun, that both crooks had rushed from the vault empty-handed. In spite of the dinning pandemonium—a racket which even now must be speeding prowl cars to the bank—the Moon Man was intent upon seizing the killers' loot… but, facing the vault, he stopped short in a paralysis of consternation.

THE MASSIVE circular door had been swung solidly into its bed. Babcock was frantically twisting the combination dial. Two tons of impregnable steel barred the Moon Man from his objective.

He spun, masked eyes searching for Sue McEwen. He caught no glimpse of her in the gloom. He sprang out the open grille gate. He crossed the foyer, a swift, spectral eddying of the darkness. Suddenly he ducked down behind the information desk in the foyer.

The Moon Man lifted off the precious glass mask—and Steve Thatcher's voice rang: "He's outside! Everybody stay back!" He jerked the black robe off and whipped it around the sphere. Concealing it against his body, he whirled out the entrance, into the faint street light. The bewildered bank workers had seen the Moon Man disappear into thin air—saw Sergeant Thatcher giving hot chase.

Thatcher sprinted into the gloom of the alley flanking the bank. He was scarcely past the corner when headlight beams lanced toward the bank—rushing squad cars. He came to a breathless stop at the side of a roadster parked in deep shadow. "Boss!" broke from the stocky ex-pug at the wheel. Thatcher slipped the bundled regalia into the rumble compartment.

"On your way, Angel, but take your time. If you're stopped, pretend you don't know what's happened. If you're recognized, chance everything on making a break. Now!"

The roadster spurted away. Thatcher, hurrying back, watched it turn into the next street. Prowl-car brakes were squealing at the curb in front of the Day and Night National. Steve Thatcher hurried into the light where uniformed men were running with drawn guns....

IN THE chief's office in police headquarters, Gil McEwen was tramping the carpet, gnawing on a cigar. He had just returned from Room 1541 of the Grand Palace Hotel, leaving the body of Stanislaw Dawst to routine handling. The Pendleton necklace was in his pocket because he distrusted the safe which the Moon Man had entered. He leveled the cigar grimly at the white-haired man slumped in the old padded swivel chair in the corner.

"We found the diamonds where the Moon Man said we would, chief, but what does that prove? Only that he was playing for other stakes. He doesn't steal jewelry anyway—only cash. All right! He robbed Dawst, then killed him. He made it look like suicide—simple!—but the fact remains that the Moon Man was in the room when Dawst got it. That spells murder—and I'm going to nail the Moon Man for it!"

The telephone zinged. McEwen snatched it up. The message that rushed over the wire drove his teeth deeper into his cigar. "Lieutenant! Signal board calling. Flash from the Day and Night National. The alarm's going off. The bank's being stuck up!"

McEwen blurted: "By damn!" He pronged the receiver and immediately the bell again exploded. An even more startling message rang over the line.

"Call just in from the Day and Night National, lieutenant. There's a gunfight in the bank—and the Moon Man's there! Three crooks and the Moon Man—"

"By damn!" McEwen waited to hear no more. The telephone crashed down. McEwen's heels tattooed. The chief's door slammed. A grim-eyed detective went out of headquarters like a cyclone....

IN THE Day and Night National, Steve Thatcher was finding it his duty, as a police officer, to handle the investigation of a crime which he, as a masked criminal had precipitated.

Burned powder still made the air pungent. The floor was scattered with broken glass and ejected automatic shells. A delirious sense of confusion filled the bank. The shock of the gun battle had numbed the perceptions of those who had witnessed it. Since his return, no one had remarked Steve Thatcher's absence during the presence of the Moon Man. He smiled grimly when, to his surprise, he heard the red-headed telephone girl gasp:

"I saw Detective Thatcher shooting at the Moon Man from the corner. He chased the Moon Man out. I saw them both rush into the street."

To this Thatcher laconically remarked: "The Moon Man was gone when I got there."

The alarm gong had been switched off. Uniformed men were keeping a curious crowd back on the sidewalk, guarding the entrance. The prowl cars, drawn by the clamoring bell, were flanked now by other dispatches to the scene by radio following the telephone flash. The stunned inaction which had followed the Moon Man's escape was yielding to fluttering nervousness. Behind the grille, Babcock was mercilessly polishing his eyeglasses. Thatcher took his arm.

"Where is Miss McEwen? She was here. Did you see her go out?"

"Miss McEwen!" Babcock mouthed. "Yes, she was here, but I'm sure I don't know. Perhaps—during the shooting—she ran into the street."

Thatcher retorted: "She couldn't have done that—I'm sure she didn't. Have you accounted for everyone else? What about the vault? Who closed it?"

"It's not only closed," Babcock answered, "but locked. One of those three men pushed the door shut. I immediately spun the combination dial, but I'm sure it had been done already, by the same man."

"Do you know," Thatcher persisted, "why it was shut? You don't know whether anyone was inside?"

Babcock stiffened. "I was protecting the bank's depositors. Why should anyone have stayed inside the vault? No, I don't know why the criminals closed it. I do know it's securely locked—and nothing was taken from it."

Worry and bewilderment shone in Thatcher's eyes as he strode to the great disk face of the vault. He crossed to the booth in which he had changed into the regalia of the Moon Man. Deeper puzzlement struck him when he found the suit box missing, his hat gone. Suddenly, taunted by a growing dread, he turned to the telephone switchboard.

A grating voice stopped him. "Well, by damn!" it said. "Well? Where's the Moon Man this time?"

McEwen had charged in the entrance. His shoes gritted on scattered glass as he strode into the space behind the grille. He turned an accusing glare on his men, scowled at Thatcher. No one answered his question. Thatcher continued to the switchboard. He dipped a plug into the socket labeled *Vault*, bent the cam, pressed the receiver tightly to his ear. Abruptly a strained, fearful voice answered—a voice traveling through a wire, out of the interior of the steel-walled vault:

"Hello—hello!"

Thatcher blurted: "Sue!"

CHAPTER V

PRISONER OF DOOM

THE LINE brought a faint whisper: "Steve—Steve."

"Listen, Sue!" Thatcher's voice tightened with anxiety. "Are you all right? How did you get in there? Darling, don't be afraid. We'll soon have you out and—"

"No, Steve—wait!" The sharp anguish in the girl's voice startled Thatcher. "Not now—not while anyone is out there. I have the things here, with me—do you understand?—your hat, and the suit box, and one black glove. If Dad is out there, and he sees them, he'll know. It will mean the end of everything, Steve. There's no way of getting rid of them—no way at all."

Thatcher sat rigid, chilled. Sue went on, her words rushing: "I took the box, Steve, because I was afraid you'd be forced out of the bank, forced to leave them behind—and I *couldn't* let them be found. I don't know exactly what happened. I was trying to get past the vault, and all at once the big door swung against me. Someone was pushing it shut. It knocked me sideward into the vault. Before I knew it, the door was closed. We can't let Dad find out the truth, Steve. Do you understand?"

Thatcher answered quietly: "Yes, Sue, but perhaps it's too late. I've got to get you out of there as soon as possible. We can't hide the fact now—that—"

He broke off, raising haggard eyes as McEwen strode close. McEwen's eyes were gleaming like burnished steel. He had heard a rapid account of the encounter between the Moon Man and the three killers. Voice rasping, he declared:

"Listen, Steve. You were here. You saw it. I'm going to check this thing." His mouth tightened. "Come to think of it, what the devil were you doing here—with Sue?"

Thatcher rose. "I told you at the hotel, I was following a hunch, Gil. I figured that Dawst had just bought the necklace; that the crooks would try to get the money under cover as soon as possible. I came here on the chance they'd turn up tonight. Evidently I was right, and evidently the Moon Man followed the same line of reasoning."

"Yeah?" McEwen drawled it. "Then what happened? Where did the Moon Man come from? He wasn't here one minute, but the next he was. In the first place, he had to get behind this grille somehow, and when he did, he wasn't wearing his mask. He must have put it on once he was in. That sounds logical, doesn't it, Steve?"

Thatcher's tight nod admitted it.

"All right," McEwen pressed on. "He came in here, behind the grille, as a customer of the bank, unmasked. This thing has given everybody such a case of the jitters they can't remember who was here when it started. But whoever it was, Steve, he was carrying his regalia in something. Do you remember seeing anyone in here with a case, or a bundle—or a box?"

Thatcher answered with an effort: "I was busy watching the three crooks, Govett and Englar and Forbs. I've already flashed headquarters a general alarm for them to be picked up on sight and—"

"Wait." McEwen's eyes were slits. "The Moon Man came in here, unmasked, with his regalia. Without anybody seeing him, he put on his robe and mask. *And mask,* Steve—of course. He must have been wearing a hat, but in order to wear the mask, he had to take his hat off. He must have left it somewhere, because he was seen to rush toward the street. It must still be here. Once we find that hat and trace it, we've got the Moon Man!" McEwen's gaze lifted. "To start with, Steve, where's your hat?"

Thatcher answered huskily: "I left it over in a booth, Gil." His hand closed hard on McEwen's arm. "Wait. You haven't given me a chance to tell you. Sue is here; you know that. She's—locked in the vault."

"What!"

Thatcher turned imperatively to Babcock. "She was pushed in when one of the crooks closed the vault door. We've got to get her out as soon as possible. Please unlock it, Mr. Babcock, and—"

THATCHER'S VOICE trailed off. He realized that his words were a pronouncement of doom upon himself. The box inside the vault with Sue, the hat bearing his initials, the black glove—evidence impossible to destroy now—would turn McEwen's suspicions directly toward him. One simple, final proof would establish Steve Thatcher's identity as the Moon Man—his thumbprint.

Early in the Moon Man's career, McEwen had obtained an impression of the Moon Man's thumb. He carried an enlarged photograph of it always with him. It was stamped on his brain indelibly. The man whose ridge-pattern matched it would be revealed, beyond all doubt, as the notorious criminal whom McEwen had been seeking so relentlessly. A single test smudge would make the electric chair a certainty. Yet, facing the inevitability, Thatcher requested:

"Please open the vault, Mr. Babcock—at once."

His blood went cold as Babcock answered: "Open it? Now? It's impossible."

Thatcher snapped: "Don't you understand Miss McEwen is locked inside it? She's in danger of suffocating. You've got to let her out as soon as—"

"Impossible!" Babcock repeated. "Just before the Moon Man appeared, I set the clocks of the time-clock. Now that the vault is closed, they are operating. I set them, of course, for the usual time. The vault cannot be opened until eight o'clock Monday morning."

McEwen rasped: "Eight o'clock Monday!"

"No power on earth," Babcock emphasized, "can open the vault until then. But—unfortunate as it is—uncomfortable as it will be for Miss McEwen—she is in no danger. She'll go hungry, but she won't suffocate. Our vault, gentlemen, is provided with a ventilator."

"A ventilator?" McEwen asked. "Is it working now? If it isn't, don't waste any time starting it!"

Babcock stepped anxiously to the switchboard. His brisk tones traveled over the vault extension. "Miss McEwen, this is the cashier speaking. Unfortunately, you must remain a prisoner in the vault for more than thirty hours. It will be most trying, but not dangerous. Please follow my instructions carefully, and the ventilator will supply you with all the air you need."

Thatcher and McEwen listened, relieved, yet still dismayed.

"On the wall to the left," Babcock continued, "you will find a metal plate. You will notice a knob on it. Simply turn the knob to the right as far as it will go. That's all. I'll make sure the ventilator is working properly."

Babcock led Thatcher and McEwen into a hallway flanking the vault. "Fortunate!" he exclaimed. "A precaution against this very emergency." He indicated a plate fixed in the wall six feet above the floor. It was pierced by two circular holes, each two inches across, one directly above the other, both covered with stout mesh. Both were blocked.

"She has not yet turned the knob," Babcock said uneasily. "Two tubes pass through the two-foot wall. They are made of very strong metal encased in special cement. They are closed now by thick, interlocking metal leaves. When Miss McEwen turns the knob—"

Thatcher, looking into the tubes, saw the leaves fall back. Immediately a strong whirring sound was set up. Air began streaming out the upper hole and in the lower, driven by a small fan. Light shone through. At the far end of the tube, Thatcher saw a blue eye appear—Sue's. He called through:

"Okay, darling—you're all right now."

Through the rushing air the girl answered: "I know, Steve. I'm not afraid."

THATCHER TURNED anxiously to Babcock. "You said you set the time-lock dials for eight o'clock Monday morning. We'd best check on that. If it's possible to get Miss McEwen out sooner, we certainly will do it."

He strode to the switchboard. Sue's voice answered his over the line. He spoke in low tones inaudible to the others.

"Listen carefully, Sue. There's nothing we can do about the box and its contents—nothing—understand? We've got to face it. What about the safe-deposit drawer the crooks had open? Can you get into it? Is the package inside?"

"Yes," Sue answered. "But Steve, these things—"

"Perhaps," Thatcher broke in, "it's not entirely hopeless. Take the package of money, Sue, and put it in the box with the other things. Then leave the safe deposit drawer open. Now, we're going to check up on the time-lock. Mr. Babcock will speak to you."

Babcock took the board. "Miss McEwen," he directed, "go to the big door of the vault. You will see three little dials behind a plate of glass. They determine the time at which the vault can be opened. There is no way of setting the dials back, but you can tell us definitely the figure which the pointers are indicating now. I'll wait."

Babcock explained to McEwen and Thatcher: "The dials are not marked with clock faces, but with figures denoting the number of hours which must pass before the combination will work. For instance, if the vault should be closed at five in the afternoon, and opened at eight the next morning, the dials would be set to the number fifteen—the interval is that many hours.

"There are three dials and three timelocks simply as a precaution against failure. One might stop—conceivably, two might— but even in that case, the third would trip the device at the proper time. Tonight, I had just finished setting the third dial to the figure thirty-two-the number of hours between midnight Saturday and eight Monday morning, when the Moon Man—Hello! Yes? What?... *What!*"

Thatcher demanded: "What does she say?"

Babcock blurted: "Two of the dials are as I set them, but the third is not. It is running now, Miss McEwen says, at about the figure forty-nine. That means—it means"—Babcock's face went white—"the vault can't be opened until—two o'clock in the morning on Tuesday!"

McEwen snarled. "By damn! There's something crazy here! Two o'clock in the—by damn, that means something. I'm sorry for Sue, being locked up in there, but—by damn!"

McEwen's metallic eyes glittered with thought. Thatcher turned tensely to the switchboard. He spoke rapidly with Sue, insisting that she verify the setting of the third dial. Her answer was the same. The pointer was indicating almost exactly forty-nine. More than two full days must pass before the vault door could be opened—a nerve-wracking ordeal for the girl. And when, at last, the mechanism yielded, it would reveal not only killers' loot, but evidence betraying Steve Thatcher as the Moon Man.

Thatcher turned despairingly from the switchboard. "Then there's nothing more we can do now—nothing."

Babcock's wag agreed. McEwen was staring at Thatcher intently. Sharp thoughts were flashing in his eyes. He said with a tight rasp:

"This means something, Steve. I've got a hunch it's going to be the finish of the Moon Man. We're going to headquarters and map it out—a trap that'll hold him. Come on!"

When Steve Thatcher strode from the Day and Night National at McEwen's side he was wearing a hat, one he had taken at random from a tree behind the grille—whose, he did not know.

CHAPTER VI

BLACK MAGIC

C**HIEF PETER THATCHER** sat nervously in the padded chair behind his ancient roll-top desk. Mark Keanan, his wounded arm nestled in a sling, watched Gil McEwen pace back and forth. Steve Thatcher, his throat dry, his face drawn, was filled with a foreboding of doom. Across and back McEwen paced, until he abruptly stopped with cigar angling pugnaciously upward.

"I've got it," he said tersely. "Listen. This is strictly under our hats—the four of us. We can't let it leak out. We've got the Moon Man exactly where we want him. This time I've got him—it can't fail—and he's going to the chair."

Thatcher asked wryly: "What about the three killers, Gil? Have you forgotten they're at the bottom of this case—not the Moon Man?"

McEwen snarled. "We know who they are. We know they're hiding out. We're doing our damndest to find 'em. We'll turn 'em up. That angle of the case will be taken care of, all right, Steve. I'm talking about the Moon Man, now. He's finished. Listen."

McEwen uttered each word with careful clarity. "This is what must have happened in the Day and Night National. The Moon Man was set to grab the killers' loot. Hell started popping. The alarm gong went off. Every second counted. The crooks were desperate to make a getaway. The package of money was too dangerous to carry with them in case they were caught. Besides, even if they made a getaway, they might lose it. One of them did some fast and slick thinking, by damn!

"Babcock had just finished setting the time-lock dials. The glass section was open and the dial key was in place. One of the crooks gave the third dial a twist from 32 to 50. He closed the door and spun the combination. That accomplished three things at the same time.

"First, it kept the money out of the hands of the Moon Man. Second, it eliminated what would be dangerous evidence in the hands of the police. Third and most important, it gave the crooks a chance to come back for the money later."

Keanan drawled: "Right."

"See it? It figures this way. The vault wouldn't open at the regular time, eight o'clock Monday morning. Nobody would know exactly when the time-lock would trip, except the crooks. The bank men would keep trying the combination, until, all at once, it would work—at two o'clock Tuesday morning. The crooks would be waiting for the deadline, As soon as the vault was opened, they'd make a surprise attack, grab the money, and run. A clever plan, by damn—and we wouldn't have an inkling of what was up if Sue hadn't been accidentally locked in."

"You've got it all right, Gil!" Keanan exclaimed.

McEwen ground on: "That's the setup. At two o'clock Tuesday morning, the three crooks are going to make a desperate play for the loot. That's only half of it. The Moon Man went after that money, and lost it. He doesn't give up. He'll try again. He has ways of learning everything. I'll bet my last dollar he knows now, or will know in time, as much about it as we do. Mark my words, he'll make a play of his own at the zero hour."

Steve Thatcher, thinking of the damning evidence locked inside the vault with the girl he loved, remarked bitterly: "I'm sure you're right, Gil."

"Damn right I'm right! And he'll show up at the bank. Why? Because he's smart enough to know the crooks might not get away with their plan. The chances are against them. When we grab them, we'll grab the money at the same time. The Moon Man will figure it that way; therefore he can't wait. He's got to get at the money as fast as the crooks do, before they even have a chance to begin a getaway. That means the Moon Man will show up at the moment the vault opens—at two o'clock Tuesday morning."

"Your reasoning," Thatcher observed acridly, "is flawless, Gil."

McEwen snapped: "All right! We've got him—if we don't make a misplay. We can't let anyone suspect we know what's up—least of all, the Moon Man. We've got to take pains to avoid letting out the slightest hint that we're laying a trap. I've got it all mapped out. Here's the way we're going to collar the Moon Man—at last!"

McEwen's eyes gleamed, and Steve Thatcher listened with tormented intentness.

"I'm going to stay strictly away from the bank," McEwen continued, "because, if the Moon Man should see me, he might smell a rat and hold back. I'm going to call every man off the bank detail, except one. One must stay there, not only so it won't seem suspicious, but because it's necessary to my plan. You're nominated, Steve. At the zero hour Tuesday morning, you'll be inside the Day and Night National."

Thatcher nodded tensely.

"Keanan," McEwen went on, "during the day, you and I are going to make camp on the second floor of the building directly across the street. We're going to smuggle in two searchlights and two machine guns—by the back way, crated, so nobody will know what's up. We'll watch through the windows. When the Moon Man shows himself, we'll use those lights and those guns. He won't be able to get away, by damn!"

Keanan asked: "Isn't anybody else going to be in on it, Gil?"

"Nobody else is going to know definitely what we're planning, but I'll have reserves ready," McEwen answered. "There'll be a dozen squad cars scattered around that neighborhood, playing possum, but set to shoot the works fast. Everybody is going to be lying low until the right second. If the Moon Man shows up first outside the bank, you and I, Keanan, will be sure to spot him. If he appears inside, Steve will see him. In that case, you're to touch an alarm button, Steve—instantly—to warn us. Well?

"There you are. That's how we're going to nail the Moon Man. By damn, it's absolutely foolproof!"

TUESDAY MORNING was one hour and thirty minutes old.

Steve Thatcher stood in a gloomy doorway. It was located a block from the Day and Night National, on the street running parallel to that where the bank was situated. The mouth of the alley which connected the two thoroughfares was nearby. Thatcher was watching it.

His nerves tightened when a roadster turned abruptly into the alley. Immediately its lights blinked off. Thatcher's eyes followed it—a shadow, melting into the gloom, pausing near a brick wall midway between the two streets. He waited a moment, made sure he was not observed, then stepped into the darkness of the alley. Pausing beside the roadster, he asked softly: "Angel?"

Dargan's voice answered breathlessly: "Okay, boss. Listen! You can't go through with this. It's too big a chance. You can't get away with it, boss. Why, McEwen'll cut you down with the machine guns the first minute you show yourself. I'm telling you—you've got to call it off. It's suicide!"

Thatcher answered grimly: "If I hold back, Angel, and let Sue walk out of that vault with the box, it will be the finish of me, anyway. It's the slimmest chance I've ever run, but I've got to take it. For Sue's sake, and Gil's, and dad's. Besides, the crooks are going to show and—"

"Boss!" Dargan protested. He slipped anxiously from the car. "You've got to listen to me! I don't want to see you shot down— or sent to the chair! God, boss, I'll—I'll do anything to stop you if you try to go ahead and—"

"Angel!" Thatcher's voice sharpened. "You're thinking only of me—but it's no use. You can't stop me now—nothing can. Stand by me, Angel. What have you found out? Did you spot the crooks?"

During the day Thatcher had telephoned Dargan instructions to attempt to locate Govett and Englar and Forbs. Though the police net had failed to bag the three killers, Thatcher had hoped Dargan, working under cover, might find a direct lead. But now the ex-pug's head wagged negatively.

"Not a sign of 'em, boss. They crawled in deep. Boss, listen—!"

Thatcher interrupted grimly: "Did you get my case from the Grande Palace, Angel? You have the robe and mask with you, haven't you? I'll take them now."

Dargan blurted: "Boss! You can't do it. I brought the mask—what's left of it—but now you can't—"

"What?" Thatcher snapped. "What the devil do you mean, Angel?"

Dargan smiled wryly. "Remember, boss, how quick you had to make a getaway out of the bank last time? You dropped the robe and mask in the back of this car. I didn't touch 'em until just before I started here tonight. I was going to put 'em in the case, but—it's no use, boss. There isn't any more mask. It's broken."

"Broken!"

Thatcher stood stunned with dismay as Dargan turned to the rumble compartment. The ex-pug reached into its dark depths. When he straightened he extended his palm. On it lay a few glittering, curved fragments of silver glass. "I don't know how it happened, boss," Dargan said huskily, "but that's all there is left of it."

For a moment Thatcher could not speak. The precious sphere of Argus glass, manufactured in France, was irreplaceable. It alone had kept the secret of the Moon Man's identity. The few shining bits on Dargan's palm were a symbol of doom to Steve Thatcher. At last, forcing the words out, he said:

"Even having no mask can't stop me now, Angel—not even that!" He turned stiffly. "Hold yourself ready, as I outlined to you on the phone. I'm going ahead—as planned."

Tight-lipped, he strode back. Despair was acid in his heart as he climbed behind the wheel of his roadster. He turned at the corner, then again at the next, scarcely aware of his own movements. He curbed the car near the shining front of the Day and Night National. An inflexible determination filled him as he strode to the entrance—an unconquerable conviction that tonight, even without his mask, the Moon Man could not turn back.

Thatcher glanced around. In the side streets beyond the bank, he knew prowl cars were cruising, apparently on routine duty, actually waiting a flash from McEwen. The second floor windows of the building directly opposite the bank were dark—but behind them, Thatcher knew, McEwen and Keanan were ready to bring searchlights and machine guns swiftly into play. The trap for the Moon Man was set, waiting to spring.

THATCHER STRODE into the bank. The tellers were working in their cages, the bookkeepers were punching their machines, but the routine activity did not disguise a mounting tension in the air. The scars of the gun-battle in the foyer promised a grim repetition. Stepping through the grille gate when Babcock pressed the lock release, Thatcher wryly eyed the closed front of the vault—a tomb of steel in which Sue McEwen was still imprisoned.

The electric clock above the vault indicated one-forty-seven. Thirteen minutes until the zero hour.

Thatcher turned at once to the nearest telephone. The girl at the switchboard connected him with the vault extension. Sue's voice answered, low and strained.

"Sue, it's only a few minutes now," Thatcher promised. "Are you all right? You have the box—and the things in it?"

She answered huskily: "I'm all right, Steve—terribly tired, that's all. Yes, everything is in the box. Darling, isn't there some way we can avoid it—everyone's learning? It will be so horrible for you—for all of us. There must be a way to—"

Thatcher broke in grimly: "Leave it to me, Sue. I have a plan that may work, but the chances are a million to one against it. There's only one thing you can do—bring the box out with you when the vault door is opened. After that—" He broke off. "Wait, Sue—only a few minutes now."

He slowly lowered the telephone, turning haggard eyes on the clock. His nerves tingled with apprehension while the big minute hand crawled on, inexorably.

He thought again of the waiting prowl cars, of McEwen and Keanan watching behind the searchlights and the guns. They were wary for the appearance of the three killers, though Mc-Ewen's plan of attack was not directed at them, but at the Moon Man. Even when the murderous trio appeared, McEwen would wait, hoping to bag the notorious silver-masked criminal—who now was thinking of the argent fragments lying on Dargan's tough palm. Thatcher thought of it all, wretchedly, while the clock hands crawled.

Babcock, standing at the combination dial, was also noting the passage of time. Thatcher again raised the telephone. He could not hear the bell which rang inside the vault. Sue's exhausted voice responded again. He told her anxiously:

"Watch the third clock on the door, Sue. The moment it trips the release, let me know. It will mean—you're coming out."

"Yes, Steve."

He waited. The line was silent while the minute hand of the clock crept to the hour mark. The deadline passed—long, empty seconds followed. Babcock tried the combination. The vault door remained closed. A full minute went by—a second. Then, suddenly, Sue's voice rushed over the line:

"Now. Steve?"

Thatcher snapped at Babcock: "Open it!"

A hush filled the bank. Every eye turned to the cashier. He stood tense in front of the great circular door, slowly turning the dial. Back and forth, with tormenting slowness, he revolved it, making sure of each mark. At last he stepped back. The great wheel twirled. The handle angled down. Thatcher assisted, straining back with all his strength to overcome the inertia of the two-ton portal.

Slowly the ponderous slab of steel swung out of its bed. The curved crack widened. Light streamed out. It fanned across the floor, streaking beyond the grille. Thatcher shouldered into the opening. Just inside the vault, Sue McEwen was standing. Her face was white, her eyes starkly alarmed. She was trembling. Under one arm she was holding the box. The way before her was open now—but she could not move.

"Steve…!" she whispered.

SUDDENLY THE swinging doors of the street entrance slapped open. Fast footfalls crossed the foyer. Every person in the bank was, at that moment, looking so intently at the girl standing in the vault door that they scarcely heard, scarcely realized the three menacing presences. A command crackled through the air.

"Throw up your hands!"

The three killers were strung out across the foyer, eyes slitted, automatics leveled. Their faces were bearded and gaunt. Desperation drew deep, ugly lines around their hard mouths. They were tensed to meet any threat, lustful for the life of anyone who defied them. In the cages, and behind the grille, hands went up—except Sue McEwen's. She stood as if paralyzed, tired eyes unseeing.

Govett snapped: "If anybody sets off an alarm, we'll start shooting to kill. If the police grab us, we'll go up for murder—that's a promise. You—open the gate. We're going in, and coming out fast—and anybody who tries to stop us will get a bullet in the brain."

Every person in the bank stood motionless, until Babcock reached for the release button. There was no sound, until the electric lock of the grille gate clicked. Instantly Govett sprang forward. Englar gripped the gate to hold it open while Govett charged through. Forbs kept his position, his automatic sweeping the cages. The killers began executing a swift, smooth plan.

Govett stopped short, staring at Sue McEwen. She was still standing inside the vault. The box was still held tightly under her arm. Govett started past her. Thatcher's hand caught her arm and drew her aside. Her eyes searched his pleadingly. His concern for her was torture, but he was watching Govett. Govett had stopped in front of the safe-deposit receptacle.

The killer jerked the drawer open. Seeing that it was empty, he straightened with a gasp. Swiftly his gaze probed corners of the vault. It stopped on Sue McEwen and sharpened. His gun leveled at her as he strode forward. The weapon threatened Thatcher into motionlessness. Govett stared at the box under Sue's arm, then jerked it away. He slipped the cover up, peered inside, then crushed it against his body.

'We've got it! Out!"

Thatcher's arm was straining to reach for his service revolver, but three guns were turned upon him. The first hint of an attack inside the bank would provoke insane retribution from the three murderers. If Thatcher so much as drew now, blazing bullets would inevitably shatter the lives of some of those who faced the sweeping automatics. He held himself tense ready to spring, as Govett and Englar and Forbs retreated to the street entrance.

Suddenly they whirled, dashed out. Instantly Thatcher sped through the grill gate. Charging to the outer door, he saw the three killers crowding toward a car waiting with idling motor. They were in plain sight of McEwen and Keanan, but the searchlights in the upper windows did not open their eyes, the machine guns did not speak. The two grim detectives were waiting for the appearance of the Moon Man.

And, as if by magic, the black-robed silver-headed figure appeared!

THATCHER STOPPED short just outside the bank peering in amazement. Sight of the phantom figure stunned him. He was the Moon Man—yet the Moon Man was standing before him, near the killers' car, with automatic gleaming. He had materialized directly in the path of the escaping crooks. They drew up stiff, too startled for an instant even to pull their triggers. During that momentary hush the Moon Man's muffled voice came:

"Drop that box!"

Thatcher sent a frenzied glance toward the windows across the street. He sensed alert movements behind them. He snapped out: "Down! Get down!"

Suddenly a brilliant beam of light stabbed across the street. It angled at the spot where the spherical-headed figure was standing. Immediately a second dazzling ray shot out. The gleam signaled swift, desperate action by the three bearded crooks, by the robed figure with the globular head.

The Moon Man's automatic cracked. Govett jolted back. The force of the bullet jarred his doubled arm from his side. The box slipped, then dropped. The three crooks sprang back, spinning toward the source of the blinding light. Two of them fired at the glaring windows. The gun of the third blasted flame at the black-robed figure. Instantly a withering fusillade crashed into the street through flying fragments of glass.

Thatcher shouted through the thundering reports. He sprang into the cover of the nearest car. The person wearing the Moon Man's regalia hunched down behind another. His automatic cracked twice, driving the three crooks away from his shelter. They scattered, shouting insanely, their mad shots flying wild. In an agony of bewildered concern, Thatcher saw the black-cloaked figure snatch up the box and whirl to face the alley.

Deliberately Thatcher straightened. He flung himself after the silver-masked being, deliberately running into the line of machine-gun fire because he realized his danger would force McEwen and Keanan to silence their guns. A few stuttering bursts followed his appearance—then silence. No bullet barred the Moon Man's way into the alley. The ghostly figure sprang into deep gloom—vanished.

Thatcher raced into the alley darkness. In the street behind him automatics were spitting. The machine guns clattered again. Demoniacal howls mingled with the flatly echoing reports. A withering attack from the windows was slashing at the three killers. Thatcher sensed that the leaden trap was claiming them. He sprinted along the alley, searching the blackness. Abruptly he paused, staring.

The black-robed figure was huddled against the pavement. A metallic clang sounded. As if by magic, the silver head disappeared. Again a resonant, bell-like note mingled with the blasting of guns in the street. Thatcher strode ahead to see the cover of a man-hole sliding into its socket. Bare hands were reaching up from below, gripping it. Thatcher dropped to his knees, peering into the cavity. He caught a faint glitter of silver.

"Angel!"

"Okay, boss!"

Thatcher jerked up, blood pounding. He thrust the heavy cover into its rim. He sprang toward the roadster which Dargan had been forced to abandon. Its motor was idling. He threw off the brakes, spurted it forward. He stopped it short when one of its front wheels was resting on the manhole cover. Then, switching off the ignition, he slid out and hurried to the street.

The machine guns had ceased clattering. The searchlights were angling down at sprawled figures. Three men lay on the pavement, huddled, their very postures declaring their deaths. From a doorway opposite the bank, two men appeared on a run. Keanan and McEwen gave the dead killers only a glance. They sped toward the alley.

"The Moon Man, Steve!"

"That way!" Thatcher shouted. "I forced him away from his car. Signal the prowl detail, Gil!"

"They're closing in now!"

Thatcher hurried into the bank. He ignored the bedlam of excitement. The grille gate was still standing open. He swung through it, toward the girl who was hunched at a table in one of the booths. She rose quickly at his step. Thatcher's arms enclosed her tightly.

"Steve, darling!"

"All right, Sue," he whispered. "I think we're all right—now...."

STEVE THATCHER drove at top speed from the McEwen house. He had rushed Sue home, had left her lying, instantly asleep, on her bed. After a long rest, he knew, she would be none the worse for her experience. Dread haunted his heart as he pushed into police headquarters. Before he opened the chief's door he heard McEwen's heels hammering, McEwen's voice rasping.

"That crook," McEwen snarled as Thatcher went in, "simply isn't human! He got the money he went after. He got under cover so fast nobody saw him. Somehow he got past twenty prowl cars. All right—we've cleaned up the Pendleton case, and we won't have to bother about sending those three rats to the chair, but—by damn!"

Thatcher asked: "What about the car the Moon Man abandoned in the alley, Gil?"

"Well, what about it?" McEwen challenged. "It's his car, that's all. We've got it, but what does it prove? What help'll it be? Ah, by damn! I might just as well dedicate my life to capturing a spook—but I'm not going to give up." McEwen's steely eyes glinted. "I'm not going to give up," he repeated, "until I see the Moon Man burn in the chair!"

A wry smile played over Thatcher's lips as he left headquarters. He drove his roadster at once to the Day and Night National. It was still a scene of excitement, though the bodies of the three crooks had been removed and the bank had closed its doors.

Squad-car men were posted around it. Thatcher took charge. A long while passed, every moment of it a separate dread, until he dared enter the alley.

He had turned his car into it. He rolled the roadster closer to the man-hole. Making sure he was not observed, he slid the cover away. "Okay, Angel!" he urged. Immediately Dargan lifted a black bundle from the depths. Thatcher swiftly—and tenderly—placed it in the rear compartment of his car. The box, containing evidence and loot, quickly followed it. He gripped Dargan's wrists, pulled Dargan up. The ex-pug hunched low in the roadster while Thatcher closed the man-hole and slid under the wheel.

"You're hurt, Angel!"

"Not much, boss. Got nicked in the arm, that's all. I guess it was a crazy play, but I had to do it. I didn't want anything to happen to you, boss."

Thatcher sent the roadster into the next street. Keeping out of the light, Dargan went on breathlessly:

"You know now your mask wasn't broken, boss. I made you think it was, hoping it would stop you. I told you I'd do anything to keep you from going through with it—I thought not having any mask would do the trick. On the way here, I stopped at a house with a big garden. I got away with the big silver ball they had on the bird bath. I broke it and—those were the pieces you saw. Lord, boss, you know I'd do anything in the world for you—and I'd rather get grabbed by the cops than see your mask broken."

A tight chuckle came from Thatcher's throat. "Thanks, Angel, with all my heart. I thought, when you told me, that the Moon Man's career was ended."

www.ingramcontent.com/pod-product-compliance
Lightning Source LLC
Chambersburg PA
CBHW072354030726
47505CB00014B/1815